# Bimbisar's Curse

Born in New Delhi, **Tanushree Podder** worked in the corporate sector for eight long years before she quit the rat race to write. A management graduate, she has worn several hats both as an individual and an army wife.

A well-known writer and a TEDx speaker, Tanushree is an avid globetrotter. She has travelled extensively and written hundreds of travel stories for newspapers such as *The Times of India*, *Hindustan Times* and *The Hindu*. She has also authored 35 books across genres, including military, historical and crime, for adults as well as young adults. Among her well-known works are *Nurjahan's Daughter*, *Boots Belts Berets*, *A Closetful of Skeletons*, *No Margin for Error*, *The Girls in Green*, *Thorns in the Crown*, *Ambapali*, *Men of Steel* and *Golden Sportspersons*.

*Boots Belts Berets* has been made into a web series titled Cadets, and *The Girls in Green* is soon to be adapted into a web series.

Tanushree lives with her husband in Pune.

# Bimbisar's Curse

Tanushree Podder

RUPA

Published by
Rupa Publications India Pvt. Ltd 2025
161-B/4, Gulmohar House,
Yusuf Sarai Community Centre,
New Delhi 110049

*Sales centres:*
Bengaluru Chennai
Hyderabad Kolkata Mumbai



P-ISBN: 978-93-7003-814-1
E-ISBN: 978-93-7003-412-9

First impression 2025

10 9 8 7 6 5 4 3 2 1



Printed in India

For my mother, Bharati Choudhury,
who opened the door to the mesmerizing universe of literature.
Without you, I would never have discovered
my passion for writing.

# Contents

# Author's Note

*'History tells us what people do;*
*historical fiction helps us imagine how they felt.'*

—Guy Vanderhaeghe

Ancient times are captivating because of the element of mystery that surrounds them. We are intrigued by the way people lived in the distant past. We are eager to learn about their culture, cuisine, traditions, and clothing. As we delve deeper into history, events and narratives become increasingly fascinating. Historians and archaeologists have relentlessly tried to uncover the mysteries of ancient times through excavations, and by deciphering cave inscriptions, analysing folklore, and studying ancient coins. However, a vast body of untapped knowledge still remains to be discovered.

I found the array of events that took place globally from the 5th to the 6th centuries BC incredibly intriguing. That was a different, exciting world.

On the one hand, there were countless invasions, conquests and power shifts, while on the other, there were remarkable advancements in the arts, architecture, science and philosophy. Alongside was a continuous reconfiguration and realignment of different regions, cultures and powers.

A succession of great empires ceded power to the Persian Empire, which dominated the Middle East. The Celts held sway over France and other regions of western Europe, while Scythian tribes spread across Central Asia and Europe.

In 537 BC, after defeating the Neo-Babylonian Empire,

Cyrus the Great granted the Jews the right to go back to Judah. Ancient Israel experienced an exhilarating era, marked by the rise of post-exilic prophets such as Third Isaiah, Haggai and Zechariah.

India had already had religious leaders like Mahavira and the Buddha who spread the message of love and compassion. Both predated Jesus Christ and Muhammad, the Prophet. Confucius, the renowned philosopher, was gaining recognition in China.

While researching for my book on Amrapali, I stumbled upon several allusions to a Magadh king named Bimbisar in Buddhist and Jain literature. He ruled over Magadh in the 6th century BC. Intrigued by the events in his life, I delved further into my research.

That led me to a treasure trove of information on the fascinating events that took place in the Indian subcontinent in the 6th century BC. The Indian subcontinent had two types of kingdoms—the Mahajanapadas and the Janapadas— depending on their size, the power they wielded and the population. In the Vedic era, there were approximately twenty-two Janapadas, but by the 6th century BC, some of these had grown into significant Mahajanapadas. Avanti, Kosala, Vatsa and Magadh were among the mighty kingdoms that were part of the Mahajanapadas.

The Magadh Empire was renowned as one of the most prosperous empires in ancient India. Between 544 BC and 322 BC, Magadh was governed by three dynasties—the Haryanka Dynasty, followed by the Shisunaga Dynasty, and finally the Nanda Dynasty.

From 544 BC to 412 BC, the Haryanka Dynasty governed Magadh, leaving a lasting impact on its historical course. Bimbisar, Ajatashatru and Udayin were three notable kings of this dynasty. Enthralled by the accounts of these kings, I persisted with my research, only to be disheartened by the lack of details.

Extensively researched and well-documented, the Gupta Dynasty has been the subject of significant scholarly attention. The Haryanka Dynasty, which governed Magadh before the Gupta Dynasty, lacks the same level of in-depth research and documentation. Despite the challenges I pressed forward, navigating through content that was accessible. As I pieced together the puzzle, a clearer and more detailed picture began to emerge.

The tales of Bimbisar and Ajatashatru offer an intriguing insight into ancient royalty. The old capital of Magadh has the remains of a magnificent fortress built by them. Textual, archaeological and sculptural evidence all indicate that these two rulers established the first major empire in North Magadh. During this period, Buddhism and Jainism emerged as two new religions. Their development has been extensively recorded in various texts. Among available records were those pertaining to the rule of Bimbisar and Ajatashatru, spanning the period from 543 BC to 460 BC. These records provide a glimpse into the lives and times of those rulers.

Born in 543 BC, Bimbisar, the son of an ambitious chieftain named Bhattiya, ascended the throne of Magadh at the tender age of fifteen. During Bimbisar's childhood, his father constantly engaged in fruitless conflicts with the cunning Anga king, Brahmadatta. Besides being defeated, Bhattiya suffered significant injuries in the decisive battle. Demoralized by the defeat, he passed on the kingdom to his teenaged son.

After the death of his father, Bimbisar vowed to avenge his father's defeat. Wise beyond his years, the young king realized that a victory needed a mighty army, so he concentrated on raising one. Since recruiting soldiers and producing weapons required considerable resources, he revamped the revenue system for a more robust treasury.

Once his army was ready, Bimbisar conquered the smaller kingdoms surrounding Magadh. These victories enhanced his reputation and increased his wealth. Later, he aggressively targeted the prosperous kingdom of Anga. Located along a bustling trade route, it reaped the benefits of a thriving commerce. Soon, Anga became a part of the Magadh Empire.

An astute and ambitious ruler, Bimbisar expanded his kingdom by conquering new territories and forming strategic alliances. Magadh flourished under his leadership and became the best-governed kingdom of the time.

Ancient texts refer to Bimbisar as Seniya or Shrenika because he was the first ruler to have at his command a well-trained standing army. Although he was an able military commander, Bimbisar was intelligent enough to recognize the disadvantages of war. So, he sought political alliances with powerful kingdoms and maintained good relations with them.

There are varying accounts about the number of Bimbisar's wives. But there can be no doubt that his first three wives belonged to powerful kingdoms and these marriages brought enormous benefits to him.

Bimbisar's first wife, Kosala Devi, was the sister of Prasenajit, King of Kosala. The alliance not only resolved hostilities between Kosala and Magadh but also granted Bimbisar the highly desired territory of Kashi, known for its abundant wealth.

His second wife, Chellana, was a princess from the Vajji Confederacy, a confederacy of many clans. Ajatashatru, who later seized the throne from his father, was born to Chellana.

Kshema, the third wife, was the daughter of Madra, while Vaidehi, the fourth wife, was the daughter of the king of Videha. Not much is known about Vaidehi, but my research has revealed some information about the first three wives.

The four marriages were strategic alliances that enhanced the

Magadh Empire's prestige, wealth and peace. Bimbisar deserves the recognition for building a powerful empire that endured many challenges.

Though Bimbisar's conquests were few, his greatest achievement was the introduction of an efficient system of governance and administration, which was followed by subsequent dynasties of Magadh. He established an efficient system of tax collection. With no less than 80,000 villages under his rule, Bimbisar decentralized the administration and appointed village headmen to administer the villages and collect taxes. It was a novel approach, which proved very beneficial for him. The policy led to a more effective judicial system and increased revenue collection.

Bimbisar was a benign king who supported monks of all religions; several religions flourished during his reign. As a contemporary of the Buddha, he wholeheartedly embraced Buddhism and frequently sought the Enlightened One's counsel on a multitude of matters.

While examining Buddhist and Jain records, I came across several contradictions. The accounts varied on multiple issues, ranging from Bimbisar's religious beliefs to his acts of violence. The identity of Amrapali's lover too remains a mystery. Opinions differ on whether it was Bimbisar or Ajatashatru. Based on specific dates and information, I concluded that Bimbisar and Amrapali were romantically involved.

While the identity of Amrapali's lover may be up for debate, historical records establish that she was romantically involved with a king from Magadh and gave birth to a son, who later embraced Buddhism as a monk.

The act of patricide was infrequent until Ajatashatru shocked everyone by murdering his own father, Bimbisar. From that moment on, patricide became the norm in the Haryanka Dynasty. Udayin, the son of Ajatashatru, assumed the throne after dethroning and executing his father. Aniruddha brutally murdered his father, Udayin, only to be killed by his son Munda. Nagadarshaka, the last king of the dynasty, was eventually overthrown by the very people he had ruled over.

Ajatashatru's actions set in motion a grim cycle of killing fathers, which endured over several generations. Every king in the dynasty suffered a terrible fate at the hands of their own sons, resulting in a chilling pattern. Although the reason for the patricides must have been greed for the Magadh throne, I have taken the liberty to fictionalize the reason as the Anga queen's curse.

*Bimbisar's Curse* is a work of fiction that draws from multiple accounts of that period. The story blends historical elements with artistic liberties. My goal is to draw attention to extant but oft-overlooked narratives and to create diverse and well-developed characters from those narratives.

Tanushree Podder

# 1

# The Dungeon

The prisoner lay in a dark, damp cell, untouched by the sun's rays. The cells were constructed to hold captive the king's most formidable enemies—rebels who plotted against him. Escape from here was impossible, condemning the inmates to a living hell.

His withered body convulsed under a threadbare blanket, his fingers icy cold despite the sweltering heat outside. The barely audible sound of his breathing and the slight rising and falling of his chest were the only signs of him still being alive. His entire body was in a state of stillness, a skill he had mastered through regular meditation. The air, too, was still but for his breathing and the occasional scurrying of mice.

The once broad shoulders and sinewy body that had set many hearts aflutter were now reduced to a mere skeleton covered in weathered skin. Bimbisar, who was once known for his golden complexion, now appeared ghostly pale. The tawny eyes that once had the power to subdue even the most courageous individuals were now dimmed by cataract. They frantically searched the tiny cell, their movements wild and erratic, desperately hoping to find a way out of this confinement. His once carefully tended crop of wavy hair and neatly trimmed beard were now unkempt and dirty—a tangled mess. Downcast, his moustache drooped below his lips. Once pampered by a masseuse, his hands had calloused skin, while the nails were not only chipped, but also had rough, uneven surfaces.

The distant sounds of music and celebration caught his attention. His ears perked up. He angled his ears, trying to hear better. Soft, barely audible music filled the cell with its gentle notes. The sound of music was joy to his ears. The haunting melody of the veena triggered a rush of memories. He could visualize the agile fingers strumming the strings. The notes had a distinct quality that only Vanmala, the court musician, could bring out. When was the last time he had heard those enchanting notes?

Bimbisar immediately recognized the familiar strains of his favourite raga. He knew each note by heart, having played it so often on his veena. He had not been mistaken. This music was indeed intended for a joyful event in the kingdom. In the past, he had been the soul of every festive gathering. Imprisoned in a cell, with his energy rapidly depleting, he had no idea about this event. No one cared to inform him. It was safer to forget deposed kings. Those guilty of overthrowing kings are so insecure, they can go to great lengths to prevent people from remembering or honouring their victims. Paradoxically, he found the situation amusing and let out a chuckle. Suddenly, the chuckle turned into a bout of coughing.

His hands shook uncontrollably as he struggled to prop himself up. An intense pain shot through his body, making him grimace as he cautiously set his scarred feet on the floor. The scars served as a constant reminder of the brutal treatment meted out by his captor. But the wounds deep in his heart remained invisible. He was no longer angry; just hurt by the injustice of destiny.

It was the curse. It hung over him like a dark cloud. Didn't the Anga queen curse the rulers of the Haryanka Dynasty, condemning them to be killed by their own sons? Resigned to his fate, he prepared to face death. The wait for the inevitable was excruciating. Each morning, he prayed for death to take away his wasted form. But death refused to oblige.

Painstakingly, he inched closer to the iron bars, the sound of his breath echoing in the dark cell. Intent on upholding his dignity, he shuffled along taking small steps, barely lifting his feet off the ground. He was careful not to do anything that would provide the guards an opportunity to humiliate him. These were the same men who had once bowed down to him and idolized him as their saviour. They had prayed for his health and happiness, but now they delighted in tormenting him.

'Is there a celebration in the palace?' His voice came out as a faint whisper, so soft that it was impossible for the guards to make out the words. 'Is there a wedding or a royal birth? Pray, tell me the occasion that calls for the celebration.'

'Did you say something?' asked the kinder of the two guards, coming closer to the bars. 'It must be important enough for you to have dragged yourself from the bed to the door.'

Bimbisar let out a heavy sigh. Gathering his strength, he licked his parched lips. 'Are those sounds of rejoicing in the palace?' He asked in his feeble, cracked voice, pointing a trembling finger towards the sounds. 'Can you hear that—the melodious tunes and the joyful laughter filling the air?'

'The old man wants to know if there's rejoicing,' the guards taunted, their laughter echoing in the corridor.

Squinting at them with watery eyes, he begged, 'Please, tell me if I'm right.'

'It is a celebration alright! You have a grandson now.'

'My grandson?' The lump in his throat grew larger, choking him. 'My grandson,' he repeated feebly.

'That is right. A prince, destined to become the future king of Magadh, was born today.'

He hobbled back to the cold wooden bed, wincing in pain.

In spite of his terrible condition, he felt an overwhelming sense of happiness. It was truly an auspicious event. He was a grandfather. The Haryanka Dynasty would continue shaping the course of history.

He raised his hands in blessing. A cloud of gloom settled on his face, his forehead creasing in anguish. Would he ever see the baby? Would they allow him to hold the prince in his arms? Would Ajatashatru give him the chance to instruct the prince in swordsmanship or to enlighten him on the obligations of a ruler? Although he knew that dreaming was impractical, he couldn't stop himself from imagining a parallel universe.

His son would never release him from prison. He sighed and shut his eyes tightly as tears began to form behind the closed eyelids.

He remembered the day his son, Ajatashatru, had come into the world. Celebrations lasted a week, complete with dance, music and feasts. People travelled from near and far to participate in the festivities in Rajgriha, the capital of Magadh. Bimbisar generously gave alms to monks and donated clothes and money to the needy. That week, no one went hungry.

Overwhelmed with love, he could not stop admiring the little prince, with his wrinkled face and perfectly formed fingers and toes. He felt indescribable happiness when his son gurgled—and intense distress when the child was in pain.

The same son had ordered his imprisonment. Such is the way of life. Never had Bimbisar imagined that the son whom he had loved beyond reason would cause him so much suffering. Humiliated and tortured, Bimbisar wasted away in a dark dungeon, while his deceitful son sat on the throne.

# 2

# The Birth of a Son

Bimbisar was flooded with memories, both joyful and sad. Just as the Buddha had advised, he tried to seek comfort in the happy memories. **'There is no path to happiness: happiness is the path,' the Enlightened One had preached. Bimbisar tried to 'seek happiness within.' It was a difficult process, but he had successfully mastered his ability to dredge up his past recollections. After all, a solitary man has the ability to experiment with many kinds of things. By filtering out the sad memories and cherishing the happy ones, he found the will to hold on to life.**

The birth of his son was undoubtedly one of the happiest moments of his life. A smile formed on his lips as he recalled the day. He was away on a visit to a distant village when the news reached him. The royal physician and midwife had assured him that the baby would not arrive for another two weeks, so the king had left for the village, promising to return before the baby was born.

When he heard about his son's birth, the king entrusted his official responsibilities to his Senapati and headed back to the palace on his fleet-footed horse, Dhoomketu. Riding swiftly with his entourage, he put hunger, thirst and exhaustion on hold. His heart danced with joy, the rhythm of his pulse matching the cadence of the galloping horses.

Eager to see his newborn son, he urged Dhoomketu to speed up. They rode on with just one stop to change horses and quench their thirst before setting off again. Bimbisar slowed down to a canter when they neared the capital's majestic walls, rising like giants, their imposing presence commanding both respect and admiration.

The city was Bimbisar's pride, for he had chosen an ideal location. Nestled in a beautiful valley, Rajgriha was surrounded by five hills: Ratnagiri, Vipalachal, Vaibhagiri, Songiri and Udayagiri.

It was dusk when they arrived in the capital. Bimbisar's heart filled with joy as he beheld the beautifully adorned city, resembling a charming maiden preparing to captivate her lover. A grand and bustling city, Rajgriha had wide roads and several watering holes. Dotted with placid lakes and lush green parks, impressive residences and dazzling shops, it lacked nothing a human could want.

Reality hit him suddenly. This was no time to admire his surroundings. He could not afford to linger.

Galloping through the gate of the Cyclopean masonry fortification surrounded by a spacious moat, the horsemen advanced towards the palace where the queen and the newborn prince were waiting for Bimbisar.

The wide avenue was lined with pillars adorned with beautiful floral decorations. Flags, buntings, and ribbons hung from the poles, beautifying the streets. To add to the mesmerizing brilliance of the city that was lit up with a million lamps, the twilight sky painted it with a delicate, celestial luminosity.

Colourful floral garlands decorated the houses lining the Rajpath, reflecting the excitement and happiness of the locals celebrating the royal birth.

Dusk was Bimbisar's favourite time of the day. It was the time when water was sprinkled on the ground to settle the dust raised by cattle returning home, and the air was filled with petrichor. The innumerable lamps, shining in the swiftly descending darkness, appeared to bathe the riders in a comforting glow. The temples reverberated with the melodic chimes of bells, rhythmic clanging of cymbals, and the sound of conch shells, creating a mystical ambiance. People sang hymns and recited sacred verses. All this, along with the enchanting scent of incense, had the power to awaken the spiritual in people's hearts.

The melodious chanting of the monks resonated from Griddhakuta, capturing Bimbisar's attention as his gaze wandered towards the caves atop the hill where the Buddha and his disciples were staying. It was the only place that offered tranquillity and solace after a hectic round of royal duties and political manoeuvring. He would go there with his son to seek the Buddha's blessings, he decided.

Bimbisar's palace stood in a sprawling estate with fish ponds and a variety of exotic trees and plants. The structure, adorned with gilded pillars intricately carved with gold vines and silver birds, was flawlessly designed. For Bimbisar, it was the most beautiful place in the entire Jambudweepa. The mere thought of being home made him beam with delight.

As the riders neared the palace, the sounds of conch shells, temple bells, and enchanting music welcomed them.

The moment they got wind of the joyous news, beggars lined up outside the entrance of the palace. They greeted the king with reverence and raised their palms in blessing for the baby. With a wide smile, Bimbisar dismounted from his charger. He folded his hands to greet everyone, before handing the horse to his groom. Then he strode briskly towards his queen's chamber.

The pillared corridor reverberated with the sound of his hurried footsteps, prompting the dasis to bow down and quickly make way for him. His dusty clothes and dark curly hair spoke of the long journey he had just undertaken, but his eyes sparkled with excitement as he walked into the queen's chamber.

He looked confusedly at the empty cradle next to the queen. A feeling of unease washed over him. Where was the baby? With raised eyebrows and a puzzled expression, he scanned the opulent chamber, desperately looking for his son. Finally he asked, 'Where is my son, Queen Chellana?'

As if in response to his query, suddenly there was a hushed silence in the chamber. Everyone held their breath. The dasis huddled close together to one side, their anxious expressions giving away their discomfort.

Bimbisar was quick to notice the fleeting sadness in the queen's eyes, which she promptly hid behind a playful smile. 'That is so unfair, Maharaj. I too have been waiting here for a long time, but all you can think about is your son. Don't you have any words of love for me?'

'My queen, I have journeyed long to see my son,' he said, his voice filled with longing and exhaustion. Then he added soothingly, 'First, let me glimpse my prince, and then I'll pour out all my love for you.'

'All lies. When you see your son, you will forget everything else,' the queen pouted.

'Don't test my patience, Chellana.' He gently rubbed his finger against the bridge of his prominent nose. There was no mistaking the sign of annoyance; the queen knew it all too well. 'Dasi,' he commanded sharply, his eyes narrowing as he beckoned the chief maidservant who had been hiding in a corner. 'Bring my son here. Immediately!' he said firmly, his eyes fixed on the woman.

The command echoed through the chamber, sending shivers down the servants' spine. He let out a fierce roar, demanding, 'Why are you delaying? Don't you value your heads?'

'Don't shout at them, Maharaj,' pleaded the queen. With some effort, she pushed herself up from the pillow, her weak body barely able to support her. Tears streamed down her face as she said, 'It is my fault. I ordered them to get rid of the baby.'

Her words struck him like lightning. He froze on the spot, horror writ large on his face. 'You got rid of the baby? Have you gone mad?' Grabbing her by the shoulders, he shook her violently. 'Why?'

'I'm sorry, Maharaj. The astrologer's prediction that the prince would cause your death worried me.' She covered her face with her palms and sobbed.

'You fool!' He spat out the words in a fit of anger. 'Did it not occur to you to seek my advice on this issue?' Turning to the frightened dasis, he thundered, 'What did you do with the baby?'

'Forgive me, Maharaj, it was the queen's order.' One of the dasis came forward and fell at his feet. 'She ordered me to kill the prince,' she wailed, 'but I could not bring myself to kill the innocent infant. So, I left him in the garbage heap just outside the palace walls.'

'Take me to him. Now!' Bimbisar thundered. 'I'll spare no one if any harm comes to my son.'

'You don't have to go,' pleaded the queen, trying to get up from the bed. Drained from the effort, she struggled to catch her breath and said, 'Kuntala will bring him here.'

'No. It might be too late already. I hope the baby is still alive.'

The dasi ran after him as he rushed out. 'Lead me to him,' Bimbisar ordered the dasi. With a silent prayer on her lips, she set off towards the back gate, fully aware that her life depended on finding the prince in good health. She knew how eagerly the king had been waiting for his son to be born.

The shrill-pitched wails of the newborn filled the air, guiding their attention to the garbage heap where he had been abandoned. Filled with rage, Bimbisar cursed the terrified dasi. Swiftly, he gathered his son in his arms, sensing the quivering of his small body, and hastened back to the secure confines of the palace.

'Summon the royal vaidya immediately!' he shouted, his voice echoing through the halls. 'My son's finger is bleeding. He needs urgent attention.'

Dhruvakriti, the royal physician, had been a part of Bimbisar's court for a significant period of time. His mother had served as a dasi to Rajmata Hemavati. Unfortunately, the woman died a few months after giving birth to Dhruvakriti due to complications caused by his birth. There were whispers about him being the illegitimate son of King Bhattiya, which made him Bimbisar's stepbrother. No one ever disclosed the truth. The Rajmata took pity on the orphaned baby and adopted him.

Although he was a few years older than Bimbisar, the two had grown up together. Together they had romped around the palace, studied, played pranks, and sought adventure. At twelve, Dhruvakriti developed a fascination for Ayurveda and showed an extraordinary talent for treating wounds and minor illnesses using herbal remedies. News of his extraordinary talent spread throughout the palace. People flocked to him seeking his services. The servants and soldiers made a beeline for his modest room. The boy's talent came to the queen's notice when he healed an ailing dasi. Rajmata Hemavati was impressed with the abilities of the twelve-year-old and requested King Bhattiya to send him to the kingdom's renowned vaidya to be educated. From there, he went to Takshila for further studies.

After ten years, Dhruvakriti, now a fully qualified physician, returned to the palace and offered his services to the royal family. By the time, Bhattiya had receded into the background and Bimbisar had been crowned king. He embraced the physician with open arms. During their early years together, Bimbisar and Dhruvakriti had developed a strong bond. The king treated the vaidya with fraternal affection and encouraged him to voice his opinions openly.

The vaidya was highly sought after by all the rulers in the region because of his remarkable power to cure the most complex diseases. In spite of being lured with greater position and wealth by them, the loyal vaidya remained devoted to King Bhattiya.

There was a flurry of activities as the sharp-eyed vaidya examined the baby's bleeding finger and applied an herbal poultice on it. Handing over the wailing prince to Bimbisar, he said, 'Maharaj, there is nothing to worry about. It is just a minor injury which will heal in a few days.'

'He's still crying,' said the anxious king. 'Do you think he's in pain?'

'The prince is hungry. Not one to wait patiently for milk, he will not be quiet till fed. He is already exhibiting the traits of a fiery monarch.' Dhruvakriti laughed, allaying the king's fears. 'The best course of action would be to deliver him to the queen so she can look after him.'

Noticing Bimbisar's reluctance, he added, 'Right now, the baby requires his mother. Her love has the power to heal and comfort him. You've had a long day, Maharaj. If you don't catch up on your sleep, I'll end up with another patient.'

The king smiled and replied, 'You never stop thinking like a physician, Dhruva, but you're right. I need a bath and some sleep since I must remain on my feet during the festivities tomorrow.' Bimbisar handed over the baby to the queen, who smiled gratefully.

'Won't you forgive me, Maharaj?' she asked tearfully. 'I want no harm to come to you, so I was willing to sacrifice my son.'

'Let's talk about this later,' he responded curtly, and walked out of the chamber with Dhruvakriti.

'What could have caused the injury, Dhruva?' he asked the vaidya as they walked down the corridor, his brows creased with worry.

'It appears like an animal bite. I think you were lucky to find the prince before any more harm could come his way.'

Horrified at the thought of an animal sinking its teeth into his son's tender finger, Bimbisar bristled with rage. 'Chellana will never be forgiven for allowing such a thing to happen to my child.' He halted in his tracks and looked at the physician. 'I know what must be done. Queen Kosala Devi will bring up my prince. She is wise and patient and has the right temperament. I'll order the prince's cradle to be taken to Kosala's chamber right now.'

'I request you to consider the circumstances in which the queen took this extreme step, Maharaj. It is not easy for a mother to abandon her baby.' Dhruvakriti's voice quivered as he uttered those words, reminding Bimbisar that the physician was an orphan who had lost his mother just a few months after his birth, and had never been acknowledged by his father. Dhruvakriti was called dasi putra by everyone in the palace.

'I think you should reconsider your decision,' continued the vaidya, after regaining control over his emotions. 'We must consider the queen's justification for her cruel action. It is possible that Queen Chellana was afraid because the astrologers predicted that the prince would do you great harm.'

Lost in thought, Bimbisar continued to walk silently for a few moments. Then he stopped in his tracks and faced the vaidya. 'I agree, I spoke harshly to Chellana, but the sight of my son's injury was highly upsetting. How is it possible for me to experience such an intense attachment to a tiny being? Does every father feel that way?'

Dhruvakriti smiled at Bimbisar, and said, 'He is not your first child. Did you not feel the same emotions when your daughter was born?'

'A son is different,' the king admitted, walking towards his private chamber. 'Daughters are nice, but they can't run an empire nor can they go to war. A king needs a son to do those things.'

'How can daughters run an empire or go to war if we don't allow them to? I'm sure given a chance, they will rise to the occasion. Your mother, Rajmata Hemavati, is a very astute woman and the strength behind the throne. Given the opportunity, I believe she would have been a capable ruler.'

'That may be true, but I'll not risk appointing my daughter to the throne. It has taken much sacrifice and bloodshed to raise Magadh to the dominant position it enjoys today.'

Dhruvakriti knew all about that. Crowned at fifteen, Bimbisar had to fight many adversaries to build a prosperous kingdom. That he was not King Bhattiya's eldest son added to his troubles when the brothers revolted against him.

'Anyway, I've been waiting for an heir for long,' the king continued. 'I can't bear to imagine my son being injured soon after birth.'

'No harm will come to your son, Maharaj. I'll check on him from time to time.'

'I know you will, Dhruva.' Bimbisar halted at the end of the corridor and turned gratefully to the physician. 'You are the most skilled physician in Jambudweepa. I know that the kings of Avanti, Kosala, Sakya, and many other kingdoms have offered you immense riches to serve in their palaces, but you have declined their offers. Magadh is grateful to you.'

'You embarrass me with your praise, Maharaj. I owe my life to your father, and nothing can compensate for the gratitude I feel for your family.'

At those words, Bimbisar enveloped Dhruva in a warm embrace. 'You have been more than a brother to me, and that should be enough.'

The two of them smiled as they recalled the happy childhood spent in each other's company.

∞

The king's day started early the next morning. He had a busy day ahead. The arrangements for a grand celebration had to be supervised, alms were to be distributed, and the monks had to be fed. But first, he had to seek the blessings of the Buddha. By sheer luck, the Buddha was in the capital at the moment. Bimbisar always visited the Buddha whenever he was in Rajgriha.

To Bimbisar's surprise, the Enlightened One arrived just as he was about to set out for the Buddha's vihara, where he was camping with the other monks. Their association went back a long time when the Buddha was a monk and had yet to attain Enlightenment.

They first met years ago, when Siddharth, the young prince of the Sakya kingdom, renounced all worldly attachments and left home in search of answers to human suffering. He travelled far and wide in search of Enlightenment. The memory of their first meeting was clear as crystal in the Magadh king's mind.

It was early morning, and Bimbisar was looking out of a window in his palace when he saw a monk begging for alms. Having witnessed many weary monks and travellers taking refuge in the gardens at the end of a tiring day, the king ensured there was enough water and comfortable seating available under the cool shade of the trees. Bimbisar was accustomed to seeing monks, but there was something unique about this one. He radiated a sense of tranquillity and luminosity. His demeanour clearly showed that he was of noble lineage. The Magadh king approached the monk with folded hands, curious to discover his true identity.

'You seem to belong to a noble family, monk,' said the king. 'Why, then, do you go around begging for alms like a common beggar?'

'What makes you think I'm from a noble family?' The monk seemed amused at Bimbisar's inference.

'I can see it in your posture and gait.'

'You impress me with your keen observation.'

'It is true, then?'

The monk responded with a smile, neither confirming nor denying the king's observation. 'It simply means that I have a long way to go. I must work harder on humility so people stop thinking of me as a royal-born and accept me as a monk.'

'I haven't met anyone who gives up a comfortable life to adopt one of hardship. It is always the other way round. You make me curious.'

Then Bimbisar humbly requested, 'I would be grateful if you could grace my palace with your presence and dine with me, so that I may have the pleasure of your company for a little while.'

After finishing the meal, the monk thanked Bimbisar for his hospitality and requested permission to leave. In that very instant, a minister walked over to the king and communicated in a hushed tone, 'Maharaj, this is no ordinary monk. He is Siddharth, the Sakya prince who has renounced his crown and riches to live the life of an ascetic.'

Astonished to learn about the monk's identity, the king requested the monk to live in his palace. 'I'm embarrassed to have treated you like an ordinary monk. Won't you allow me to atone for my mistake?'

'You have made no mistake, Maharaj,' the monk reassured the king with a gentle smile. 'I'm just an ordinary monk, passing through your kingdom. I will not be able to stay in the palace, but I would be delighted to have a meal with you in the future.'

'I enjoyed being with you. It made me feel peaceful. Will you not stay here for a couple of days at least?'

'That will not be possible. I have to leave tomorrow.'

'Why don't you stay in Rajgriha? I'll have a monastery built for you,' said Bimbisar. He felt a strong urge to spend time with the monk.

'I can't stay here long, Maharaj, but one day I'll return to Rajgriha and remind you of your offer for a meal.' With those words, the monk departed from the palace.

Time went by, yet Bimbisar could not shake off the memory of the monk and the meal they had enjoyed together. One morning, the king was informed that the monk, accompanied by his followers, had arrived at the palace gate. Having attained Enlightenment, the monk was now referred to as the Buddha. This was the second time he was visiting the king's palace. The king, filled with joy, quickly went to welcome him with folded hands.

The Buddha smiled. His face shone like a thousand suns as he said, 'I have returned for the meal that you had offered.'

'You have not forgotten, O Buddha!' Bimbisar beamed with joy as he welcomed the Buddha and the monks into the grand palace.

The king served the Buddha with his own hands and stood watching as the monks ate the meal. Once they had finished, he called for his son and requested the Buddha to bless the prince.

Placing his hand on the baby's head, the Buddha asked, 'What have you named your son?'

'I considered naming him Ajatashatru—one without enemies—but everyone is already referring to him as Kunika since his little finger was injured right after birth. We will be grateful if you give him a befitting name.'

'A name does not define a person's character. The goodness of a person with a compassionate heart remains unchanged, irrespective of the name. Ajatashatru is a good name and so is Kunika. I don't see the need to suggest any other name.'

Bimbisar was reluctant to let the Buddha leave. With folded hands, he said, 'O wise one, I want you to stay here forever. I humbly offer you half my kingdom as a gesture of reverence.'

'You are a generous king, Bimbisar, but I have no use for your kingdom,' the Buddha said. 'I wander around on foot, begging for alms, and spend most of my time in meditation. What will I do with a kingdom?'

'In that case, let me offer you my pleasure garden, Veluvana. I'll construct a monastery for you, so you can have a comfortable stay while in Rajgriha.'

The Buddha accepted the gift with humility, saying, 'I can't keep refusing your offers, can I?' With those words, the Buddha left the palace with his monks.

Soon after, the nobles and kings who were invited to the celebrations arrived, carrying gifts, and showered their blessings on the newborn prince. The entire palace was abuzz with activity. Kosala Devi, the eldest queen, had taken charge of organizing the feast, and Kshema, the youngest queen, oversaw the entertainment and decorations. The two queens worked tirelessly with the ministers to ensure that the best of cooks, dancers, musicians, jugglers and mimicry artists were summoned for the occasion. Nothing but the best would do.

The four gates leading to Rajgriha wore a festive look with fluttering flags and floral garlands. Floral arches had been set up all around the city. The streets were swept clean and watered to settle the dust. Pillars festooned with flowers and banners lined the Rajpath. Not to be outdone, people adorned the entrance of their houses with flowers and rangoli. Donning their best clothes, they joined the crowd to dance and rejoice. Bands of minstrels wandered around the streets, singing paeans to the king. Not since the wedding of Bimbisar and Kosala Devi had the city seen celebrations on such a grand scale.

# 3

# A Crucial Battle

Tears escaped Bimbisar's eyes as he recalled his blind love for Ajatashatru. He had never imagined the son he loved so much would imprison him one day.

*Is it ambition that provokes a son to imprison the father? Would I have done the same? Since I was not the eldest son, I never harboured ambitions of ruling as a king. Ajatashatru knew he would wear the crown, so what was the hurry?* Bimbisar wondered silently.

*I should have handed over the throne to my son, as the Buddha had suggested. Even though I heard the Buddha's sermons on detachment, I could not let go of the temptation of power. I should have followed in my father's footsteps.*

Bimbisar's face lit up with a wistful smile as he remembered his father, Bhattiya. Magadh was fragmented into small territories, each governed by a chieftain. There was a continuous struggle to expand the territories. Despite ruling over a small area, Bhattiya had grand ambitions. He dreamt of a kingdom that would extend from one end of Magadh to another, and further beyond.

His also dreamt of conquering Anga, a kingdom that lay on the eastern border of Magadh. Its capital, Champa, was strategically located on the confluence of the Ganga and Champa rivers, from where ships sailed down the Ganga to the south and returned with spices and jewels that were much in demand in the region. Bhattiya longed for the gold mine, but he lacked the resources to claim it.

The conflict between the two rulers had deep roots. The

soldiers of Brahmadatta frequently crossed the river at night to pillage the nearby villages under Bhattiya's control. They raped the women and carried away cattle and the crops stored in the granaries. As a result, there were multiple minor battles between Magadh and Anga, and the latter always won.

Then the Anga soldiers launched larger attacks on the border villages. They wreaked unprecedented havoc. A massive contingent of bedraggled survivors marched to Bhattiya, calling for vengeance.

Deeply moved by their heart-wrenching stories, Bhattiya embarked on another battle. Once again, he returned vanquished. His eyes reflected despondency, and his shoulders drooped in resignation. He appeared to age suddenly.

Though not the eldest son, Bimbisar had displayed his ability to rule from a very early age. While his siblings were busy with frivolous activities, he dedicated himself to the court proceedings and perfecting his skills in warfare. This had drawn him closer to his father. Each time his father returned from a battle, he shared the details of the battle, analyzing their strengths and weaknesses that ultimately determined the outcome. Those were important lessons in warfare, and Bimbisar soaked them up like a sponge.

Despite the passing weeks, Bhattiya could not shake off the sadness of his defeat. As the king's support, Queen Hemavati who was known for her strength, couldn't bring her husband out of the all-encompassing darkness. The physician's attempts to improve his mood with herbal drinks, and the priests' efforts to comfort him with sermons about life's difficulties, remained unsuccessful.

One evening, after dinner the son observed his father walking back and forth in the garden, lost in thought. As a young boy, Bimbisar had seen his father strolling in the garden after dinner. During this hour, his father would relax and deeply reflect on the difficulties confronting the kingdom. The queen would always join him for the walk, sharing her thoughts with him.

These were the winding paths where Bimbisar had taken his first steps, with his father's hand guiding him during his hesitant initial attempts. Later, his father used the garden as a classroom to teach him about constellations, focusing specifically on the North Star. Eventually, Bhattiya made it a routine to take Bimbisar for the walks. After completing their stroll, the two would sit on the stone bench beside the small pool brimming with lotus flowers in bloom, enjoying the evening breeze. The days of peaceful strolls ended after Bhattiya's defeat.

One evening, Bimbisar spotted his father sitting on the bench. He could no longer restrain himself.

'I have noticed that you walk alone these days,' Bimbisar remarked. 'I long for the times when we used to stroll in the garden, exchanging stories and advice.'

He waited calmly for a reply, but when his father did not react, he enquired. 'May I accompany you?'

'The air is getting chilly. I'll not sit here for long,' Bhattiya responded. Noticing the dejected expression on his son's face, he moved aside to accommodate him. 'Well, join me if you want,' he said.

'Father, it pains me to see you in this condition,' said Bimbisar after a couple of minutes. 'I have never seen you demotivated after a defeat. I'm curious to know what has led you to this point of extreme sadness.'

Bhattiya reluctantly ended the long silence. 'Son,' he sighed, 'nothing is the same anymore.' The mere idea seemed to cause him so much pain that he shook his head. 'I'm no longer the person I used to be.'

'Please don't say that, father. You are the same strong and valiant man in my eyes.'

'You are a loyal and loving son. One day, you will avenge

your father, I know.' Bhattiya shifted his gaze to his well-built and good-looking son. He was proud that his son was like he had once been—ambitious and determined. Those things would pave the way for his success.

'I'll seek vengeance for your humiliation, and I'll stop at nothing,' Bimbisar insisted.

On hearing his son's words, Bhattiya seemed to feel better. 'Alright son, I'll narrate the story of my humiliation and loss to teach you something about Brahmadatta, the Anga king.

'He has been steadily expanding his territory, and his soldiers frequently attack our villages. We have engaged in many battles with no decisive outcome. Anga's wealth and powerful army render the battles relatively insignificant for them. Whereas I'm losing invaluable soldiers and exhausting our meagre resources. The cost of a large-scale war is something I just can't afford.

'Brahmadatta's greed knew no bounds this time. Under his leadership, the soldiers committed terrible crimes in our villages, and the tearful villagers came to me seeking vengeance. There was just one way to bring an end to the ongoing harassment. I planned an impactful battle that would teach Anga a lesson they would not easily forget.'

Bhattiya's eyes filled with sorrow as he narrated about the battle. 'My plan was to carry out a quick and decisive battle by springing a surprise attack on Anga and killing Brahmadatta. Our soldiers successfully crossed the Champa River and arrived in the forested region of Anga that evening. The attack was to be launched after midnight while the enemy was asleep.

'Sadly, a vagabond camping in the forest spotted us right after we touched down in Anga territory. Immediately, he set out to inform the Anga senapati, who relayed the news to the king.'

Bimbisar was completely engrossed in what his father was recounting. 'The news enraged Brahmadatta. Without wasting time, he rounded up his army in the middle of the night and set out for battle.

'Just as our troops were preparing to move towards the palace, the Anga military launched a sudden attack. Our strategy, which depended on the suddenness of our attack, failed. The situation was reversed. Before long, we found ourselves under a full-scale attack by heavily armed Anga soldiers. They surrounded us from every direction, buzzing like furious hornets. A fierce battle broke out; our troops scattered in a disorderly manner. A part of my small army took shelter deep in the forest, while the majority tried to escape by swimming across the river. The Anga soldiers on the riverbank rained arrows on them; they fell one by one.

'As a king, I refused to retreat in shame and instead pressed forward with only a handful of soldiers. We fought gallantly, knowing there was no choice. It was a life-or-death situation where we had to choose between killing or being killed. Our approach included the successful separation of the Anga king from his army. Finding him isolated, I gave him chase. He is puny and not as brave without his army, while I'm much bigger and pride myself on being a skilled swordsman and a fearless warrior.' Bhattiya paused momentarily.

The loyal son squeezed his father's hand and stated, 'You're the bravest man I know.'

'The moment Brahmadatta saw me leading my troops in a charge, he immediately fled into the nearby woods.' A wan smile flitted across Bhattiya's face as he recalled the scene. 'I followed him into the woods, resolved to kill him. Instead, we found ourselves caught in a meticulously laid trap. With just four soldiers by my side, I found myself being ambushed. About thirty Anga soldiers had us surrounded. Our struggle proved futile as the enemy forces vastly outnumbered us. In no time, they disarmed us and forced us to our knees. Then I saw Brahmadatta coming towards me with an evil smirk.

'"You had the nerve to attack me on my territory," he snarled. "Did you think you would conquer Anga with a handful of cowardly soldiers who were quick to desert you?"'

The memory of that incident caused Bhattiya's face to redden. Bimbisar moved closer, straining to hear his father's strained voice. 'They tied the five of us together and forcefully dragged us towards a glade where their colleagues had set up camp. What followed was too humiliating to bear.

'The Anga soldiers were in jubilant mood. They gathered around us like a pack of dogs, brandishing their swords and thirsting for our blood. The Anga senapati unsheathed his sword and advanced towards us. With a cruel twist in his thin lips, he said, "Maharaj, should we behead the prisoners along with their king?"

'"No!" said Brahmadatta, raising his hand to restrain the senapati. "I want to teach the arrogant Bhattiya a lesson. I want to parade him and his men through the streets of Champa, so people can jeer at them, spit on them. We shall then tie them to the stakes and execute them in the public square in full view of the citizens."

'The Anga soldiers cheered enthusiastically in response to their king's remarks. Once the cheering subsided, Brahmadatta smiled and continued, "It is too late to return to Champa now. We shall camp here for the night and leave for Champa tomorrow morning."'

The memory caused Bhattiya's face to crumple in pain. After a brief pause, he said, 'Brahmadatta raised his hand and his troops fell silent. "You have done well and deserve a reward for your victory, so enjoy yourselves tonight. There is enough madira and food. Tomorrow, you will be handsomely rewarded for your efforts." And his troops cheered once more.

'Exhausted from battle, the Anga soldiers were happy at the idea of enjoying themselves and resting after that. The Anga senapati, a skilled leader, had thoughtfully planned for all eventualities. He had made sure there was plenty of food, drinks, and even a grand tent for the king to stay in.

'Everyone was in a cheerful mood. Brahmadatta had retired to the hastily assembled royal tent, while the troops engaged in dancing, singing and drinking. Our captors fastened us to the trunk of a substantial peepul tree at the periphery of the glade, assigning three armed soldiers to stand guard while the others revelled. After running out of ways to entertain themselves, the drunken soldiers boldly came up to the peepul tree to verbally and physically assault us. One of them had the nerve to urinate on one of our soldiers. I could do nothing but lash out verbally, which amused the lot.'

Bhattiya stopped speaking. The scars of his defeat still hurt. They would never heal.

'None of it matters now, father,' Bimbisar consoled Bhattiya. 'I'm happy you are back. We can settle scores later. I'll be by your side the next time.'

'There will not be a next time for me, son.' His father shook his head sadly. 'I'll leave it to you to defeat Brahmadatta.'

'Father, I have been speaking to your soldiers. They spoke of Virata's daring plan to rescue you that night.'

'Yes, my son. He is exceptionally brave and loyal. I owe my life to him.'

'Please tell me about the rescue.' Bimbisar's eyes sparkled with curiosity. He had heard the story from the others, but he wanted to hear the account from his father's perspective.

'Amid the chaos of the retreating soldiers, Virata trailed a group of my soldiers who were fleeing toward the river. A soldier told him that the Anga soldiers had captured me and four of my soldiers. "You can't desert the king and the other prisoners," Virata told the small group of soldiers. "We must free our king."

'The soldiers were aghast at the suggestion. "That's impossible!" they declared. "How can a handful of us challenge so many Anga soldiers? They'll kill us in no time."

'He tried to galvanize them into action, saying, "We can do it. The key is for all of us to work together in complete synchronicity. Besides, do you think you will be successful in escaping when the Anga soldiers have killed so many of our fleeing soldiers? Isn't it better to die valiantly, then to be killed like a coward?"

'"It's too dangerous," they declared.

'True to his nature, Virata refused to back down.' Bhattiya's face creased into a smile as he recollected the obstinacy of his commander. 'The chap continued his effort to persuade them. Many of the soldiers had friends or relatives among the prisoners. He shamed them by pointing out their cowardice.

'"Isn't your brother among the prisoners? Will you allow him to be killed?" he asked Govinda.

'"And Purendra, isn't your best friend also in that group of prisoners? Will you abandon them now? I'll give my life to save our king. What about you? Didn't you take the oath of loyalty when you joined the Magadh army, or have you forgotten everything in a hurry to save your scrawny necks?" he rebuked them.

'Virata added an incentive for action. "I'll ensure the king doesn't forget to reward those who risk their lives to rescue the prisoners."'

'I did not know about Virata's powers of persuasion,' Bimbisar chuckled as he thought of the burly, silent warrior who accompanied his father everywhere. The chap rarely cracked a smile. 'I can't remember when I last heard him speak.'

'Well, I didn't know either, but he goaded the others into joining his audacious mission. Anyway, the inducement, shaming, or whatever he did had the desired effect. I couldn't have done a better job of motivating the soldiers.' Bhattiya chortled and continued, 'When the others pointed out that they were outnumbered, he told them that numbers were not important. It was his foolproof plan and its flawless execution that mattered.'

'Yes father, the soldiers recounted Virata's words when I spoke to them later. "Remember, the enemy is in a complacent mood after the victory. They don't expect us to regroup so quickly and attempt a rescue. Besides, they are in a celebratory mood, so they must be drinking. Soon, they will be too drunk to do anything. We will have to seize that opportunity and risk our lives to save our king."' Bimbisar imitated Virata's voice.

With a smile on his face, Bhattiya recounted the rest of the story.

'It was a rousing speech that convinced our exhausted and demoralized soldiers to come to my rescue. Sneaking silently through the dense forest, they arrived at the enemy camp. The revelry over, many Anga soldiers lay sprawled on the floor, snoring loudly, while a handful stumbled about in a drunken state. The Magadh soldiers quickly silenced a few sleeping Anga soldiers and moved them to a hidden spot made of bamboo, where they stripped them of their uniforms.

'Within minutes, our soldiers appeared from the thickets, donning the attire of Anga soldiers. They put on a drunken act as they stumbled towards the three tired soldiers standing guard over us. Virata and his companions approached the guards, who were waiting to be relieved by their colleagues.

'"We are here to relieve you," Virata told the guards. "Enjoy the feast of succulent roasted meat and madira before getting some rest."

'Unable to see the faces of their relievers in the dim light, the three guards were only too happy to pass on the baton. It had been a long day, and they were eager to enjoy some food and drinks before resting their tired bodies.

'Virata and his companions got to work immediately. They knew that time was running out.

'We were initially unsure about the soldiers freeing us from our bondage. We wondered if Brahmadatta had changed his mind and ordered them to kill us. It was then that I identified Virata as he humbly bowed and motioned for me to stay silent. "We have come to rescue you, Maharaj," he whispered in my ears.

'Swiftly, they freed us from our captivity and signalled us to follow their lead. We rubbed our sore hands vigorously to increase the blood flow, and soon after, we hurriedly headed towards the river. Regrettably, the worst was yet to happen. Suspecting something was amiss, one of the Anga guards went back to the peepul tree to check on us. He knew their heads would roll if we escaped. Shocked to find we had fled, the fellow raised an alarm. The senapati realized we would have to swim to safety, so he ordered his soldier to intercept us at the riverbank. Arrows began flying at us, most of them hitting the water even as we swam to safety. The archers were drunk, and we had gained quite a distance under the cover of darkness. We got away with one dead and three wounded.'

Fuming with rage, Bimbisar clenched his teeth. 'Brahmadatta will suffer for his cunning tactics. I swear I'll wring his neck with my bare hands.'

Bhattiya smiled and said, 'You are a brave young man, but I don't think we should attack Anga right away. We need many more soldiers, arms and money. Besides, I'm a spent force, and you are too young to go to battle with the sly Anga king.'

'We will recruit more soldiers and arm them…'

The father gently placed his hand on the agitated son's arm and sighed. 'I'm touched by your optimism. I'm certain that one day you will encounter Brahmadatta. Bear my advice in mind when you do. The Anga king is a treacherous and cowardly man. His unorthodox fighting style makes it difficult to defeat him in a straightforward combat. The only solution is to outsmart him. Choosing an ethical path will not lead to success.' Bhattiya looked hopefully at his son. 'When you fight him, you must remember he is left-handed and his right flank is weak. Take advantage of his weakness and you will defeat him.'

Bimbisar was taken aback. His father, who had always emphasized the importance of ethics in peace and war, was now advising against it.

Bhattiya correctly interpreted his thoughts and said, 'I understand what you are thinking, my son. Over the years, I've learnt a few lessons. Fairness doesn't exist in war. If your opponent lacks in ethics, it may be necessary for you to adopt the same attitude.'

Touching his father's feet, Bimbisar promised, 'I'll never forget your advice.' He realized that his father was more affected by the humiliation of the defeat than by his physical injuries. The physical wounds would heal, but the scars on his soul would remain forever.

As days turned to weeks, and weeks to months, Bhattiya sank deeper into his gloom. He started avoiding his duties, leaving his ministers to handle the affairs of his territory. The ministers tried to revive the sagging spirits of the soldiers and citizens, but the king's absence gave rise to many rumours. The king's illness was a topic of conversation among the people, and rumours were rife that he had gone mad. A territory without a king is vulnerable to invasion. Troubling reports emerged from the border areas. The neighbouring chieftains wasted no time in seizing significant parts of Bhattiya's land, and the Anga soldiers carried out fresh attacks.

A king never stops being a leader, no matter the state of mental or physical health. His responsibilities are paramount. When Bhattiya realized the situation was quickly slipping out of control, he emerged from the depths of his wretchedness and started attending the court. Shocked, the courtiers watched the grey-haired and bearded ruler limping into the court to dispel the menacing dark clouds hanging over his territory. The sight of him filled his subjects with hope, and the court erupted in loud cheers. Their happiness was short-lived. Within a couple of days, it was apparent their king had lost his appetite to rule.

The ministers tried their best to goad Bhattiya to take crucial decisions, but he remained dispirited.

'It is time I appointed my successor,' the king told his wife one night.

'There's no hurry. You have many more years to go. Besides, your eldest son, Agatsya, is too young to be a ruler,' said Queen Hemavati. Over the past few months, she had observed her once brave husband slowly diminishing into a mere shadow of his former self. She knew that her oldest son was an indolent individual, unfit to rule.

'My youngest son will make a capable king. I'll keep providing guidance and advice to him,' said Bhattiya.

'You are thinking of crowning our youngest son? That is wrong. The eldest son has the right to the throne,' said Queen Hemavati.

"No, my dear, you must stop shielding your son. Not just Agatsya, Kashyap is also a hedonist who thinks of nothing but his pleasures. Think like a true queen and you will realize our eldest son is unfit to be crowned king, and so is his younger brother, Kashyap.'

No matter what Hemavati said, Bhattiya's decision remained

unchanged. She felt devastated at the thought of the territory being ruled by the youngest son. She knew Bhattiya's decision would lead to conflict and bloodshed.

The next morning, Bhattiya ordered Bimbisar to be present in the court.

The day was filled with unforeseen events. Bimbisar was startled when his mother woke him up early in the morning and commanded him to take a bath in the sacred pool near the temple. Thereafter, he followed her to the temple, and she offered a special puja to the family deity seeking the divine being's blessings for her son.

An hour later, he accompanied his father to the court, where the ministers and courtiers had gathered for a crucial meeting. The king ordered Bimbisar to remain by his side as he addressed the assembly.

'I take great pleasure this morning in appointing my son, Bimbisar, as the new king,' Bhattiya declared to the stunned courtiers. 'He will lead this kingdom to glory.'

The declaration struck everyone like a thunderbolt. The three princes sitting in the court were equally stunned. Bimbisar was aghast. Not for a moment had he expected his father to hand him the throne.

A collective protest erupted, breaking the stunned silence.

'But Rajan, Bimbisar is too young to wear the crown,' said the mahamantri. 'He lacks the experience to govern the kingdom. Also, he is not the rightful successor to the throne.'

The mahamantri's words emboldened the eldest prince, who stood up and protested, 'It is my right to inherit the region. You can't bypass me and crown Bimbisar.'

'Sit down!' Bhattiya's voice boomed like thunder. 'You have proved yourself incapable of handling the duties of a ruler.'

'Just because you are the oldest son does not give you the

right to be king. You are eighteen and your only accomplishments are chasing women and gambling. On the other hand, Bimbisar is a courageous soldier and an intelligent young man. I have faith that my son's intelligence will make up for his lack of experience. I have ruled for long, and now it's time for me to hand over the reins to my son.'

Bhattiya raised a hand to silence the voices rising in protest. 'I have arrived at this decision after much deliberation. Nothing you say will change my mind.'

Upset, Bimbisar's brothers abruptly left the assembly to consult with one another. Some of their close friends also stormed off in anger. Queen Hemavati's face showed signs of distress as her brows furrowed. She hoped her older sons would not defy their father, but Bhattiya remained unfazed. Although he knew they would cause difficulties, he had faith in Bimbisar's competence to handle them efficiently.

The astrologer's declaration of a propitious date and time for the coronation triggered a whirlwind of activities. Bhattiya wanted the best for his youngest son. Word quickly travelled to the neighbouring kingdoms; friendly chieftains and rulers were invited to the event. Magadh's friends greeted the news with caution. The hostile chieftains were excited about the prospect of an inexperienced prince becoming king. They saw it as an opportunity to conquer Magadh.

Bimbisar's coronation was an impressive event, with a multitude of guests in attendance. The temples resonated with the tolling of bells and priests reciting sacred verses. The crowd erupted in joy. Finally, a beaming Bhattiya placed the crown on his son's head and led him to the throne.

An exuberant crowd cheered loudly. Soon, the air was resounding with chants of 'Long live Bimbisar, the ruler of our lands!'

Tearfully, Bhattiya observed his son Bimbisar as he greeted the crowd with folded hands, and promised to live up to their expectations. He knew that royal obligations carried far more weight than the crown placed upon the head of the teenage ruler. On Bimbisar's shoulders now lay the burden of a crumbling realm.

# 4

# The Weighty Crown

Despite the sudden, overwhelming responsibility, Bimbisar approached his duties with utmost seriousness. But first, he had to deal with his mutinous brothers, who had joined hands with the hostile neighbours to launch a battle against Magadh. Queen Hemavati watched with consternation as her three sons went to war. Her efforts to bring about a reconciliation met with failure.

Fuelled by unyielding determination, Bimbisar ventured forth to confront his two brothers. The early days of the battle were tough on the Magadh army, but everything changed when Bhattiya joined the fight, determined to resolve the issue definitively. Encouraged by a powerful speech delivered by the ageing king, the brave soldiers of Magadh fought valiantly. For the first time, Bhattiya and Bimbisar were leading the charge together in war.

The battle raged on for an entire week, with fluctuating outcomes. Facing a larger enemy force, the Magadh soldiers were getting demoralized. They knew that if the battle dragged on, they would be defeated.

On the seventh day of the battle, Bimbisar's patience finally ran out. As the sun faded in the sky, the anxious king paced back and forth, searching feverishly for a solution. After a while, he walked towards his father's tent with purposeful strides.

'I was expecting you,' Bhattiya smiled at his son. He too had sensed the low morale of his soldiers.

'Father, we must end this battle tomorrow,' Bimbisar said as he sheathed his sword and settled down.

'I've been thinking along the same lines,' Bhattiya nodded in agreement. 'But first, let's have dinner. No one can think rationally on an empty stomach.'

After a frugal dinner of karambha, ghee, and a few pieces of roasted meat, the two sat down to strategize their battle plan for the next morning.

'With our limited troops, our only option is to depend on an element of surprise. The success of the strategy will determine the outcome of tomorrow's battle.' Using a twig, Bhattiya began to draw a rough plan of the ground. 'The enemy forces, believing in their superior numbers, have been carrying out frontal attacks. They are confident about their victory tomorrow, so they are not likely to change their strategy. We will use a pincer attack strategy by attacking them from their flanks.'

'Their complacence will lead to their defeat,' Bimbisar declared triumphantly. 'My treacherous brothers will have to face the consequences.'

They held a detailed discussion and ultimately settled for a meticulously devised plan for their attack. At sunrise, Bimbisar and his troops attacked from the flanks while Bhattiya launched a simultaneous attack from the opposite flanks of the enemy. The offensive caught the enemy soldiers off guard, causing them to disperse haphazardly. Those who could, fled the battlefield. It did not take long for the Magadh soldiers to defeat them.

On receiving the news of his oldest son's death in the battle, Bhattiya was shattered. This was not the outcome he had wanted. Bimbisar's happiness at his victory turned to grief when he received the news.

'How will I face my mother?' He let out a loud wail.

With drooping shoulders, Bhattiya patted his youngest son.

'This is the sad truth about war. Some die and some survive. Your eldest brother, Agatsya, died doing what he felt was right. Seek comfort in the knowledge that your other brother, Kashyap, has returned to the family fold.'

It was important to reorganize the Magadh army before they faced any more attacks. Bimbisar began breathing new life into the army, determined to reclaim the territories captured by the neighbouring rulers.

The territory inherited by Bimbisar was not extensive, but it had large fertile stretches. Regrettably, Bhattiya had focused more on defending his territory against repeated onslaughts from the Anga forces than on streamlining revenue collection. For a long time, the Lichchavis and Anga forces had been steadily nibbling away at parts of his territory. They now encroached on a larger part, forcing him to engage in constant battle with them in order to reclaim what was rightfully Magadh's.

The Magadh region was fragmented, with many chieftains possessing small territories. This led to ongoing conflicts over borders, resulting in endless fighting between the chieftains, and serving only to compound Bhattiya's existing problems.

Bimbisar's early years were defined by his father's frequent and lengthy absences because of his ongoing battles with the neighbouring territories. He would often return battle-weary, only to depart once more. There had been no respite for Bhattiya. Bimbisar wanted to put an end to the continuous warfare by conquering and integrating the smaller territories into a large kingdom. He understood that solely relying on diplomacy and negotiation might not yield the desired result. The only effective approach would be through battles. His mission included not just conquering the chieftains, but also taking measures to defend Magadh against the Lichchavis and Anga forces.

Bimbisar realized that in order to expand his kingdom, he

would have to engage in battle. Battles demanded an army, weapons, and, above all, sufficient financial resources. Since taxes were the sole source of income, he needed to implement an efficient tax system. To accomplish this, the revenue system would need total restructuring. On ascending the throne, one of the first initiatives he took was to reorganize his cabinet. Bhattiya had appointed men who were valiant soldiers and could fight the battles that he waged from time to time. But none had administrative capabilities. Bhattiya's ministers and advisors were ill-equipped to formulate administrative reforms.

While relying on the counsel of Vishnudasa and Anantsena, who had been like fathers to him, Bimbisar desired to enlist men who possessed both military prowess and administrative capabilities. He selected multiple military generals capable of putting together a formidable army, but his pursuit of knowledgeable ministers took him in different directions. It was at Takshila, a renowned seat of learning, that he found Udaydatta, a man of great intelligence with vast knowledge of the scriptures, science and philosophy. Madhavadatta, who had dedicated years to studying at Takshila, was a scholar renowned for his deep understanding of politics and policymaking. Both men, though not warriors, would be assets for Magadh. Soon, the two men established themselves as trusted advisors to the king.

Next on the young ruler's agenda was the production of weapons and the recruitment of soldiers. Agnimitra, who had proven his mettle in many battles, was selected as the commander of the army and given full authority to recruit his soldiers.

Bimbisar offered tempting remunerations for the best of young warriors and metalsmiths. He dispatched royal messengers and drummers throughout the kingdom to spread the word. Throngs of young men eagerly lined up to enlist in the army and the arms factories. These factories handled the production of weapons, while skilled metalsmiths crafted bows, arrows, spears, swords and daggers.

The commanders trained the recruits while the factories worked extra hours to meet the demand for weapons. All this required financial resources. With the treasury rapidly running out of funds, Bimbisar promptly began implementing fresh tax reforms.

From the sidelines, Bhattiya watched his son going about the task in an orderly manner. Skirmishes with the neighbouring chieftains had encouraging outcomes, with many tribal leaders surrendering to Magadh. Within a couple of years, Bimbisar brought much of Magadh under his rule. White banners bearing the striking image of a garuda flew proudly above the vast and fertile lands that were once governed by different chieftains. Thanks to this, the revenues increased and the pace of work picked up.

'Did I not say that he would make an able ruler?' Bhattiya said to Queen Hemavati as they discussed the progress Bimbisar was making. 'He is doing things that never entered my head. I'm a warrior and I ruled because of my physical strength. Scholarly pursuits, administrative reforms, regulations and procedures played a minor role in my life. But now I can see the benefits of such things in the expansion and governance of a kingdom. How and where did he learn all this?' Bhattiya's eyes lit up with wonder.

'Mark my words, queen, our son will bring glory to the Haryanka Dynasty,' he declared with pride.

'You were right, my lord. The ministers who once opposed the idea are now singing praises of our son. I only wish he would go slow with the battle plans.' The queen's eyes were full of concern.

'A ruler must be prepared for all eventualities. He can't sit in the palace and twiddle his thumbs. Don't you recall the battles I've fought?' asked her battle-scarred husband, who looked older than his years.

No one knew it better than Queen Hemavati. 'I agree, my lord. You have faced more than your share of battles, and I have lived in the constant fear of losing you. Bimbisar is too young to die.'

'You are a warrior's wife and mother. Such words don't behove you, queen. Our son is a brave warrior. He will survive, just as I have.' There was pride and confidence in Bhattiya's voice. He had trained his son in warfare.

It was during a military campaign against a neighbouring chieftain that Bimbisar met a fearless warrior. The rains had turned the ground to sludge. While traversing a dirt road, the wheels of his chariot sank deep into the mud. Despite repeated attempts by the charioteer and the other soldiers, they couldn't extract the chariot. The more they tried, the more the chariot sank into the mud. By now, the chariot tilted dangerously to one side, with the frightened horses whinnying and beating their hooves in their desperation to break free.

Bimbisar ordered the charioteer to untie the horses so that the chariot could be heaved out. He realized it would take a couple of elephants to get the job done. At that moment appeared a young man, balancing a bundle of wood and twigs on his head. Without wasting time on greetings, he pushed everyone out of the way and placed a dense layer of twigs on the muddy ground, then tried to lift the wheels of the chariot. His muscular arms and back were covered in sweat as he put all his energy into the task. Soon, the charioteer and soldiers joined him. Together, they pushed and pulled by turns until the wheels were free and the chariot could be brought out of the sludge, back to an upright position.

Impressed by the quick thinking and strength of the young man, Bimbisar called him aside.

'Pranam, Maharaj!' the young man wiped his sweat and bowed before the king. 'I'm sorry for not having greeted you earlier. I had to act swiftly before the wheels sank further into the sludge. Inadvertently, the charioteer and soldiers were pushing the chariot in a manner that would make the wheels sink further.'

'What's your name, young man?' Bimbisar asked. 'And what do you do?'

'I'm Devavrata, Maharaj. It is a lofty name for a poor woodcutter. I wanted to serve Magadh as a soldier, but ambitions can't alter one's destiny.'

Bimbisar laughed at the young man's words. 'Fate can change sometimes, Devavrata, and ambition is a good thing. Do you want to be a warrior?'

The king's question took the young man by surprise. Was he jesting? Having fun at his expense?

'No, I'm not jesting,' Bimbisar responded to the young man's unspoken question. 'I'll instruct the senapati to enrol you in the Magadh army. But you will have to undergo rigorous training. Let me warn you, young man, it will not be easy to please the Magadh senapati.'

'Thank you for the opportunity to serve Magadh, Maharaj,' Devavrata fell at the king's feet. 'I'll lay down my life for this kingdom.'

Over the next few months, Devavrata consistently proved his worth and gained the king's trust. Finally, he was appointed Bimbisar's personal bodyguard.

Over the next few months, Bimbisar used unconventional methods to get a group of young and devoted men to work for him. These were men who would lay down their lives at the snap of his fingers. Sumana, a gardener, started by providing eight measures of jasmine flowers to the royal palace, but quickly became a trusted assistant because of his unwavering loyalty and hard work.

Later, Bimbisar selected an able minister named Koliya from a neighbouring kingdom after his successful conquest. Kumbbaghosaka, the treasurer, was appointed in an unconventional manner, like many others. The wise minister Udaydatta was given the responsibility of handling the crucial portfolio of mahamantri.

Consumed by jealousy, the other ministers expressed their disapproval at these appointments. They had served Bhattiya for long. Most of them were ineffective and their ideas were no longer relevant. Bimbisar was slowly phasing them out of his group of trusted ministers.

The disgruntled ministers took their grievances to the old king, who appeased them, saying he would have a word with his son. One evening, during dinner, Bhattiya brought up the topic. Bimbisar always ensured that he had a meal with his father, even during busy times, and Queen Hemavati would serve them food. He had learned from his father that family came first.

'Son, a few days back, I received a complaint from a contingent of ministers,' Bhattiya said as the queen served him some more millet gruel and fried meat. 'They claim that you have given important positions to inexperienced individuals, neglecting those who have served the kingdom faithfully.'

'That's true,' agreed the son, picking up a piece of succulent meat. 'They have enjoyed important posts, but have grown complacent over time. In fact, they have proved themselves inefficient in most matters. The kingdom can't prosper without being infused with fresh energy. We require innovative concepts to drive progress. The individuals I have chosen are brimming with creativity and vitality.'

'While that may be true, one must accommodate experienced

hands too. We can't ignore these ministers,' said Bhattiya.

'I haven't ignored them. In fact, I have given them portfolios that require conventional wisdom. Over the past few months, I have focused my efforts on revamping all the systems so that Magadh can keep up with the powerful kingdoms. Our land is highly fertile and produces excellent yields. Our people are hardworking, yet the revenues are inadequate and prosperity hasn't reached everyone. Upgrading the systems in every department is of utmost importance and needs to be done urgently.'

Bhattiya was aware of the reforms that were being introduced. The perceptive young king prioritized the villages, recognizing them as the primary sources of revenues. Under Bimbisar's rule, village chiefs were appointed to oversee village councils, which oversaw tax collections. They took care of the grievances and acted as intermediaries between the villagers and the central authorities. Bimbisar was a forceful advocate of decentralization. The system was highly effective.

'No doubt, the systems introduced by you have yielded excellent results. I know that tax collection has gone up manifold, and that it has also eliminated corruption, but there will always be resistance to new ideas. I'll advise you against displeasing the old ministers,' Bhattiya said.

As the days passed, Bhattiya found it difficult to keep pace with his son's enthusiasm and energy. The constant effort to keep up with the changes left him drained.

Bhattiya knew that the old order had to yield to the new one, but accepting this bitter truth proved challenging for many. 'Show some flexibility and try to accommodate the senior ministers, my son,' he said wearily.

'It shall be as you wish,' said Bimbisar, touching his father's feet. His thoughts were consumed by the construction of a grand new capital, which he had named Rajgriha—Abode of Kings.

An expert engineer by the name of Mahagovinda had already built a detailed maquette of Rajgriha. The new capital would be a more modern and advanced iteration of Girivraja, which had functioned as the capital for a significant duration. The city had abundant water supply and many luxurious mansions, but he desired to expand and renovate both the city and the palace.

The successful overhauling of the tax collection system led to increased revenue in the treasury. There was enough money to strengthen the army and give shape to Bimbisar's dream capital.

Over the past few months, Bimbisar had spent much time with the engineer, discussing the details of his dream capital. His goal was to surprise his parents, so he was determined to finish the construction quickly and have his father inaugurate the palace.

'Rajgriha will be built along the principles laid down in the Arthashastra. There will be a strong focus on its defence. We are fortunate to be surrounded by a range of towering mountains. These will offer a natural defence against our enemies,' Mahagovinda declared, presenting his scaled-down model to the king. 'The mountains will be our natural ramparts, and the parts that are not covered will be ringed by high fortification made of burnt brick.'

Pointing with a stick at the outer wall of the maquette, he continued, 'The fortification wall will take the shape of an irregular pentagon, primarily because of the hilly terrain, and will be accompanied by a wide moat. Four gates leading in different directions will be incorporated into the fortification, along with watchtowers, guard rooms and bastions. The Uttarapath in the north and Dakshinapath in the south will connect Rajgriha with Uruvela, Kasi, Takshila, Shravasti, Pataliputra, Tamralipta and other important cities.'

Bimbisar was absorbed in the engineer's description. 'Tell me about the layout inside the fortification,' he insisted.

'The capital city will stretch from east to west and become narrower from north to south. The palace will be built in the heart of the city, featuring a spacious Rajpath leading to the palace which can accommodate four carriages side by side. Pedestrians will have designated walkways. Wide roads, arranged in a grid, will connect the Rajpath to various parts of the city. On both sides of multiple avenues in the city, we will plant trees like parijat, gulmohar and palash that will bloom with fragrant orange, golden and purple flowers. In spring, the blossoms will turn the city into a wonder in gold and purple. We are fortunate to have several hot springs in our territory. My goal is to construct water channels that will transport water from the hot springs to different parts of the city. This will enable people to use the water for therapeutic purposes.'

'That is an excellent idea,' Bimbisar's face lit up with a smile. His love for plants was legendary. 'Have you considered royal pleasure gardens and public parks?'

'There will be many public parks, along with viharas,' the royal engineer promised. 'People will have access to a wide range of amenities. The city will have sports arenas, music halls, parks, neatly planned squares, stunning architecture, and well-organized marketplaces with strategically placed stalls for vendors. I have planned to install tall pillars topped with lighting arrangements to illuminate the thoroughfares in the city.'

'As for the royal palace, it will be one of the grandest in the region,' Mahagovinda continued. 'We will use the finest timber for its construction, and also equip the palace with effective fire-prevention measures.'

Bimbisar was thoroughly impressed by the engineer's meticulous planning. 'You have done a wonderful job, Mahagovinda. I can't wait to see the results. Requisition for all the funds you require, and they will be allotted. I want my father to inaugurate the royal place on the auspicious Vasant Utsav.'

'It will be completed by Vasant Utsav,' Mahagovinda promised the king.

# 5

# Father's Death, and a Vow

Bimbisar's wish for his father to inaugurate his dream capital didn't come to fruition. Bhattiya passed away three years after his son assumed the throne. His last words to his son were, 'Beware of your brother Kashyap. He will strike when you least expect.'

Kashyap had returned to the family fold after the battle, and Bimbisar had assigned him an important portfolio. Despite his outward display of remorse, Kashyap was seething with rage within. He hadn't forgotten the humiliating defeat and the death of his eldest brother in battle.

The loss of his father had a profound impact on Bimbisar. He held Brahmadatta, the Anga king, responsible for hastening his father's demise.

As the flames leapt from Bhattiya's funeral pyre, they kindled a fire within Bimbisar. He applied ash from the pyre to his forehead and renewed his vow with a steady and firm voice, 'Brahmadatta's days are numbered. I'll avenge your death, father.'

Bimbisar had vowed to kill Brahmadatta, but he hadn't expected that the day would come so soon.

A king does not have the luxury of wallowing in grief. Rulers may come and go, but the responsibility of governing a kingdom remains the same. Two weeks after completing all the funerary rites, Bimbisar summoned his ministers to a crucial meeting. Heated discussions filled the sabhagriha as ministers deliberated on the agenda. The king's vow during his father's cremation was clear to all. The feasibility of an attack on Anga was the topic of discussion. Would it be wise to launch an attack on the enemy now?

A hush fell over the sabhagriha. Everyone stood up with hands folded in greeting as the king walked up to his throne. The determined air about him confirmed the fears of the ministers. Wasting no time on preliminaries, Bimbisar started speaking. 'The preparation of three full years has yielded satisfying results. The Magadh soldiers have undergone rigorous training. There are many weapons at our disposal, and our coffers are filled to the brim. There will be no better time to go to war,' he told his ministers and army commanders. 'I'm confident of victory and expect you to inspire the soldiers. There's no place for defeatist thinking in Magadh. If my father, with scant resources, could challenge Brahmadatta, I am certainly better placed to do so.'

The ministers, who had been expecting the king to speak of his plan, met his words with stoic silence. Udaydatta, who had assumed the responsibilities of a mahamantri, hesitated briefly before standing up to give his response.

'Maharaj, it might be prudent to extend our kingdom by recapturing the lands we have lost to the neighbouring kings,' he advised. An experienced hand, the astute minister realized that the young king, carried away by his emotions, was impatient to attack Anga. 'This will help us expand our territory and improve Magadh's image. Not only their territories, we will have the army of the neighbouring kings under our control. This will augment our military might, and then we can easily conquer Anga.'

It was a sensible suggestion, and the ministers agreed to it unanimously. Agnimitra emphasized that the Magadh army was prepared for small skirmishes, but they would need to be more prepared if they were to engage in a war with Anga.

'Everyone in Magadh knows you have vowed to kill

Brahmadatta,' said Vishnudatta, Minister of War Strategy. 'We fully support your decision, which is driven by your love for your father. We also understand the significance of conquering Anga.' His words drew approving nods from the ministers. 'The prosperous kingdom of Anga, positioned strategically near the Bay of Bengal, dominates both trade and the pathways to the seaports. A victory over Anga will bring enormous advantages to Magadh. However, the timing needs to be right.'

His statement received unanimous approval. Bimbisar was youthful and ambitious, yet he possessed enough intelligence to understand the importance of caution. He had handpicked his ministers for diligence and wisdom, and he respected their counsel.

'It would be unwise to engage in a hasty battle with Anga,' Rajmata Hemavati supported the ministers' perspective during their dinner that evening. 'You have many lessons to learn from your father's experience. I would advise against any impulsive reaction to your father's death. Lack of planning has led to many defeats.'

Bimbisar had immense respect for his mother's advice and always sought her approval before embarking on any significant undertaking. While his father played a crucial role in his life, it was his mother who had taught him the fundamentals of sword fighting and archery. He considered her to be the most fearless woman he had ever met, excelling in horse riding, archery and swordsmanship, surpassing many men in these skills. With her extraordinary political acumen, she could always identify any chink in her opponent's armour. So great was her wisdom that her husband always sought her counsel before undertaking any mission.

'Learn your lessons from life. What should people do when they are very hungry but the food is too hot to eat?' she asked.

'Wouldn't it be unwise to pounce on the hot food and burn their mouth?'

He knew there was a lesson in her conundrum. 'Why don't you suggest the solution?'

'If you are wise, you'll spread out the food and begin eating from the outer edges, which will cool first,' his mother continued. 'Likewise, it would be wiser to expand your kingdom by vanquishing the small territories that lie just outside your kingdom. That will augment our resources and our army. Also the soldiers would taste smaller victories and be better prepared for the larger battle.'

The more he pondered on his mother's words, the more he became convinced of their wisdom. 'I'll do nothing without giving good thought to your advice,' he promised.

Bimbisar realized that times were uncertain and rulers in newly formed territories were engaged in a constant tussle for supremacy. Mistrust and insecurity plagued the neighbouring kingdoms as they sought to expand their borders. He would have to tread cautiously.

Heeding his mother's counsel, the young king put on hold his plans to attack Anga. Instead, he launched rapid and decisive attacks on the chieftains in the surrounding areas. The Magadh soldiers, who had undergone rigorous training for the past three years, easily defeated the disorganized enemy soldiers.

The chieftains either died or were conquered, and their soldiers became part of the Magadh army. It wasn't long before the Magadh banner could be spotted flying everywhere. Bimbisar's kingdom continued to expand, but there was one problem that continued to rankle him.

For a while now, the Lichchavis had been gradually encroaching on Magadh lands, pilfering metals from Magadh mines, and appropriating the crops and fodder gathered by farmers. Each time they were repelled, they returned in larger numbers. It seemed impossible to keep them away. Despite his countless battles, Bhattiya's efforts to safeguard his lands and people had remained unsuccessful. Now, Bimbisar was engaged in a war against the raiders.

One day, exhausted after a battle with the Lichchavis, Bimbisar was having a meal under a tree. The battle had been bloody and disheartening. The Magadh forces had suffered significant casualties. He knew the enemy would come back, but he couldn't do anything to prevent them from returning, because of their strategy of stealth attacks and their superior numbers. The only redeeming feature was the confiscated thoroughbred white stallion, which had refused to desert its slain master. The king instantly fell in love with the horse.

'You will be the most cherished horse in the stable,' Bimbisar took the reins and patted the horse gently, but it bucked. He had a deep-rooted passion for horses, and one valuable skill he had acquired from his stable attendant was the art of taming a horse. He pulled down hard on the lead shank till the front feet returned to the ground. After pulling down the shank, he took a few steps back with the horse to assert control. 'From today, you will be called Dhoomketu and you will learn to love me,' he whispered into the horse's ear.

As his weary troops found respite under the trees, Bimbisar observed one of his soldiers feeding the nearby crows by throwing food at them. In a swift motion, a murder of crows resting on a nearby tree swooped down on the food. A stray dog that had wandered into the area joined them. Soon enough, they found themselves locked in a fierce battle for food.

With their united and aggressive stance, the crows frightened away the dog. The lesson left a lasting impression on Bimbisar. He realized that a unified force could triumph over a larger one. The secret behind the Lichchavis' win lay in their ability to stay united. To defeat them, he would need to create powerful alliances.

His mind was firmly set on a course of action. Before attacking the Lichchavis, he would form alliances with influential allies. Bimbisar decided to avoid unnecessary casualties by refraining from engaging in futile battles, opting instead to wait for a more opportune time.

⁂

The construction of the newly built capital of Rajgriha was completed exactly as Mahagovinda had promised. It was a magnificent sight, just as Bimbisar had imagined. His only remorse was that his father had died before being able to see his dreams realized.

Enclosed with sturdy walls, the city had twenty-two gates and fifteen posterns that were closed in the evening. Thereafter, no one could enter the city.

Avenues lined with trees laden with fragrant bright blossoms ran parallel to each other, crisscrossed by streets inhabited by different sections of society. Prosperous members of various guilds constructed lavish palaces in the most affluent parts of the town, while artisans, shopkeepers, labourers lived in the more modest parts. With rows of flower-bearing trees, the Rajpath was an impressive and spacious thoroughfare. Temples, gardens, public halls, markets, taverns and open grounds completed the city. The residents of Rajgriha had every amenity imaginable at their disposal.

The royal palace, elegantly furnished under the watchful eye of the Rajmata, was a magnificent structure with lavish interiors. The corridors leading to the royal chambers were adorned with marble sculptures of apsaras and other celestial beings, with brass vases filled with fresh flowers placed in between.

The white marble assembly hall was a stunning sight. Luxurious silk rugs adorned the floor. The hall boasted grand decorations, including elaborate arches at the entrance and thirty-one intricately carved wooden pillars that supported a roof with gilded embellishment. Stunning and exotic murals ornamented the walls.

Years passed. The king was now firmly in control. The indecision and brashness of his early years had given way to a confident and calm outlook. He openly admitted to being nervous when he had embarked on his first battles. Despite having competent commanders and advisors, Bimbisar was solely responsible for leading his troops and making critical decisions. Rajmata Hemavati's soaring ambitions, and her high expectations of Bimbisar, weighed him down. He couldn't confide in anyone, not even in his mother, about his anxieties. There were a few friends, but none to whom he could reveal his true feelings. The course of one's life is often determined by destiny. This was certainly true of the young king.

# 6

# Romancing a Ganika

During his most vulnerable and isolated phase, one day, Bimbisar encountered a remarkably attractive woman named Kadambini, under the most unusual circumstances. Early that day, Bimbisar had set out to the nearby forests on a hunting expedition after a long time. Despite his strong affinity for hunting, the affairs of the kingdom consumed all his time, leaving him hardly any time to pursue his passion. That morning, his spirits were high as he had killed a tiger and a couple of deer. The sun shone bright above as it approached midday.

Exhausted but satisfied, as Bimbisar and his companions rode back to the palace, they came across a chariot that was stuck near a tree. Standing beside it was the most beautiful woman he had ever seen, wringing her hands helplessly.

Bringing Dhoomketu to a halt, he raised his hand to signal his party to stop.

'Devi, are you in trouble?' Bimbisar asked as he dismounted and handed the reins of his horse to a groom.

The lady clasped her hands in greeting. 'Maharaj, one of my horses has lost a shoe, so it is in pain.' Tears filled her eyes. 'Witnessing the suffering of something dear to me is truly distressing.'

On the king's signal, a soldier inspected the horse's hoof. 'Maharaj, the horse can't move until we fix the shoe,' he confirmed.

'Can you ride?' the king asked the woman. 'Returning with the chariot to Rajgriha will take time, and it is not advisable for you to stay in the forest that long. It will be better if you ride with us to the city.'

The soldier unhitched the healthy horse from the two-horse chariot and gave its reins to the woman. Bimbisar assigned another soldier to care for the injured horse and handle its shoeing.

'You are very kind, Maharaj,' she said. 'Please do not inconvenience yourself. I can ride back on my own.'

'Your safety is my responsibility, lady,' he said gruffly. 'Do you think I'll abandon you in the forest? My men will replace your horse's shoe and bring back the chariot to your doorstep.'

As Bimbisar rode alongside the woman, he grew curious. She seemed to sense his thoughts and introduced herself, 'I'm called Kadambini, Maharaj.'

'What were you doing in the forest?'

'I had gone to gather some herbs required by the vaidya.'

'You are a vaidya's assistant?'

As she cast her gaze downward, a faint blush spread across her porcelain-like cheeks. 'I'm a courtesan, Maharaj. The vaidya is old and feeble. He has no help, so I lend him a hand by gathering herbs from the forest. Sometimes I help him prepare the concoctions.'

'You are interested in herbs?' Bimbisar was surprised. He had never heard of a courtesan collecting herbs.

'Yes, Maharaj! My father was a vaidya too. A series of unfortunate events led to my family's downfall, pushing me into this profession.'

He left her at her mansion, which was tucked away in a secluded part of the city, but thoughts of her refused to leave Bimbisar. That night, he tossed and turned restlessly on his bed, unable to sleep. Kadambini's captivating face kept haunting him.

With the monsoon months over, it was more pleasant and comfortable. Love was in the air. The young king had been so consumed with the affairs of the kingdom that thoughts of romance had been far from his mind. Meeting Kadambini had triggered a peculiar awakening within him.

Bimbisar's heart skipped a beat as he vividly recalled the tingling sensation that overwhelmed him when he touched the ganika's slender body. He found himself irresistibly drawn to her, consumed by a powerful longing.

The sun was yet to rise the next morning, when he harnessed Dhoomketu and stole out of his palace to visit Kadambini. The lush gardens surrounding her mansion, with their vibrant blooms and meticulously trimmed hedges, offered a serene sanctuary amidst the heavy weight of his responsibilities.

Bimbisar found the ganika bathing in the pond behind her house. She emerged like an apsara from the water, her white antariya clinging seductively to her body. The wet kanchuki was a scant cover for her breasts. Drops of water sat like dews on her trembling lips. He froze on the spot. The vision had left him transfixed. His body tingled with desire, as if every pore was on fire. A strange tightness gripped his chest, making breathing difficult.

Kadambini smiled shyly, her eyes sparkling with warmth, and he followed her into the house.

She let her clothes fall to the floor and stood before him, her cheeks flushed. Her fingers, skilled and desperate, wandered over him with a sense of urgency, seeking, searching and urging. Their breaths merged in a feverish embrace. He let out a groan. Their bodies entwined, they rode the storm of passion, their senses overwhelmed by its intensity until it gradually abated. Eventually she leaned back, a satisfied smile on the brink of her lips. Emotions flowed over him like an unstoppable avalanche.

Bimbisar propped himself up on his elbow and looked affectionately at the woman beside him. He understood she had given him more than her body. She now held his heart in her hands. He wished the moment would not end.

He was young and lacked experience in matters of the heart. Fuelled by feelings of isolation and a newfound desire, he sought solace in the arms of the ganika. The skilled enchantress taught him all about a woman's body, and about lovemaking. The king found the experience completely new and intriguing, prompting him to return to her repeatedly, driven by his desires and curiosity to explore the complexities of physical pleasure. Over time, he spent more and more nights in her company, often not returning to the palace until after sunrise.

That autumn, they met many times. Each time, he wanted more from the woman. For some time, Bimbisar set aside the plans for battles and the matters of the kingdom. He delegated the administration to his capable ministers, allowing himself to indulge in the pleasures of madira, women and hedonism.

The Rajmata took note of his affair, but she remained unfazed, certain it would not endure. Her son needed an outlet for his sexual urges, and a ganika was safer than a woman who would demand a more rewarding relationship. But she took the precaution of engaging a spy to report on her son's visits. She wanted to keep the affair within manageable boundaries.

A couple of months passed. The Rajmata realized her son's deep involvement with the ganika. Lost in his romantic world, he neglected the affairs of the kingdom. It was then that she resolved to put an end to their affair.

Bimbisar's waywardness ended when the ganika suddenly disappeared from the kingdom. Heartbroken, the young king sent soldiers in search of Kadambini, but to no avail. He had been serious about his love for her and wanted to make her the queen of Magadh, but he never found her.

Then, one day, a minister, who had known about the

dalliance, whispered that the ganika had found a more powerful patron and moved to Avanti. Filled with rage, he swore to find her and kill her with his own hands.

But life carries on, and Bimbisar moved on too. His ministers reminded him that there were urgent matters that required his attention. Love had made him shirk his responsibilities for quite a while. Now, with a vengeance, he was back to focusing on the kingdom, immersing himself completely in matters of the court.

# 7

# The Battle with Anga

Bimbisar believed that an efficient network of spies was as valuable as an army of well-trained soldiers, so among the first things the king did was set up a formidable intelligence system. In just a few years of becoming king, he successfully established a highly efficient intelligence network operating in Anga, Vaishali, Kaushambi, Kashi and Avanti.

The Magadh intelligence network had enlisted many travellers, ganikas and acrobats as spies. A few of them successfully established themselves as traders, whereas others disguised themselves as workers, labourers and beggars. Some spies strategically opened madira shops in various locations across the city. These locations were ideal for gathering information, as people spoke more freely under the influence of liquor, and intoxicated officials and soldiers often unintentionally revealed classified information.

The Magadh intelligence network also had a significant number of women working as ganikas in different parts of the city, and they too provided valuable information.

The Magadh intelligence unit based in Anga's capital, Champa, was highly efficient. Bimbisar received regular intelligence updates on Anga through a spy named Shalambha who ran a large tavern in Champa. Shalambha informed the Magadh king about the festivities that were being planned to celebrate the birth of a son. The birth of the boy, following a string of daughters and many prayers, filled the Anga king with immense joy. To celebrate the birth of his heir, he declared a week of festivities.

The festivities would include drinking, feasting, dancing and singing. The organizers had also scheduled several sports events and competitions. Artists from different parts of the kingdom, including musicians, poets, actors and acrobats, were all brought together. A vibrant atmosphere prevailed in the capital, Champa, as individuals flocked to take part in the festivities and behold the grandeur of the events. Hordes of beggars, monks, dancers and magicians also made their way here. The king's benevolent mood was a great opportunity for everyone to earn some quick money.

❧

Bimbisar issued an ultimatum to his commanders. They had to prepare to set out for Champa in three weeks.

The plans were meticulously drafted and discussed in detail. The attack on Champa would take place while the city was in a stupor after mindless feasting and drinking. Bimbisar devised a plan for a three-pronged attack. He, along with a platoon of approximately one hundred soldiers, would launch an attack on the palace from the left, while his senapati with his platoon would approach from the right. A smaller platoon would infiltrate the palace from the front. The three platoons would converge at the royal palace.

'This will be the decisive battle,' Bimbisar had told his mother while leaving for Anga. 'Either Brahmadatta or I will live to tell the tale.'

'Vijayee bhava!' blessed the Rajmata. Braving her tears, she watched her son going to war with an enemy who had remained invincible till now.

Bimbisar had learned several lessons from his father's battles. His spies had carried out their tasks effectively. They had gathered all the information about the festivities, including the locations of the ceremonies, the Anga king's itinerary, and his complete schedule for the week-long celebrations. Luckily, the spies, along with their trusted men, could complete a tunnel from a temple outside the palace walls to a grove at the rear of the palace garden.

With the most recent updates, Bimbisar began his journey with his army. They moved through the forests towards Champa in small groups. Forewarned, the spies mingled with the groups of revellers, waiting for the Magadh soldiers to arrive. The secret tunnel allowed weapons to be smuggled in small lots into the palace. These were hidden in tree hollows and bushes in the vast palace garden by the Magadh spies who had infiltrated the Anga army.

The week-long festivities started; Champa was in a celebratory mood. People were dancing, singing, eating, drinking and merry-making through the night. The timing was perfect to strike.

With utmost precision, the Magadh Senapati flawlessly executed the plan. Bimbisar advanced with his army and halted in the forest's depth ten miles short of Champa.

As planned, two spies from Magadh met their comrades in the forest at night. They guided the first group of armed soldiers disguised as civilians along a secluded route into Champa. The Magadh soldiers had no problem getting into Champa. They then joined the revellers outside the palace gates, and danced with the crowd while waiting for darkness to descend. When the timing was right, the senapati would command them to mount the assault on the palace.

At sunset, Bimbisar divided his remaining troops into two groups who made their way towards the city. One group approached from the north, while the other took the southern route, guided by spies through secluded areas that led them as close to the palace as they could get. It was difficult to make progress in the darkness. Quietly and stealthily, they followed the spies to reach their designated locations.

Until that moment, everything was proceeding according to plan. The two groups remained concealed in their hideouts, observing people who were enjoying themselves. In the midst of the uninterrupted merrymaking in Champa, the people requested the king's attendance.

In a magnanimous mood, Brahmadatta obliged by emerging from the palace in his royal chariot. He halted in front of the imposing gates and threw gold coins as he passed through the crowds in his majestic chariot, before returning to the palace. The excited crowd cheered thunderously as he passed by.

Hidden away, Bimbisar observed the events unfold in front of him. Despite wanting to rush out of his hiding place and behead the Anga king, he kept his emotions in check. That would be foolhardy. He had to be patient and wait for the right moment. His well-equipped soldiers were eager and ready for the fight. They studied the crowd and made a note of the enemy soldiers posted at various places, and of those deployed to protect the king.

The liquor consumed exceeded all bounds. Before long, the crowd was dancing to booming music that echoed through the entire city. Seeing the citizens in a frenzy, the guards at the gates threw all caution to the winds and grappled with the civilians to claim the coins and join the drinking.

As the clock struck midnight, the merrymaking gradually subsided. Some revellers lay sprawled at the gate, too intoxicated to move. Those who managed to stand, struggled to remain upright. The women were using all their strength to drag their inebriated menfolk back home.

Observing from the sidelines, Bimbisar and his men recognized that the conditions were perfect to mount their attack. It was necessary for them to enter the magnificent palace that loomed before them. Keeping the Magadh troops in check became a formidable task for Bimbisar; they were raring to go. He needed to exercise caution. There was no scope for failing this time. He had firmly resolved to learn a lesson from his father's error. His patience paid off. By that time, the Anga guards were so drunk that they couldn't move even a finger.

Well past midnight, when the spies reported that Champa was as good as dead, Bimbisar gave the signal. The troops attacked the Anga soldiers posted outside the palace gates. The drunk Anga soldiers sprawled on the ground were completely unaware of the presence of the Magadh soldiers.

With determination, Bimbisar and his army pressed forward to the palace, leaving behind a trail of fallen enemy soldiers. The Magadh soldiers overpowered and killed the few guards who fought back. Two Anga guards quickly sprinted towards the palace to alert the king about the impending attack. Their lives were cut short before they could reach their destination.

Bimbisar was completely focused on pursuing his goal. He wanted to capture the king alive. He headed for the royal palace with his group of armed soldiers.

Gaining access to the fort was difficult. Only the most skilled soldiers who refrained from consuming alcohol guarded the palace gates that night. Bimbisar ordered two of his soldiers to approach quietly and eliminate the three guards stationed at the palace entrance. The sentinels were attentive and quickly alerted others when they noticed two armed men moving close to them. All the guards at the gates showed up and successfully encircled the two soldiers that Bimbisar had dispatched. The distraction provided an opportunity for a full-scale attack, but the two Magadh soldiers were in imminent danger.

Bimbisar quickly emerged from hiding with his men, and engaged in a fierce fight with the palace guards. An intense battle followed. Soon, more soldiers from the palace joined the ongoing fight. Just then, the second group of Magadh soldiers from the south joined the battle. The conflict was intense, with both sides evenly matched. There were many casualties on both sides.

In an unexpected turn of events, Bimbisar started gaining the upper hand. Relief overwhelmed him as he observed his troops, who had successfully infiltrated the palace through the tunnel, launching a sudden assault on the guards from the rear. The element of surprise in the two-pronged assault resulted in panic among the palace guards. Bimbisar halted their progress, while the Magadh soldiers stationed behind them hindered any possibility of retreat. The attackers swiftly overpowered the guards. Most of the palace guards were killed; only a handful were able to escape.

Once the troops had made their initial entry, they encountered almost no resistance. The passageways of the palace were illuminated by the dancing flames of mashaals. There were no guards in sight. They had all been killed or had fled the palace. Bimbisar had no difficulty finding his way. Moving with swift, determined strides, he led a dozen soldiers towards the royal chamber. There was an eerie calm in the palace, disturbed only by the hurried footsteps of soldiers.

The Magadh soldiers took the two soldiers guarding the king's chamber by surprise. The Anga guards couldn't withstand the might of Bimbisar and his army. Bimbisar and his troops executed them before they could even reach for their weapons. Finally, Bimbisar arrived at the royal chamber.

# 8

# A Victory and a Curse

Bimbisar burst into the king's chamber, his sword still dripping with blood. Drunk from the wild festivities, a naked Brahmadatta lay snoring, his arms draped protectively around Queen Vipasha Devi.

'Get up, you coward,' the Magadh king prodded him with the tip of his sword.

In an instant, the Anga king and his queen were wide awake. Seeking to hide his embarrassment, Brahmadatta said sarcastically, 'You are a coward, Bimbisar, to steal into my bedchamber like a common thief. Even thieves have ethics. Brave warriors face their adversaries on battlegrounds, and not steal into palaces in the dead of night. Your father was a coward and so are you.'

Filled with anger upon hearing his father's name, Bimbisar roared like an injured tiger and forcefully thrust the sword into Brahmadatta's right arm. Knowing that the Anga king was left-handed, he wanted to ensure that he had a fair opportunity to defend himself. Vipasha Devi let out a loud scream and rolled nervously to one side of the bed.

'You talk of cowardice,' roared the Magadh king. 'You, who defeated my father by deceit?'

'I gave him a fair chance to defend himself.' Brahmadatta let out a painful groan and clutched his wounded arm. He felt helpless and vulnerable in his naked state. It was humiliating. 'Let me get dressed, and then we can engage in combat.'

Bimbisar used the tip of his sword to pick up Brahmadatta's

antariya and hurled it at the king. 'Wear this and fight,' he ordered.

'Please spare our lives,' begged the queen. 'You can't kill an unarmed man and woman. Our son will be orphaned if you kill us.'

'Don't beg for your life, Vipasha,' ordered the Anga king. He concealed his nervousness with a cunning grin. His shrewd mind devised escape plans while he tried to buy time. 'A king will not stoop to disgrace himself by killing an unarmed person. As for you, queen, it is hardly likely that he will kill a woman.'

The challenge in Brahmadatta's words was unmistakable.

'You did not give my father a fair chance, but I'll give you an opportunity to defend yourself,' Bimbisar snarled. He grabbed the jewel-encrusted sword from the edge of the bed and threw it at Brahmadatta, taunting the king. 'Let's see how you handle this challenge.'

Without hesitation, he leapt away from the bed and took a stance, patiently waiting for what was to come. Faced with a challenge, the Anga king drew his sword and skilfully defended himself against Bimbisar's vigorous attacks. Brahmadatta's hedonistic lifestyle had left him with little desire to engage in a sword fight against his youthful and vigorous adversary. With blood streaming from his wound, he bravely charged at Bimbisar, fuelled by a mix of desperation and intoxicated resolve. Bimbisar swiftly sidestepped, letting out a mocking laugh. Filled with anger, the Anga king charged once more at the young opponent, but this time, the opponent employed a different strategy. He ducked and the sharp blade intended for his chest ended up slashing the air. More than his inability to wound the young king, it was his laughter and mirth that infuriated the older man.

Bimbisar was thoroughly relishing every moment of this duel. He intended to tire out his opponent by employing skilled lunges and feints. Bhattiya had spent long hours training his son, who learnt to fend off his father's moves with remarkable dexterity. Even as a child, Bimbisar amazed his father with his ability to shift his weight onto the balls of his feet, granting him the advantage of swift lateral movement. He cleverly used that to gain advantage over his opponent.

'When confronting Brahmadatta, avoid using horizontal middle strikes. His strength lies in those strikes. You should resort to low horizontal attack by swinging the sword from below and aiming towards his arms, or by using diagonal rising cuts directed to the right leg. A man is most vulnerable when angry. No matter what the provocation, try to remain calm.' Bhattiya's words echoed in Bimbisar's ears.

His father's instructions always had the desired effect. Bimbisar had won many battles using the tactics taught by Bhattiya.

Swords clashed in the dim light of the chamber, their steely sound striking deadly fear in the queen's bosom. The adversaries circled each other like puppets in a macabre dance, their eyes alert to movement. Bimbisar, full of youth and agility, taunted and dared the Anga king, keeping his eyes fixed on his adversary. He sprang, pirouetted, and crouched like an expert warrior, his movements orchestrated in a strange symphony. Unpredictable and swift, Bimbisar's intricate manoeuvres heightened Brahmadatta's agitation.

The noise outside kept getting louder as the Magadh soldiers captured the fleeing Anga guards.

Suddenly, Bimbisar's sword flashed like lightning. There was a crack and Brahmadatta's weapon flew from his hands. Gripping his injured hand, the Anga king moaned in pain and dropped to his knees. Bimbisar's sword struck the fallen man's neck with precision, leaving the queen in shock. 'Spare his life, Maharaj,' she cried as he made a move to slash the neck of her husband. 'I promise we will go away from this kingdom.'

Brahmadatta, the Anga king, knelt humbly before Bimbisar, the young king of Magadh, pleading for mercy. Abandoning his arrogance, with folded his hands he whimpered, 'Spare my life, Bimbisar. Take this kingdom, take my crown and my riches. I'll leave Anga forever.' Fear shone in his eyes as they darted from side to side, desperate to find an exit. There was none. His attacker stood in front of him like an impregnable wall.

Bimbisar hesitated briefly, closing his eyes for a fleeting moment. Then the moment of hesitation passed. He was reminded of his father's suffering. The Anga king didn't spare him any mercy.

There was no hesitation in Bimbisar's action when he opened his eyes. With a single swift stroke of the sword, he severed Brahmadatta's neck. His body fell on the floor. The cloth hastily wrapped around his waist came undone; he ended up in a humiliating heap on the ground. Within minutes, the unequal combat was over.

With a loud wail, the queen rushed to her husband's side. Overcome with sorrow, she cradled his lifeless body in her arms. With eyes blazing, she turned to the king of Magadh. Her shrill curse pierced the stillness of the night, echoing ominously in the air. 'You have killed my husband is an utterly shameful manner. I curse you with a death brought upon by your own son in an equally shameful manner. Each king of your dynasty will die a horrible death at the hands of his own son. My curse will hound you and the Haryanka Dynasty forever.'

Feeling a chill run down his spine, Bimbisar rushed out of the royal chamber, the curse ringing in his ears. The words of the Anga queen clung to him, defying all his attempts to shake them off.

# 9

# A Journey to Kashi

The wind whispered joyous tidings. The Rajmata lent willing ears to the tidings. Pride filled her eyes as she gazed into the distance from the terrace of her grand palace. Whenever she laid eyes on the white banner with the magnificent garuda, flying over every building as far as she could see, her heart would race with excitement. It was not a mean achievement, nor had it come easy. Countless lives were lost, and many hardships endured, before the Magadh flag finally found its rightful place. The son worked tirelessly and faced many challenges to achieve success. Her husband would have been proud to see Bimbisar ruling over the mighty kingdom with a sagacity well beyond his years.

It is time he was married, she thought, as she shortlisted eligible princesses from neighbouring kingdoms. In her list were the princesses of Kosala, Vaishali and Avanti. She had heard many stories about the beauty of Kosala Devi, Chellana and Vasavadatta, and she wanted one of them to grace the throne by her son's side. There was a time when she would have found it overly ambitious to imagine establishing an alliance with influential kingdoms, but that was no longer the case. Her son had successfully conquered multiple small kingdoms and expanded the Magadh Empire to a size much larger than her husband's insignificant kingdom. The very name of her son was enough to strike terror in the hearts of rebels.

Swiftly and silently, time had flown like birds in a tempest. Bimbisar had been too busy, too long, consolidating and extending his empire to think of marriage. The Rajmata knew how important it was for a king to have capable sons to ensure the continuity of the royal lineage. A king needed at least one heir, if not more. The greater the number of sons, the higher the likelihood of a dynasty's survival. Her husband had started the Haryanka Dynasty and Bimbisar was taking it to lofty heights. She felt a strong desire to hold a grandson before she passed on, else her soul would not find peace. She wanted Bimbisar to give in to her request quickly, but to accomplish that, she needed to find a suitable bride for him. She refused to accept just any woman; she wanted only the most stunning princess from a mighty kingdom.

She had been the backbone of the palace for a long time, but now she desired to step back from the overwhelming responsibilities of the far-flung empire. However, her priority was to fulfil her vow to visit Kashi. Two years ago, when her son had gone to war against the Anga king, she had vowed to offer prayers in Kashi on her son's return. The Rajmata decided to discuss the matter with her son. She wanted him to accompany her on the journey to the holy town.

Overseeing her son's dinner that evening, the Rajmata brought up the matter. 'Son, I want you to escort me to Kashi,' she said as she placed a bowl of his favourite dessert—kheer—in front of him. She decided to cook the dish for him herself because she believed that no one else could make it as deliciously and precisely as he preferred—with the ideal aroma and flavour.

Bimbisar knew she prepared kheer whenever she wanted to get him in a mellow mood before broaching an important subject. It was a clever, time-tested ploy.

'Why the sudden decision to travel to Kashi?'

'Don't counter my statement with a question,' warned the mother. 'You will come with me. And that is not a request.'

Bimbisar's eyes crinkled with mirth, and he smiled indulgently. 'All I want to know is the reason for your sudden decision.'

'Although I don't offer explanations for my decisions, I'll make an exception this one time. Son, it has been a few years since your father died, and I want to organize a special havan in his memory. That is not the only reason. I had vowed to feed five hundred brahmins at Kashi if you returned victorious after the battle of Anga,' said the Rajmata as she ladled some more kheer on his platter. 'Do you need any more explanations?'

'That is fine, mother. I'll make all arrangements for your journey, but it will not be possible for me to accompany you. There are several crucial matters that need my immediate attention.'

'The havan can't be conducted without the presence of a son. All other matters can wait until we return. There is no dearth of capable ministers who can take care of those crucial matters, as you refer to them. The visit to Kashi is of utmost importance.'

Bimbisar was conscious of her unyielding demeanour. Once she decided on something, the Rajmata was not likely to give up; the one virtue missing in her arsenal was patience. She didn't believe in mincing words when it came to her demands. Knowing his soft spot for her, she tactfully used it to her advantage.

'Is it possible to postpone the journey by a month, at least?' He tried to buy himself some time.

The Rajmata directed a scathing look at her son. It conveyed her response far more effectively than words. Bimbisar smiled and raised his hands in surrender. He could deny her nothing.

'It shall be as you desire. But a certain amount of delay is unavoidable. We can't travel to another kingdom without informing the ruler. I'll send word to the Kosala king and wait for his reply before we set out on the journey.'

'Do you think I'm not aware of the protocol? I have been

a queen longer than the number of years you have spent on this planet. Send the fastest rider with a message to Prasenajit immediately,' the Rajmata snapped back. 'This is the month of Bhadrapada and the rivers are in spate because of the monsoon, which makes it impossible to go by boat. It will be Ashwin by the time we receive Prasenajit's reply—a perfect time to visit Kashi.' As always, the Rajmata was quick to come up with solutions. 'That will give you time to resolve the crucial matters which need your attention.'

The message from the Magadh king reached Prasenajit while he was conducting a gathering of ministers in his court at Shravasti, the capital of Kosala. The Kosala minister carefully opened the luxurious silk scroll adorned with the golden crest of Magadh. The message, written in beautiful calligraphy, was sent by Bimbisar. The mahamantri read out the message to the Kosala king.

'The King of Magadh is writing to inform Your Majesty that his mother wishes to visit Kashi. She plans to perform a special havan for the peace of her husband's soul. The king will accompany the Rajmata. He conveys his greetings, and he also hopes to meet you.'

A soft murmur followed the reading. Prasenajit contemplated the issue a moment before turning to his mahamantri, 'What protocol would you recommend we adhere to?'

'Maharaj, Magadh has come a long way since the days of Bhattiya. Bimbisar has conquered many kingdoms, including Anga, since he came to power. This has led to prosperity in his subjects. It has also created a sense of unease in many kingdoms, like Avanti and Vaishali. The Lichchavis, who once attacked Magadh with impunity, now live in fear of an attack from Bimbisar.'

'That is true, Maharaj,' Senapati Nagasena stood up and

bowed to the king. 'Our spies have brought news of Magadh's preparations to attack Vaishali. Bimbisar has invested a lot of resources and effort into expanding his military might, and that is at the core of Magadh's victories. Due to his large army, he is now addressed as Seniya Bimbisar.'

'So, what do you think would be an appropriate approach?' Prasenajit looked at his mahamantri.

The mahamantri's opinion caused visible concern among the ministers. 'With due respect, Maharaj, it will be wise to extend a hand in friendship to the mighty Magadh king. Having him in our camp will benefit both kingdoms.'

'That is true. A powerful ally is worth more than a dozen weak ones,' quoted the rajpurohit.

'So be it,' said Prasenajit. 'Send a message of welcome to the Magadh king. Tell Bimbisar we will host him in our palace in Kashi.'

It was a beautiful Ashwin morning when the exhausted Kosala messenger reached Rajgriha, bearing with him a message for the Magadh king.

Minutes later, Bimbisar burst into the Rajmata's chamber. The Rajmata, accompanied by her loyal maids, was engrossed in preparations for the puja that would mark the end of her Ekadashi fast. Since Bhattiya passed away, the Rajmata had begun fasting on a multitude of occasions. The caring son had repeatedly cautioned her about the grave outcomes of fasting excessively, but his words had fallen on deaf ears.

'Don't tell me you are fasting again,' he chided, disturbed by her pale face. Her skeletal frame gave her a gaunt appearance, making her clothes hang loosely. Taking her hands in his, he led her to the low bed in the centre of the chamber and asked, 'Pray, which are the days when you don't fast? At this rate, you will soon be bedridden.'

'Don't fret about my fasts, son,' the Rajmata smiled fondly at Bimbisar. 'You have enough to worry about. I'll not die without holding my grandson.'

'King Prasenajit extends a warm welcome to Kashi. He also requests that we grace his palace during our Kashi visit. I have already made arrangements for our stay, but we could accept the Kosala king's offer.'

'That is how it should be. We will accept his kind invitation, of course. It is time for us to embark on the journey.'

'I have made all preparations in advance. We will set out in two days.'

Dawn was breaking when the Magadh Rajmata, along with her son and entourage, sailed for Kashi in a dozen beautifully adorned and adequately equipped boats.

At Shravasti, the Kosala king paced his chamber in agitation, his mind troubled with thoughts of his beloved sister, Kosala Devi.

'There can be no better way to extend our friendship,' remarked Queen Mallika, as she lolled among the silk cushions on a low divan. 'Kosala Devi should have been married a long time ago. In your search for a perfect husband, you have delayed her marriage too long. Let me assure you, you will not find a better man than the Magadh king. Bimbisar will make a perfect match for your sister.'

'You say that because you are not her mother,' retorted Prasenajit. He was aware of Mallika's astute grasp over state affairs, but he had no intention of yielding so easily. 'I am in no hurry to get her married.'

'I may not be her mother, but I love her as much as you do. If I suggest this alliance, it is because we must grab every opportunity for the sake of the kingdom. Did you not teach me that kingdom comes before self—always and each time? I was a humble gardener's daughter, but you made me your queen and taught me everything about politics. Whatever I suggest now is the result of those lessons. Oh King, everyone knows how fond you are of her, but every princess must get married one day. I assure you, this alliance will strengthen us, and we will face no threats from Bimbisar. He is an ambitious person and soon his eyes will fall on our lands. Who knows what may happen then?' she glanced craftily at her husband.

Prasenajit had lost his appetite for battles and skirmishes; no one knew it better than her. Quick to believe in charlatans and prophesies, he was no longer confident of a victory in a battle.

There was no place for bloodshed in his hedonistic life. Liquor and women were all he desired.

Her words found their mark. He stood staring thoughtfully out of the window overlooking the palace garden where his sister was walking with her maids. The sight of her radiant face pulled at his heartstrings.

As always, Mallika was confident that he would concede to her suggestion. He always did.

'Let me think about it,' he said, turning around to face her.

'Well, we better hurry with the decision. It might be a good idea to invite the Rajmata and her son to Shravasti.' Once again, she looked archly at Prasenajit. 'Besides, Bimbisar is not yet married, so Kosala Devi will be his chief queen.'

'It would be good to know Kosala Devi's mind before we do anything.'

'My lord, she is young and shy.' Mallika got up and joined her husband at the window. 'Do you think she will share her thoughts with you?'

'In that case, you must speak to her. Since she is close to you, you can ask her about her thoughts on the matter. Honestly, I can't think of anyone more suitable for the task.'

'I'll try, but I don't think a princess's desires carry much weight in marriage alliances. They are married off for political advantages, never for love. Is it not expected of them to put the kingdom's welfare above their own?'

'That is true, my queen, but I'll not sacrifice my sister's happiness for the kingdom's welfare. I married for love and will allow her to do so, too. Don't you remember how we met?' Prasenajit's eyes lit up as he recalled his first encounter with Mallika.

She was a lovely and innocent sixteen-year-old daughter of the royal gardener. One beautiful, clear day, she packed a lunch of rice gruel and set out for the flower garden to join her friends. As she made her way to the garden, she encountered the Buddha and a group of monks collecting alms from people passing through. Enchanted by the tranquillity the Buddha exuded, she humbly presented him with her modest meal and prostrated herself in reverence at his feet. A wave of joy inundated her when the Buddha graciously accepted the gruel and smiled. Ananda, who accompanied the Buddha, was aware that there had to be a reason for the lord's smile and was eager to discover it.

Ananda remarked, 'I perceive a meaning to your smile, my lord.'

The Buddha replied, 'You are right, Ananda. This humble girl will become the queen of Kosala this very day.'

That seemed impossible as Mallika was of low caste and it was unlikely that King Prasenajit would choose a girl of low caste as his queen.

On his way back from a battle he had lost, the delightful singing in the flower garden caught the king's attention. Captivated by the melodious singing, he ventured into the garden, where he discovered a stunning girl gracefully dancing and singing in utmost delight amidst the vibrant flowers. Prasenajit instantly fell in love with her. Dismounting from his horse, he asked her if she was married. When Mallika replied she wasn't, he decided to make her his queen. He gently placed her on his horse and brought her back to her parents' house and expressed his wish to marry her.

In the evening, he sent an entourage to fetch her to the palace and made her his queen.

The entire capital was lavishly decorated and Prasenajit hosted the finest of feasts. Mallika came to be known as 'the flower girl queen'. The story of their love and marriage continued to be told in Kosala and beyond. Mallika turned into a devout follower of the Buddha and goaded the king to become one, too.

As time passed, Prasenajit married thrice, but his affection for Mallika persisted. She was wise and honest, and he trusted her judgement.

As he watched her leave his chamber, his brows furrowed, and he was certain that she would not fail him.

In her private quarters, Queen Mallika remembered her fateful encounter with Prasenajit.

*I'll find out if Kosala is in love with someone, and conduct her marriage with that person, no matter which caste or class he comes from. The king is right. Love is all that matters.* Queen Mallika's mind was made up. She got up and went in search of the princess.

# 10

# Kashi

A grand welcome awaited the Rajmata and Bimbisar when they reached the Dashashwamedh Ghat in Kashi. The ghat near the Vishwanath Temple wore a festive look. Pillars festooned with flowers and leaves stood on both sides of the ghat steps, which were strewn with fragrant flowers. Musicians seated near the steps played joyful ragas on the veena, the melody adding to the cheerful atmosphere.

The Magadh king stepped down from the royal barge and helped his mother disembark. The clear sky stretched out above, while the sun beamed down with a radiant smile. A few dasis stood nearby with decorated umbrellas to shield them from the elements. A group of women honoured the Rajmata and Bimbisar with garlands and performed the customary welcome by applying vermilion and sandalwood paste on their foreheads.

King Prasenajit had spared no effort or expense to welcome them. He had dispatched several high-ranking ministers to greet the Magadh ruler and his mother. They greeted the visitors with folded hands and guided them towards the beautifully adorned chariots that were ready to take them to the Kashi palace. The Rajmata's face glowed with pride as they headed towards the majestic palace. Never had she dreamt that the mighty Kosala king would one day receive them in such grand style. If only her husband were alive to witness this day, she thought. He had long believed that he was a small and unimportant ruler of a tiny kingdom, despised by the mighty kings of Jambudweepa. She cast a sidelong glance at her handsome son; he seemed to take it all in his stride. *He deserves it all, and more*, mused the proud mother.

The Kashi palace turned out to be far more magnificent than what Bimbisar or his mother had expected. Ornate and imposing, it was a triple-storeyed wooden structure with sunlit verandas, jharokas and balconies that overlooked the Ganga River. The walls were decorated with exquisite paintings depicting scenes from the Ramayana, as well as frescoes of Krishna and Radha. Enormous pillars sculpted with flowers, vines and peacocks supported the roof of the sprawling main hall on the ground floor.

The black marble floor in the hall was polished to a shine, creating a mirror-like effect that reflected the breathtaking interiors. The gilded roof was supported by 108 wooden pillars exquisitely carved with intricate floral patterns and exotic birds.

The passages leading to the opulently furnished chambers on the first floor, where the Rajmata and Bimbisar would stay, were adorned with polished brass urns filled with fragrant flowers. The palace was decorated in a way that harmoniously melded aesthetics with luxury.

After a sumptuous meal, the royal guests from Magadh retired to their chambers to rest. It was dusk when the Rajmata summoned her son and expressed a desire to walk along the riverside.

'This is the best time of the day,' she breathed deep, taking in the vibrant colours of sunset. 'Soon, the temple bells will begin ringing and the air will echo the verses chanted by priests as they perform the evening aarti. Can you imagine the beauty of hundreds of diyas afloat in the river as people pray on the ghats?'

'I can imagine.' Bimbisar's eyes crinkled with mirth at his mother's romantic description. He gazed at his mother, who, even at fifty, possessed a flawless complexion. She appeared ethereal in the gentian blue twilight. If only his father had lived for some more time. He knew how much his parents had loved each other.

'You will come with me, of course.'

'I...'

'I'll not listen to your excuses. You are currently on holiday. Seize this opportunity to break free from the tiresome routine of managing a kingdom. Just unwind,' the Rajmata said. 'We will not take the bodyguards along. I want a quiet stroll to enjoy the magical evening. I don't want you to carry your sword either.'

'It would be unwise to go without the bodyguards. Walking around without my sword would be foolish. What if any unfortunate incident were to take place?'

'Do you really believe, my dear son, that I'm foolish?' the Rajmata laughed. 'We will shed our royal attire and assume the appearance of common folk. The town is full of pilgrims, and we will easily blend in.'

Dressed in ordinary garments, the Rajmata and her son slipped past the guards and left the palace a few minutes later. Hidden in Bimbisar's garments was a sickle that had been custom-made. Though compact, it had the potential to cause significant damage. He was ready to face any unforeseen danger that came his way.

The stroll by the river was just as delightful as his mother had promised. Bimbisar enjoyed her observations as they walked past the temples, which were now filled with the sounds of chanting and prayers. The sweet music of kirtan reached their ears, leading them to a small temple in a secluded location.

They felt rejuvenated and full of energy as they headed back to the palace after their walk. As they reached the palace, they heard the sound of horse hooves and saw a chariot coming to a halt at the entrance.

King Prasenajit stepped down from the chariot and walked towards them with a puzzled expression on his face.

It was his old charioteer, who often visited relatives in Magadh—he recognized Bimbisar and apprised the Kosala king. It took a fraction of a moment for King Prasenajit to recover his wits and then he approached Bimbisar with folded hands.

'Greetings, Magadh Naresh,' he said, his face breaking into a broad smile. His sudden presence caught the Rajmata off guard She stopped. Her eyes widened, and she raised her eyebrows.

'Pranam, Rajmata!' his eyes twinkled with mirth as he greeted Hemavati. He seemed amused by the effect caused by his sudden arrival.

She folded her hands and beamed at the king. 'Ayushman Bhava.'

'Pranam, Kosala Naresh.' Bimbisar responded warmly as he strode towards his host with folded hands. 'We were not expecting you. No one told us you were arriving in Kashi,' he added.

'That is because no one knew of my plans. In fact, it was a sudden decision. To be honest, I didn't expect you to be in disguise. I hope the arrangements are satisfactory and you are comfortable.'

'Thank you for the invitation to stay at the palace. We are very comfortable.' It was the Rajmata who responded. 'You really should not have taken the trouble to come all the way from Shravasti.'

As they were walking towards the hall, another carriage halted at the entrance. They turned to see a couple of women alighting from it.

'I'm not the only one who wished to meet you,' said the Kosala king. 'Queen Mallika Devi is a perfectionist. She does not have faith in any of the ministers or dasis where royal guests are concerned. Mallika has been fretting about the arrangements ever since she heard of your visit to the holy city, and insists on supervising the arrangements to ensure you are comfortable.'

The two women, followed by their dasis, walked towards the Rajmata and folded their hands in greeting.

'Pranam, Rajmata,' said Queen Mallika Devi. 'I expected the king to have already influenced your opinion of me.' Her beautiful eyes twinkled with mischief as she looked at her husband.

'Putravati Bhava,' responded the Rajmata, placing her hand on the queen's head. 'I had heard enough stories about your beauty, but you are more beautiful than the descriptions.'

'You flatter me, Rajmata. The tales of your wisdom and kindness have held me in awe of you.'

'Now I see why the Kosala king is so taken by you. Not only are you beautiful, you have a way with words.'

'This is my sister-in-law, Kosala Devi,' said Queen Mallika, pulling the girl who was hiding behind. A faint blush slowly spread across the young princess's cheeks as she folded her hands. 'She wanted to pray at the Vishwanath Temple, so I took her with me.'

'You did the right thing.' The Rajmata held Kosala Devi's chin and tilted her face upwards. 'You are more beautiful than I had imagined,' she said. Removing her kanthahaar, she fastened it around the young woman's slender neck. 'This looks so much better on you.'

The Rajmata's sharp eyes didn't miss the expression on her son's face. Bimbisar couldn't tear his eyes away from the stunning princess. Busy with his battles and administrative reforms, it had been some time since he had been with a woman. The sight of the princess with her graceful neck bent under the weight of shyness, its smooth milky white expanse dotted with a dark mole at the nape, stirred some deep-seated emotion in him.

Bimbisar's interest in the princess didn't escape Queen Mallika's notice either. She quickly glanced at King Prasenajit from the corner of her eye, but he was too busy speaking to Bimbisar, so he failed to notice her subtle gesture.

*Kosala Devi will make a perfect wife for Bimbisar*, mused the Rajmata. *She is the woman I want for him. Exquisite, gentle and refined.* She wondered whether to bring up the topic or await a sign from the Kosala royals, which she imagined would come sooner or later. King Prasenajit, his queen, and the princess must have had a good reason to travel all the way to Kashi. The Rajmata was too smart to be fooled by the feeble excuses given by the Kosala king. Regardless, she was thrilled that things were going well.

Both the Rajmata and Bimbisar recognized King Prasenajit's enthusiasm to strengthen ties between Magadh and Kosala. Bimbisar was equally determined to contribute to this effort. It was an unexpected delight to encounter the enchanting princess. He resolved to develop a friendly relationship with her.

During dinner, King Prasenajit discussed his plans for the next two days. Temple visits, picnics, hunting trips, and more. 'I'll make sure your schedule is filled with exciting activities,' he declared.

'You've gone through the trouble of planning so many things, but my age limits me. I'm sorry, but I must excuse myself,' the Rajmata said. 'While you enjoy your adventures and hunting trips, I intend to visit the temples.'

'You will not be alone, Rajmata. I'll accompany you to the temples.' The princess raised her eyes and smiled shyly.

'Oh no, I would not dream of depriving you of the exciting adventures.' The Rajmata took Kosala Devi's hands in her own. 'I have done it all. Now it is your turn to enjoy life.'

'I plan on savouring every moment of this much-needed respite from the chaotic affairs of the kingdom,' remarked Bimbisar, exchanging a significant glance with the princess. He hoped she would not stay behind with his mother. 'I have heard that the forests near Kashi offer fantastic hunting opportunities.'

'That is true.' King Prasenajit took a sip of the fragrant sura from his cup. 'Would you like to set out for the hunt at dawn tomorrow?'

'Not tomorrow,' the Rajmata intervened before her son could respond. 'Let's defer the plan for the day after.'

She noticed Bimbisar's raised eyebrow and clarified, 'I plan to have a special havan at the Vishawanath Temple tomorrow, and Bimbisar's presence is necessary. You are free to make plans for the evening, of course.'

'There is no hurry, Rajmata,' Queen Mallika reassured her. 'You have come here with a purpose, and we would not dream of imposing our plans on you. Hunts and other activities can wait.'

After dinner, the Rajmata retired to her chamber, while the others made their way to the hall for an entertainment programme featuring dancers and musicians.

At midnight, Bimbisar decided to turn in, claiming fatigue from a tiring day. Soon, everyone retired to their chambers. Alone in his chamber, the Magadh king tossed and turned restlessly on the bed. No matter what he did, he couldn't shake off the memory of the Kosala princess. He got up and walked towards the window, which had a beautiful view of the garden. The silk curtains fluttered gracefully in the refreshing, fragrant river breeze. Parting them, he leaned over and stared at the garden that appeared almost magical in the silvery light of the moon.

The garden was a stunning canvas of flowers, fountains, pavilions and ponds. Bathed in moonlight, the marble sculptures glowed with an ethereal beauty, as if they had been infused with life. A deep yearning for Kosala Devi's companionship took hold of the king. He had felt a similar longing only for a woman named Kadambini a few years ago.

Suddenly, he noticed a woman sitting on a marble bench by the pavilion in the garden. At first sight, she seemed like a mythical being who had gracefully descended into this world. Bimbisar wondered if his eyes were playing tricks on him. Did his imagination bring to life the woman who had been on his mind since they first met?

It was Princess Kosala Devi.

In a trice, he hurried down to the garden and trod softly towards the lady, unwilling to break the spell. Her eyes shut, she sat immobile. Mesmerized, he observed the lady. She looked fresh, soft and bewitching, as though a skilled artisan had meticulously sculpted her flawless features. The glossy black hair cascading down her back shimmered like a lake in the moonlight. A mischievous strand of hair danced freely on her forehead. Bimbisar felt an overwhelming urge to restore it to its rightful place. Abruptly, her eyes opened as if she had sensed his presence. Immediately she leapt up, like a startled deer.

'Don't be frightened, Kosala,' he said to her soothingly. 'I couldn't sleep, so I came down for a stroll in the garden. May I sit next to you?'

She nodded silently and lowered her head. After a moment, she stole a quick look at him, her eyelashes creating a gentle shade over her eyes.

'Let me not drive you away from this beautiful garden. Won't you sit down and speak to me for a few minutes?'

Kosala Devi sat nervously at one end of the bench. He smiled and remarked, 'You can relax. I'll not bite you.'

They remained quiet for a couple of minutes before he broke the silence. 'Kashi has captivated me. If it were not for my responsibilities, I would have preferred to remain here permanently.'

A hint of a smile played on her lips, and her fingers toyed with the fringe of her odhni.

'Do you play the veena?' he asked.

The question seemed to catch her off guard. She responded by nodding slowly. 'Your fingers gave you away,' he added. 'They are long and shapely, like those of an artist.'

He waited for a comment, but she remained silent. 'Are you observing a vow of silence, or is there a specific reason why you are not speaking to me? Are you frightened of me?'

His words prompted a reaction from her. Raising her head, she met his gaze and smiled. Her eyes shimmered like two sparkling gemstones. They tantalized him. Speaking in a gentle voice, she reassured him, 'I'm not afraid.'

Pausing for a moment, she sighed and said, 'This garden is where I feel most at peace.'

'There is no doubt it is a stunning sight. I am thinking of kidnapping your gardener to the Magadh palace so he can create a garden like this there too.'

At his words, Kosala Devi burst into laughter. 'In that case, you will have to kidnap me because I am the landscaper and architect of this garden.'

He chuckled and said, 'That would be even better. I'll lock you up forever so you could create a paradise in Magadh.'

Suddenly, the uneasiness disappeared, and she became relaxed with the man sitting beside her. Time flew by. He realized they had been sitting in the garden for a long time when she shivered because of the growing chill and wrapped her arms around herself.

'I should not hold you up any longer,' he said, helping her to her feet. 'We both have a busy day ahead of us tomorrow.'

Leaving her at the door of her bedchamber, he walked towards his own, feeling light and joyful.

The two days at Kashi passed swiftly as the Magadh king and the Rajmata performed havans, offered pujas, attended entertainment programmes, experienced moonlit boating, and enjoyed lavish feasts. There were musical soirées and hunting expeditions.

The hosts made sure their guests were comfortable. The Rajmata and Queen Mallika schemed to bring Bimbisar and Kosala together. After having an extremely pleasurable time, it was time for the royals to depart and return to their respective capitals.

The Rajmata expressed gratitude to the hosts after dinner. 'Like all good things, this visit will end tomorrow.' Folding her hands, she continued, 'I'm thankful to you for making our visit memorable. I'll not forget your generosity.'

'You should give us an opportunity to return the favour by visiting Magadh,' Bimbisar added.

'We are grateful for the opportunity to host you,' King Prasenajit joined his hands together. 'Please extend your stay by a few days and allow us the pleasure of hosting you in Shravasti.'

'Rajmata, I join my husband in requesting your benign presence at our capital,' Queen Mallika appealed. 'I am confident you will not decline our invitation.'

'I wish it was possible,' Rajmata let out a sigh. For the past two days, she had patiently waited for King Prasenajit and Queen Mallika to discuss Kosala Devi's marriage. She wondered whether it would be a good idea to agree to visit Shravasti. It would provide an opportunity to discuss a potential marriage alliance between the two kingdoms. 'I have no hesitation in extending my visit, but my son is a busy man.' She looked meaningfully at Bimbisar and waited for a cue from him.

She was aware of the increasing fondness between her son and the princess. Love and duty seemed to pull him in different directions.

'Rajmata, my brother and I would be honoured if you would allow us to host you in the capital of Kosala,' the princess requested in a respectful voice. Her beautiful eyes looked hopefully at the Rajmata. 'Having come so close to Shravasti, please do not go back without visiting the Kosala capital. I request the Magadh Samrat to spare a few more days for us.'

Neither the Rajmata nor Bimbisar could say no to her request. The Rajmata touched the princess's shoulder and replied, 'How can I refuse you, my dear?'

As the princess's eyes met Bimbisar's, a faint blush spread across her face.

'Well, it is impossible for me to decline an invitation that the Rajmata has accepted. It will be a pleasure to visit the Kosala capital.'

Everyone was pleased with the outcome.

Queen Mallika was pleased with Bimbisar agreeing to visit Shravasti. She had considered bringing up the matrimonial alliance with the Rajmata that evening, but now she could postpone it until they arrived in Shravasti. It would provide her with a greater opportunity to talk to the princess. The past two days had been too busy to take up the topic. She was curious about how Bimbisar would react to marrying Kosala Devi. Observing their interactions, she was convinced of the young king's interest in the princess.

The Rajmata, who gave her approval to the princess, was pleased to see her son besotted with the young woman. She knew he would say yes to a marriage proposal.

King Prasenajit was happy about the prospect of impressing the king of Magadh with his extravagant palace in Shravasti. He was sure his ministers would appreciate the friendly bond between the two rulers. It would also give him the opportunity to propose a marriage alliance between them.

As for Bimbisar, he was happy to spend more time with the princess, getting to know her better.

Kosala Devi found it difficult to understand her developing fondness for the young king. The hours spent with him were some of the most beautiful ones she had ever spent with a man.

# 11

# A Royal Wedding

With its polished wood construction, columns and ornate carvings, the royal palace in Shravasti stood out as an impressive four-storeyed structure. The lower levels were slightly larger, resulting in a visually impressive effect.

They entered the palace through one of the grand gateways and rode past serene gardens, pavilions and ponds filled with graceful swans and ducks swimming peacefully among pink and white lotus flowers in bloom. Peacocks displayed their magnificence while deer moved fearlessly and swiftly. Colourful parrots and other brightly plumed birds found their perch on the fruit trees.

Surrounding the grand entrance hall was a gallery, its columns embellished with intricate carvings. The hall was beautifully decorated with carefully placed brass figurines, vases filled with flowers and embellished with jewels, and stunning artefacts.

The palace was more magnificent than anyone, including the Magadh king and his mother, could have imagined. It was not surprising, given that the Kosala kingdom had an extraordinary succession of kings dating back to the Treta Yug, including those from the Ikshvaku Dynasty. According to legend, King Prasenajit hailed from the same lineage. One of the most powerful kings in Jambudweepa, he controlled a vast kingdom filled with immense riches. In contrast, the Haryanka Dynasty, of which Bimbisar was a part, was only a generation old and had much ground to cover before rivalling Kosala. The young king was determined to surpass the beauty of Kosala and make his kingdom exceptional.

*That day is not far away*, the Magadh king mused. *I'll reach there sooner than expected. All I have to do is to conquer the Vajji and Malla kingdoms. Perhaps Kashi too. It is a city rich in revenues.* He had an insatiable ambition and unwavering confidence in his abilities.

Inspired by King Prasenajit's magnificent palace, Bimbisar decided to include some grand elements in his palace. Although the ambitious project of constructing a new capital was finished, there was still a significant amount of work remaining to enhance the palace's aesthetics.

Meanwhile, the Rajmata focused on getting to know the royal family members. The more time she spent in Shravasti, the more resolved she became to arrange her son's marriage with the Kosala princess. She also wanted to determine if there were any imperfections in her character. She knew there was no better way to extract information than to have a conversation with a dissatisfied family member. It would be necessary to be both tactful and clever when investigating. Gradually, they would start complaining and reveal their most confidential secrets.

Vasabhakhattiya, the junior wife of King Prasenajit, was the daughter of a Sakyan slave. The Rajmata was familiar with the tale of how the Sakyans had tricked King Prasenajit into marrying a slave's daughter rather than a Sakyan princess because of their belief in their superior caste. When the Kosala king found out about their deceit, he cut off ties with the junior wife and treated her like the other neglected wives.

For this very reason, King Prasenajit refrained from declaring Vidudabha, the offspring of Vasabhakhattiya, as his rightful heir.

The astute Rajmata cleverly avoided attending the feast hosted by Queen Mallika, citing exhaustion from the long voyage. 'I'm not young any more,' she smiled. 'I'll have a quiet meal in my chamber, if you don't mind. Tomorrow, when I'm rested, I'll join everyone for the morning meal.'

Once the queen departed, the Rajmata sent a dasi to invite the junior wife to join her for the meal. Vasabhakhattiya, she learned, lived in the rear section of the palace with the king's concubines and other women. This was a punishment for her role in the Sakyan plot.

'Pranam, Rajmata,' Vasabhakhattiya stood before her with folded hands. The king's neglect had taken a toll on her. Her frustration led to overeating, causing her to gain weight. The beautiful face was now buried under a layer of fat. 'Forgive me, but I can't accept your invitation to share a meal, because of my low birth,' she said tearfully.

The Rajmata ordered the dasis to retreat from her chamber after they had laid out the food and drinks.

'Come and sit with me, Vasabha,' the Rajmata commanded. Taking out a beautiful necklace from a jewellery box nearby, she presented it to the younger queen. 'Allow me to secure the clip at the back,' she remarked. 'Ah, it looks beautiful on you.'

'You are too kind, Rajmata, but I can't accept such an expensive gift. I don't deserve it.' Vasabhakhattiya made a move to remove the necklace from her neck. Tears flowed down her plump cheeks. 'I'm a rejected queen and have no right to be sitting here with you.'

'Shhh! The most important thing is that you are a queen. Don't let anyone tell you otherwise. I believe the goodness of people matters more than the caste they were born into.' The Rajmata patted her shoulders affectionately.

'Not everyone is as generous, Rajmata. Ever since the king found out the truth about my caste, I have been treated poorly. Not only me, but my son is also facing undeserved punishment.'

'Timing is crucial for things to unfold. Your son will

eventually ascend the throne. Is he not the sole heir to the king?'

'So he is, but Vidudabha is unfit to wear the Kosala crown. He is young now. I fear he will resist the injustice as he matures. Also, the king may have more sons in the future.'

'Sometimes, we have no choice but to wait for things to settle down,' the Rajmata sighed. 'For the moment, let us not talk about those things. It would be unfair to let this feast go to waste.'

'I…'

'No. I don't want to hear any more excuses,' said the Rajmata, ladling out a heap of the fragrant rice on Vasabhakhattiya's plate.

'Let me do this, please.' The junior queen took the ladle from the guest's hand and apologized. 'I may have been cast out by the king, but I have not forgotten my duties as a host.'

In no time, Vasabhakhattiya felt at ease with the Rajmata. Once they finished eating, the Rajmata summoned the dasis and asked them to clear the dishes. The two of them enjoyed a game of chaturanga while the dasis entertained them with evening ragas on their veenas.

The cunning Rajmata skilfully extracted information from Vasabhakhattiya, who was too focused on the game to realize she was being interrogated. The Rajmata was skilled in playing chaturanga, and she never failed to defeat her opponent, but she let Vasabhakhattiya win one game when she was on the verge of giving up. It was an infallible strategy—to allow opponents to win when they had lost interest after a string of defeats. It ignited a renewed passion in them to achieve another victory.

In the next one hour, the Rajmata extracted enough information from the junior queen to satisfy herself. She learned that Kosala Devi was indeed an innocent girl with many virtues. She was a patient, dutiful, obedient and compassionate person with an unblemished character. Everyone, from the royal family members, ministers and courtiers to the dasis, loved the girl. Once she was satisfied, the Rajmata yawned to convey her fatigue.

'How inconsiderate of me,' exclaimed Vasabhakhattiya. 'You must be exhausted. I have been too engrossed in the game to notice.'

Following Vasabhakhattiya's departure, the Rajmata devised a plan to motivate Queen Mallika and King Prasenajit to seek a marriage alliance with Magadh. It needed to be executed subtly.

While the Rajmata was polishing her plan, Bimbisar requested Kosala Devi to show him around the gardens she had mentioned during the feast.

The next morning, before the Rajmata could execute her plan, Queen Mallika brought up the topic. The two of them were returning after a visit to the temple when the queen suggested they take a walk in the garden. With the dew drops still fresh everywhere, and the sun lazily ascending the sky, the air was filled with the melodies of singing birds, creating a heavenly atmosphere.

'This is the best time of the day to walk in the garden. I like to take off my shoes and walk barefoot on the grass so I can feel the dew under my feet.' Queen Mallika removed her shoes and, tossing them aside, grabbed the Rajmata's hand. 'Would you like to try walking without shoes?'

'It seems improper. I couldn't….'

'Oh Rajmata. You are not old enough to stop enjoying life,' reminded Queen Mallika.

The Rajmata hesitated for a moment, then throwing caution to the wind, she tossed aside her shoes. As the grass tickled her feet, she sighed with delight. Dropping all pretences, she embraced her natural self. She felt young and carefree. Queen Mallika burst into giggles and the Rajmata joined in the fun.

The Rajmata who loved vibrant colours had been leading

a dull, washed-out life for many years. It had been some time since she had lowered her defences. Her husband's death had caused her to age prematurely. It was difficult for her to recall the last time she had burst into laughter or abandoned herself to emotions. Not too far in the past, she had joined her husband on a hunting expedition and aided him in formulating his military strategies. Together, they had travelled incognito in villages and towns to understand the problems of their citizens. Now, it was her son who sought her counsel.

The title of Rajmata had given her gravitas, calling for an unsmiling countenance. People expected wisdom, balance and sobriety, not giggles from the queen mother. She yielded to their demands and buried her dreams for the well-being of the subjects. Queen Mallika's company helped her embrace her age as a woman in her fifties, rather than feel like a relic of the past. She was a woman denied the joys of life and burdened with excessive responsibilities.

Side by side, they took a leisurely walk on the wet grass while deer and peacocks trailed behind them. Snatching grains from a basket carried by a dasi, Queen Mallika playfully hurled them at the peacocks. Their jubilant cries echoed in the air.

'I like Shravasti,' said the Rajmata, feeding grass to a fawn with the most appealing eyes she had ever since. 'In this garden, away from prying eyes, I can be myself without caring too much about everyone's opinion.'

'Then stay here for a while,' Queen Mallika caught her arm and turned to look appealingly at the unlined and youthful face. 'We will indulge in all your favourite activities, with no fear of criticism.'

'That is not possible, and you know it. We all live within the boundaries created by our circumstances. But the dreams don't die. Do they?'

Queen Mallika led the Rajmata near a pond full of lotus blooms. They sat down on a beautifully crafted marble bench. The swans glided effortlessly on the water, occasionally diving down to catch their prey.

'I have been wanting to discuss an important matter with you,' the Kosala queen spoke after they spent a few minutes admiring the beauty of the surroundings. 'It is something that can lead to a strong and lasting relationship between us.'

The Rajmata was prepared for what was coming. She had been expecting Queen Mallika to broach the subject of marriage. She looked at Mallika encouragingly and said, 'Don't be afraid to voice your thoughts. Let there be no secrets between us.'

'Do you think it a good idea to have a matrimonial alliance with Kosala?' The words rushed out of Queen Mallika's mouth before she knew. Realizing her indiscretion, she swiftly silenced herself by pressing her hand against her mouth. 'I am sorry…'

'You don't have to feel sorry.' The Rajmata swiftly comforted the apologetic queen. She was happy that the Kosala queen had come up with the proposal. It would not have been right of her to bring up the topic. 'I too have had similar thoughts on the matter.'

'It is such a relief to know that.' Queen Mallika gazed eagerly at her guest. 'What do you think should be done? The Kosala king believes it is best to consult his sister before discussing marriage, but I sense that Kosala Devi is attracted to your son.'

'I have noticed it too. I think my son will have no hesitation in marrying the princess.'

The two co-conspirators smiled at each other.

Meanwhile, in another part of the palace, King Prasenajit was considering the idea of a marriage alliance with Bimbisar. They had wrapped up a satisfactory discussion on the political situation in the region and understood the significance of maintaining cordial relations between Magadh and Kosala.

'Don't you think it is about time you gave a queen to Magadh?' asked King Prasenajit.

Bimbisar had expected this question. He replied cautiously, 'I have entrusted the task to the Rajmata. She is the best person to find a suitable queen for Magadh.'

'That is the right approach, though I married for love. Despite knowing its foolishness, I let my heart guide my decisions.'

Embittered by his experience with Kadambini, Bimbisar had pledged to stay away from women. The years that followed were highly productive as he worked on expanding his empire. Over time, the bitterness diminished. Being in the presence of the Kosala princess reignited his passion. He longed for a woman in his life—someone he could trust completely and love without worrying about being betrayed.

While the Magadh king pondered over a fitting reply, the Rajmata and Queen Mallika entered the hall. Their cheeks flushed after an invigorating walk, the two women appeared thrilled with the morning's experience.

King Prasenajit and Bimbisar got up to welcome them. It was only when they had taken their seats that the Kosala king cleared his throat and started to speak, 'Now that the Rajmata is here, I'll speak about an important matter that has been on my mind for the past few days.'

The Rajmata and Queen Mallika exchanged a knowing smile.

'For a long time, Kosala has been seeking an alliance with Magadh, and nothing is more powerful than a marriage alliance.' King Prasenajit glanced meaningfully at his queen and continued speaking, 'After careful consideration, I have concluded that there is no one more suitable for my sister than the Magadh king. May I humbly request the Rajmata to consider my proposal?' He turned to the Rajmata.

The Rajmata glanced at her son, who nodded. 'Kosala Naresh, we are honoured by your proposal. I hope my son doesn't disagree,' she said.

Bimbisar realized the direction in which things were going. He turned to the Rajmata and said, 'I agree to follow your wishes.' Captivated by Kosala Devi's naivety, he was excited at the idea of marrying her. An alliance with the Kosala king would be a welcome outcome. It was something he had yearned for since some time.

'My son will marry Princess Kosala Devi,' the Rajmata joyfully announced the news.

'Excellent! In that case, I'll start making the preparations for the events.' Prasenajit stood up and hugged Bimbisar.

'We could perhaps return at a later date,' Bimbisar stated.

The Rajmata was resolute in her decision to return to Magadh, accompanied by her son's wife. 'Why do you want to delay the matter?' she asked her son. 'I don't think it will be possible for us to return to Kosala in the next few months.'

King Prasenajit said, 'I agree with the Rajmata. Please enjoy our hospitality for a couple of days more, so we can solemnize the wedding at the earliest. I'll ask the royal astrologers to suggest an auspicious date and time for the wedding.'

The astrologers consulted the almanac. There were no suitable dates for the next few months, so the wedding had to be scheduled within the next two days. Thereafter, they agreed on an auspicious time for the royal wedding. They also proclaimed it to be a very auspicious match.

After consulting the Rajmata, King Prasenajit declared that the wedding would be held the day after, prompting the commencement of the preparations. Drumbeaters travelled through the kingdom to inform the citizens about the upcoming auspicious event.

Bimbisar sent a messenger to the Magadh senapati, instructing him to reach Kosala.

Despite the hurry, the decorators adorned Shravasti like a bride. The wedding of the Kosala princess and the Magadh Naresh was going to be anything but ordinary. The rich and the poor, everyone began beautifying their houses with garlands of flowers.

The palace and town were decorated with vibrant arches covered in flowers and silk banners displaying the crests of Kosala and Magadh. Racing through the streets, the royal announcers declared a public holiday, inviting everyone to join in the merriment.

Dancers, musicians, jugglers, acrobats, bards and snake charmers from various parts of the kingdom flocked overnight in response to the royal wedding announcement. With great enthusiasm to capitalize on the event, they assembled in the town, delighting the locals who eagerly spent money on their performances. The taverns overflowed with merry-makers, and even the street vendors enjoyed brisk sales.

Dressed in their finest, people carrying children on their shoulders blended with the crowds. The streets were filled with the joyful sounds of singing and celebration. Many indulged in gambling and drinking, while some enjoyed quail and bull fights, betting on their favourites. Women flocked to colourful stalls set up in an open area, selling clothes, trinkets, utensils, decorations and sweets. Children gathered around jugglers, magicians and snake charmers. The festive ambiance showed the king's widespread popularity.

On the scheduled day, at dawn, the Magadh king departed from the Kosala mahamantri's palace to the royal palace in a spectacular procession, including a hundred elephants with golden tusks, followed by fifty chariots adorned with flowers and drawn by white stallions, and then a hundred soldiers and musicians in vibrant silk attire. Carrying the banners of Magadh and Kosala, the Kosala royal guards marched behind them. As the royal guards proceeded, a procession of twenty-four dasis in exquisite clothing followed, scattering flower petals in their wake. Thousands of spectators lined the streets to watch the impressive pageant. With their hands folded, they excitedly shouted joyous greetings to the bridegroom. Bimbisar's senapati tossed gold and silver coins at the crowds in acknowledgement.

The majestic procession wound its way to the royal palace and reached at the auspicious hour. Bands of musicians serenaded them from the palace terraces as the Magadh king dismounted and King Prasenajit came forward to receive him with fanfare. Together, they walked towards the marriage pavilion with cymbals and drums heralding their arrival. The queens and members of the royal family were resplendent in sparkling jewels and rich clothes. The splendour was a testimony to Kosala's wealth and prosperity.

Bimbisar felt an overwhelming desire to get away from it all. All he wanted was for the wedding to be over, so he could return to his capital with his queen. The purohits tasked to carry out the wedding formalities were, however, not in a hurry. They performed extensive rituals, chanted dozens of verses, and conducted a lengthy havan before declaring them a married couple.

A lavish feast that seemed to go on endlessly, followed. The highlight of the feast was when King Prasenajit announced he was giving Kashi and its income as a dowry to his sister. The unexpected bonanza pleasantly surprised the Rajmata and her son. It foreshadowed a well-intentioned relationship.

The celebrations concluded with a procession through the beautifully decorated Shravasti. The pathways were strewn with flowers as the newlyweds were welcomed by a jubilant crowd.

❧

It was late night when the newlyweds found themselves in a bedchamber done up with flowers. The room was filled with the intoxicating smoke of incense burning in the filigreed silver censers, besides all kinds of fruits, nuts and sweets. Peeking coyly from beneath her veil, the bride looked at Bimbisar as he extended his hand towards her.

It was an auspicious beginning to a powerful alliance, thought the Rajmata as they travelled back to Magadh, followed by boatloads of gifts which spoke of the Kosala king's generosity. Her plan had succeeded, and she heaved a sigh of relief. Magadh had become a prominent force among the Mahajanapadas.

From Kosala to Magadh, the festivities seemed unending. It was late evening when the royal contingent finally reached Rajgriha. The Magadh capital nestled in a valley, encircled by five hills: Ratnagiri, Vipalachal, Vaibhagiri, Songiri and Udayagiri. News of the king's wedding had spread rapidly, so the ministers had organized a magnificent reception for the newlyweds. The city was adorned in a way that resembled the divine dwelling of Vishnu. There was a festive ambiance, with music, fireworks, and a sense of joy.

The royal palace was adorned magnificently to prepare for the king and his new wife. Fragrant flowers were used to decorate the exquisitely carved pillars, while the arches were adorned with silk and brocade. The marble floors were laid over with luxurious silk carpets, and hundreds of lamps provided beautiful lighting.

After the grand reception, the exhausted couple retired to the bridal chamber. But the feasting and merry-making continued way past dawn.

# 12

# An Illegitimate Prince

The capital of Magadh continued to experience a joyous period as the king, deeply in love, courted his queen. A period of prosperity followed the fourth successful monsoon in a row. The reforms and improved administration resulted in a boost in revenues, with Kashi contributing significantly to this positive outcome. An era of peace prevailed, except for the sporadic raids by the Lichchavis.

People attributed the new queen's arrival to the change in their fortunes. She was referred to as 'Magadh Lakshmi' by the people. The Rajmata's happiness knew no bounds. Kosala Devi was a learned, calm, obedient and wise woman, and she lived up to the Rajmata's expectations. Adding to the joyous atmosphere was the announcement of the queen's pregnancy. From the Rajmata to the king to the courtiers, everyone looked forward to the birth of an heir.

Bimbisar was ecstatic. All he required to bolster his kingdom was the birth of a son. Although he had not shared it with anyone, the curse of the Anga queen would often haunt him.

Little did he know that his son, born out of his relationship with Kadambini, was already being raised in the palace. Only the Rajmata, her devoted servant, and a couple of senior ministers knew the truth.

Every day, a continuous flow of people in need queued up outside the palace, seeking an audience with her. The Rajmata was known for her generosity, but she was not without her boundaries. Two years back, Kadambini arrived at the palace to seek an audience with the Rajmata. Believing that the woman sought monetary aid, she firmly turned down the appeal, but the woman stayed resolute. Every single day, she persistently returned and pleaded to see the Rajmata, until the Rajmata eventually granted her an audience.

'What do you want, woman?' asked the Rajmata.

'I'm Kadambini, Rajmata,' said the woman.

The Rajmata knew her son had been involved with Kadambini. She was taken aback when she realized the ganika was quite young. Her innocent face and proud posture were clear indications of her privileged background. She tossed a purse filled with gold at the ganika and said, 'Take this and go away. Never return to the palace. I'll be forced to order the guards to throw you into the forest if you return.'

'You misunderstand me, Rajmata. I'm not here for money,' said Kadambini.

'Then why are you here? You are in a profession that calls for providing physical gratification to men and you have no right to demand anything beyond your price, which I'm sure my son has paid. Besides, I have no sympathy for women of your kind.'

'I don't have any such expectation, Rajmata. Your son has paid much more than I expected.'

'Then why are you here?'

With tears in her eyes, Kadambini confronted the Rajmata. 'I'm carrying your son's child,' she said.

The ganika's words left the Rajmata speechless. It took her a couple of minutes to regain her composure. She narrowed her eyes and frowned.

'And you believe you are carrying the king's child? You are a ganika, woman. You entertain hundreds of men. Any of them could have fathered the bastard you are carrying.'

The ganika looked stricken at the accusation. 'I have entertained no man since I met the king, so I'm certain it is his child I carry.' She stood up haughtily and continued, 'Rajmata, I have no expectations from you. I can bring up my son on my own.'

'How dare you hold my son responsible for your baby?' the Rajmata snarled at the ganika.

'I'm telling the truth, Rajmata. I'm going to be a mother to your son's child. All I want is for him to acknowledge the child,' the woman pleaded, with desperation in her voice.

'Impossible! You're trying to blackmail us. You are displaying the attributes of your profession.'

'I'm doing nothing of the kind. I'm pleading for the child's legitimacy. But I don't think I'll get justice here.' Kadambini bowed, straightened her shoulders, and turned to leave.

Something in her expression convinced the Rajmata that the woman was telling the truth. It would be unfair to abandon Bimbisar's child. She was a devout woman and believed in the fairness of things. 'Wait!' she called out to the ganika. 'I hope you know a ganika can never become a queen. You cannot even live in this palace.'

'I don't have any ambition of being a queen, nor do I want to live in this palace. All I want is my child's right to the father's name.' Kadambini paused at the door and flung the words over her shoulder.

'What do you want?' the Rajmata sounded exasperated. 'Spell it out, woman. Do you want me to take care of your confinement?'

'I want the child to grow under your care.' The ganika returned to sit close to the Rajmata's feet. 'So he can have a fair chance to learn the things he should. As the son of a ganika, he will get nothing more than the title of a bastard.'

'Let me get this straight. You will give up the baby, so it can be brought up in the palace?'

'Yes. That will give me much happiness.'

'Let me think about the matter.' The Rajmata stood up to leave the room. 'Come back tomorrow morning for my decision.'

That night, the Rajmata lay tossing in her bed, a hundred thoughts jostling in her mind. She could banish the ganika, and never see her again, or she could get her killed so the woman could no longer create trouble. The baby would die with the mother and that would be the end of the problem. The solution was simple, but her conscience warned against it. Could she live with the sin of killing an unborn baby? It belonged to the Haryanka Dynasty.

Would it be better to buy her silence with gold? First, she had to find out everything about Kadambini.

A faithful spy gathered details of the circumstances that had led the young girl to the profession. Kadambini was born into a wealthy family, but in her teens, she fell in love with a man from a lower caste. They eloped to get married, but tragically, before they could wed, the lover was murdered by unscrupulous individuals who also stole their belongings, leaving Kadambini devastated beside her lover's lifeless body.

With no food or shelter, she wandered into a ganika's mansion. The ageing ganika greeted the young girl with a loving embrace. The girl was beautiful and talented, and her insurance for life. She taught Kadambini various skills, including the art of charming and attending to her customers.

The ganika passed away a few years ago, leaving behind a grand mansion and all her belongings for her protégé.

By dawn, the Rajmata's mind was made up. She knew the right thing to do. The baby deserved a chance to live.

Kadambini was brought before the Rajmata after she had

returned from the temple following her morning prayers. The Rajmata was filled with compassion upon seeing the vulnerable woman.

'Pranam, Rajmata.' The ganika stood patiently—her hands clasped together—awaiting the verdict. Throughout the night, she had been on edge, consumed by thoughts of what would happen to her unborn child. The woman understood that Bimbisar would never marry her. He had to enter into matrimony only with a princess. Love had little to do with royal marriages, which were dictated by political ambitions.

'Sit down, Kadambini,' said the Rajmata gently. 'After much deliberation, I have come to a decision.'

The woman waited, her eyes filled with hope.

'I have made suitable arrangements for your delivery. An experienced midwife will accompany you on your journey to a distant location, ensuring a safe delivery. Once you are there, a suitable house will be rented and all necessary preparations will be made to ensure that you have a pleasant and comfortable stay. Since you have to leave early tomorrow morning, make sure to complete all the preparations tonight.'

'But…' the ganika began. The Rajmata held up her hand to silence her.

'You have no choice. Either you agree to my terms or we end this discussion.'

The ganika dropped her head and fixed her gaze on the ground, concealing her tears.

'The midwife will bring back the baby to the palace, and you will leave Magadh forever.' The Rajmata continued after a pause. 'I'll bring up the child and be its guardian. It will get a comfortable life, education and training. In return, I expect you to keep away from the palace and never disclose the identity of your child to Bimbisar or anyone else.'

The ganika looked stricken as the Rajmata's words sank in. She stood mutely, wringing her hands as tears flowed down her cheeks.

'Do you agree?' asked the Rajmata. 'Give it a thought. You can give your decision in an hour.' She felt sorry for the woman who had to make a tough choice. It is never easy for a mother to give up her child. 'It calls for an enormous sacrifice. All I can do is promise that I'll bring up your child with love and provide the training and education appropriate for a prince.'

The ganika wiped her tears with the back of her hands and squared her shoulders. 'I'll do whatever you want. All I want is for my child to grow up without the label of a bastard. People call you a generous and just queen, and I know you will do justice to your first grandchild.'

Six months later, the midwife returned with Bimbisar's illegitimate son. The Rajmata's heart melted at the sight of her first grandson. One look and she had no doubt about the identity of the father. She named him Abhay, the fearless one.

The illegitimate child grew up amidst the dasis under the watchful eyes of the Rajmata. An affectionate toddler with a cheerful nature, he won the hearts of all, including his grandmother. Bimbisar couldn't help but smile as he watched his mother play with the little one in the garden.

'This is Abhay,' the Rajmata introduced the child to her son, one day. 'Isn't he a lovely boy? He will make a delightful companion for your son.' Turning to the child, she asked, 'Abhay, have you forgotten how to greet the king?'

'Planam, Mahalaj,' lisped Abhay. Bowing, he joined his chubby palms.

'So, you have already found a playmate for your grandson? Abhay is adorable.' Bimbisar ruffled the child's hair lovingly.

'He has royal blood in him.' The Rajmata watched the effect of her words on Bimbisar.

'Really? And who are his parents?'

'His father comes from a royal family.'

'You mean he's an illegitimate child?'

'Unfortunately, yes.' The Rajmata scrutinized Bimbisar's expression, but he seemed clueless about the child's parentage. She heaved a sigh of relief and continued, 'I intend to raise him like royalty, ensuring he receives a fair and just treatment.'

'So he is one of your charitable projects?' Bimbisar arched his eyebrows, his gaze searching for answers.

'You could put it that way,' replied the Rajmata. 'I'll pass Abhay to his father once he reaches the age of ten.'

'Would it be justifiable to surprise the unsuspecting father with such a tremendous responsibility? The crucial question is whether or not he will believe the son is his.'

'Do you think he will question the genuineness of my words?' the Rajmata countered. She was testing Bimbisar's reaction to the situation.

'It depends on how much he values your words.'

Having received a satisfactory reply from Bimbisar, the Rajmata went back to playing a game with the child. Bimbisar couldn't help but be amused and perplexed by her sudden fascination with the boy. This was the first time he had ever noticed his mother giving so much time and attention to a child.

## 13

# A Princess Is Born

Chaitra gave way to the auspicious month of Pausha. It was a doubly auspicious occasion for both Magadh and its people. Queen Kosala Devi gave birth to a beautiful baby girl, filling the palace with joy and excitement. Despite the celebrations, the Rajmata couldn't shake off her sense of disappointment. Her heart yearned for a grandson who would carry forward the legacy of the Magadh throne.

Bimbisar's heart was a battleground of conflicting emotions. The curse of the Anga queen was still fresh in his memory. He thought it wise to not burden his mother or Kosala with the curse. The Rajmata had hoped for an heir, but he had experienced an unspoken dread. The birth of his daughter filled him with joy and relief. He was convinced that his daughter would not be a party to the curse.

Exhausted from the delivery, the queen felt her heart sink with fear as she imagined the king's reaction at the news of their daughter's birth. She knew the weight of disappointment that would silently suffocate him. For the past few months, Bimbisar had only discussed his plans to train his son in warfare and teach him the art of ruling a kingdom.

'My son will be the greatest warrior and the most just ruler in the entire Jambudweepa,' he had said to the queen. 'I'll train him to be the best.'

In all their conversations, they had never discussed the possibility of having a daughter. With a sense of trepidation,

Kosala Devi watched the king enter her chamber, his presence filling the room. Just as she was about to sit up, the king swiftly raised his hand, motioning for her to lie down.

The sight of his daughter's innocent face stirred a strange tenderness in Bimbisar's heart. He never expected to be so deeply touched.

With a faint smile, Kosala Devi extended her hand. Bimbisar's hand clasped it as he proudly proclaimed, 'Our daughter is a true beauty, Kosala.'

'Do you want to hold her, Maharaj?' she asked.

'I have never held a baby. She appears so fragile. What if I drop her?'

'I have never held a baby, either,' Kosala Devi smiled wanly. 'It is easy. All we have to do is go with our instinct.'

Picking up the swaddled princess, the midwife said, 'Allow me to place the baby in your arms, Maharaj.'

Carefully, he extended his arms, and the midwife delicately placed the baby on them. It was a magical moment. His eyes welled up with tears as he held his daughter close. He had never experienced such a powerful emotion in his life. At that moment, he realized the overwhelming love and responsibility that comes with being a parent.

With the newborn in his arms, he sat near the queen and whispered, 'Thank you, Kosala, for this wonderful gift.'

Kosala Devi nodded shyly, tears welling up in her eyes. Her voice weighed down with regret, she said softly, 'I'm sorry I couldn't provide you with an heir.'

'Hush!' Bimbisar wiped away the tears from her eyes, and said, 'I don't want you to mention it again.

'We can have sons later. A king requires daughters too.'

As if following a script, the baby began wailing. 'She's hungry, Maharaj,' said the midwife.

Although he longed to continue holding his daughter, Bimbisar handed over the baby to the midwife and left the chamber.

The following day, a brahmin youth named Vassakar arrived in Magadh. He sought an audience with the king, hoping to present his case. The brahmin's gaunt figure and fragile posture indicated a tough, impoverished existence. Finding his appearance unimpressive and his insistence bothersome, the praharis refused him entry.

'You've arrived at an inconvenient moment,' they sneered. 'The royal family is celebrating the birth of a princess, and the king is busy. Come back after the full moon and try your luck.'

The man waited for a fortnight until the festivities for the royal birth were over, before returning to seek an audience with Bimbisar.

Prostrating himself before the Magadh king, Vassakar spoke with sincerity, 'Pranam, Maharaj! I'm truly fortunate to be in your benign presence. I have been hearing legends of your courage and righteous rule for a long time.'

Bimbisar looked at the young brahmin with his dishevelled clothes and hair tied in a topknot. Despite his appearance, the man's eyes sparkled with profound intelligence. Curious to know more, Bimbsar enquired, 'Are you seeking alms, brahmin?'

'No Maharaj! Although I'm a poor brahmin, I don't need alms,' Vassakar replied humbly. 'I'm confident of using my intelligence to earn a living.'

'Then what is it you want, brahmin?' the king asked, carefully examining the man in front of him.

'Maharaj, I travelled a long distance to pay my respects to you. All I want is to serve you.'

'Are you insane?' A minister standing close to the king shouted. 'The king has no time to waste. Go to the amatya, who deals with such matters.' He nodded at the guard standing near the door and said, 'Take this man away.'

Vassakar fought back when the guard tried to remove him from the court. He turned towards Bimbisar and pleaded, 'Give me a chance, Maharaj, so I can prove my worth to the Magadh kingdom. You will not be disappointed, I promise.'

'Guards, throw him out of the palace,' commanded the minister.

'Wait!' Bimbisar raised his hand. 'You said you could prove your worth,' he addressed the brahmin. 'How do you propose to do that?'

'Maharaj, give me an opportunity to work in any of your departments, and I guarantee I'll bring about positive changes in just a few months.'

The king deliberated for a few moments before summoning the minister. 'Amatya, take him to the revenue department and assign him a clerical position,' he ordered.

'But Maharaj...' objected the minister. 'He's a stranger. We know nothing about him. What if he is a spy, or an assassin sent by your enemies?'

'I'm not a spy, Maharaj,' protested Vassakar. 'Nor am I an assassin. I'm a poor brahmin who has travelled a long distance to serve you. All I want is an opportunity to prove myself.'

'Brahmin, I'll grant you two months to showcase your abilities, but remember, you will be under constant observation. Take the man to the revenue department,' the king commanded.

'Thank you, Maharaj,' the brahmin said with a respectful bow. There was an earnestness in his voice as he assured Bimbisar, 'You will not regret your decision.'

The minister instructed a guard to take Vassakar to the revenue department. He looked concerned as he urged the king, 'Maharaj, we need to be cautious. The stranger might have a hidden agenda.

I'll employ a guptachar to investigate the brahmin's background. In addition, I'll instruct the treasury head and a soldier of the revenue department to keep an eye on him.'

'That is a wise decision,' agreed Bimbisar. 'The young brahmin should be placed in the position of a toll collector under the shulkadhyaksha. Amatya, I entrust this task to your care. You can perhaps decide after consulting the shulkadhyaksha.'

'Leave it to me, Maharaj. It is my responsibility to ensure that the matter is dealt with correctly.'

Two months passed in the blink of an eye. Lost in the matters of the kingdom, Bimbisar had completely forgotten about Vassakara. He was surprised to see the shulkadhyaksha named Ranveer and the young brahmin at the court one morning.

Chosen directly by the king, Ranveer assumed the role of shulkadhyaksha at a young age. Almost all employees in the revenue department went through a rigorous screening process before being hired. Guptachars were employed to meticulously scrutinize the details of their backgrounds and past activities. Like his colleagues in the revenue department, Ranveer was known for his unyielding integrity and his untiring commitment to his work, always putting the kingdom's needs first.

The mahamatya gestured for Ranveer to step forward, while Vassakar remained at the back.

'Pranam, Maharaj,' the young tax collector bowed reverently before Bimbisar and stood hesitating.

'Maharaj, the shulkadhyaksha has shared some information about the young brahmin, which I believe you should know.'

The mahamatya nodded at the man. 'Tell Maharaj what you told me.'

'Speak without fear, young man,' said Bimbisar. The king was aware of Ranveer's unblemished reputation, and the shulkadhyaksha's presence in court showed he had something significant to disclose. 'What is it you want to say?' the king asked.

'Maharaj, it is about the young brahmin you placed under my observation,' replied Ranveer. 'I submitted my report to the mahamatya, but he thought I should share it directly with you.'

'Well, it must be important enough for him to feel so,' said the king. 'Has the young brahmin proven himself untrustworthy?' he asked, recalling the lingering doubts of his Amatya. Bimbisar looked across at Vassakar, who was standing at the back. There were no visible signs of anxiety or impatience on the young brahmin's smooth face. Instead, he carried himself with an air of unwavering confidence.

'No Maharaj,' said Ranveer. 'On the contrary, he possesses an impeccable sense of integrity. In the last few weeks, I have put him through several tests, and he has come out in flying colours.'

'So, what is the problem?' Bimbisar asked, a trifle irritated. 'Is it of sufficient importance for you to ignore your work and inform me about the credibility of your claim?'

'Maharaj, the young brahmin possesses an extraordinary memory for figures. After reviewing the figures once, he can effortlessly remember hundreds of transactions. Also, he possesses an incredible talent for solving any problem encountered in revenue collection. I have never met someone like him before,' the Shulkadhyaksha's tone revealed admiration. 'Within a very brief period, the brahmin has offered several innovative solutions to streamline tax collection methods. I have studied those and found them excellent. In addition, he meticulously reviewed the records and created detailed reports showing that a high-ranking official had embezzled a significant amount of revenue.'

'But that's impossible. We have multiple mechanisms in place to ensure that any wrongdoing is promptly identified and addressed.' Bimbisar leaned forward on his throne and fixed his eyes on Ranveer. 'How did the theft take place?'

'Maharaj, the matter has been attended to. We have identified the embezzler and arrested him. The shulkadhyaksha is too junior to question the high-ranking officer, so the chief of security is questioning him, as we speak,' the mahamatya intervened. 'During the preliminary interrogation, he admitted to the theft and informed us about his methods.'

He paused for a moment and then continued, 'The discovery of the embezzlement has put pressure on the investigating team to recover the money quickly.'

'Has there been a careful examination of the matter?' asked the king. 'There might be more than one person involved in the theft. The investigation must be conducted in utmost secrecy, ensuring that no information is leaked out. We can't afford to let this matter become known to the public.'

'Just a couple of people are involved in the investigation, and I'm one of them, Maharaj,' said the mahamatya. 'Also, Maharaj, given Vassakar's capabilities, dedication and honesty, I suggest we assign him a more crucial position in the revenue department.'

'I leave that to you, mahamatya. Offer him a position wherever you think is appropriate.'

Vassakar remained faithful to his commitments. Regardless of the department—revenue, security, or finance—he swiftly became invaluable in any role he was assigned. Through a skilful combination of sharp wit, careful manoeuvring, and ingratiating behaviour, he swiftly ascended the hierarchical ladder. Progressing through various positions, he went from being the revenue head to the chief of security, and ultimately was assigned the esteemed role of finance minister within the king's most trusted group.

Due to the brahmin's fearlessness, which enabled him to voice his opinions boldly to the king, most ministers despised him. They were fascinated by his ambition. He was devoid of both a family and a longing for riches. The pleasures of good food, madira and women didn't interest him. He dedicated over eighteen hours of his day to work, leading a spartan life. His courage was unimaginable. The only thing on his mind was proving his indispensability to the king. Although the king had great faith in Vassakar, the ministers found it difficult to have confidence in him.

They couldn't quite put a finger on it, but there was something odd about a man who appeared to lack in any vice, greed, or material possession. *What was his motivation,* they wondered.

When the old mahamatya announced his retirement a year later, citing his declining health, Bimbisar wasted no time in designating Vassakar to take his place.

# 14

# Enemy at the Gate

Vaishali was a thorn in Bimbisar's flesh. The border villages of Magadh lived in constant fear as the Lichchavis raided them repeatedly. They looted the villagers' possessions and ravaged their crops, leaving behind destruction and despair.

As days passed, Bimbisar grew increasingly restless. News of renewed Lichchavi raids on Magadh's mines and fields were trickling in. They had become more daring while he had been romancing his queen. Fearing no action from the Magadh army, the raiders had expanded their area of operation and were advancing farther into Magadh territory. Just last week, they had intruded upon a mine and killed a few of Bimbisar's soldiers who were keeping guard.

The Magadh ruler had been patient for long, but the enemy's raids on his mines were the last straw. Besides, the Rajmata was an ambitious lady. She goaded him into launching an attack on Vaishali.

'The Magadh Empire's territories have not seen expansion for some time,' the Rajmata broached the subject during her son's visit to her chamber.

Bimbisar and Abhay were busy competing. Both were drawing a bird that sat on the balcony. Abhay's quick wit and boundless energy breathed life into the atmosphere. The boy, now three years old, was showing signs of an intelligent mind, so the Rajmata put him under the tutelage of a brahmin.

The king enjoyed spending time with the boy and found it

relaxing after a hectic day of work. 'What do you have in mind, Rajmata?' he asked.

'I want the Magadh Empire to prosper, grow in strength and reputation. Your marriage to Kosala has created a profitable source of income from Kashi, but we could use additional revenues and a more robust reputation. Shouldn't you think of another conquest to add to your list of successful campaigns?' she asked.

'Your bird does not have a tail,' Abhay pointed out and laughed.

'Let me add a long tail to my bird,' Bimbisar declared with a mischievous grin. He turned to his mother and said, 'You are right, Rajmata. I have been thinking on the same lines. In fact, I was thinking of a battle with the Lichchavis.'

His mother's face lit up as she exclaimed approvingly, 'That's an excellent idea! Vaishali is a prosperous capital. Bringing it under Magadh dominance will put the Lichchavis at our mercy, and substantially enhance our riverine trade.'

'Defeating the Lichchavis is no simple task. As you know, the Vajji Confederacy comprises many minor kings and clan chiefs, each commanding a formidable army and enjoying substantial wealth. The united might of the Vajji Confederacy is Vaishali's strongest defence. Taking on the combined army of all the princes seems like an insurmountable task for the Magadh army.'

'Nothing is impossible if you have the right strategy,' chided the Rajmata. Her son had become soft after his marriage with Kosala. It was time to convince him to go to battle with the Lichchavis. 'I think you should work on a strategy.'

The Rajmata's words had the intended impact. Bimbisar wasted no time and immediately summoned Vassakar, the mahamatya. Bimbisar paced the council chamber in Rajgriha, his brows furrowed in irritation. With each passing second, the muscles in his tall and well-built body grew increasingly taut, reflecting his impatience.

The doors opened. A soldier heralding the arrival of the Magadh mahamatya echoed through the hall. Vassakar, known for his shrewdness, had strategically manoeuvred his way to the top by relying on his intelligence and cunning. His devious manipulations had led to several wars, yet also prevented them from spiralling out of control. Known for his influence and power within the Magadh kingdom, he was both respected and loathed by many.

'Pranam, Maharaj,' Vassakar bowed reverentially. The king's agitation didn't escape his notice.

'I'm sure you have heard of the recent forays of the Lichchavis. They are getting bolder with each passing day.' Bimbisar didn't waste any time and immediately came to the point. 'It is time to teach them a lesson.'

'I agree with you, Maharaj. However, there are a few points...'

Interrupting Vassakar mid-sentence, Bimbisar said impatiently, 'I'm aware of all the points that you are likely to make. Mahamatya, are you attempting to deter me from my mission?'

'I would never dream of trying to dissuade you, Maharaj,' Vassakar said humbly, bowing his head. Tactful that he was, he had a knack for navigating delicate situations with ease. 'Your decision will be acted upon promptly and with no hesitation on my part.'

'In that case, let's get on with the battle plans. Summon all the ministers so we can plan our strategy.'

The Magadh ministers swiftly devised and presented a detailed plan of attack to the king.

It was the perfect season for a campaign. With the retreat of the rains, winter began its quiet entry, bringing with it a gentle chill in the air. The Magadh army made its move that night. Darkness provided cover as a multitude of boats, filled with soldiers and essential resources, silently glided down the Ganga, making their way to the gates of Vaishali, the resplendent and thriving capital of the Lichchavi Confederacy.

The Lichchavi guards on the watchtowers observed a huge Magadh army setting up camp and relayed the news to their king. Bimbisar had arrived with a large army and this time he was determined to subjugate Vaishali. It was an unexpected attack. The Lichchavi spies had missed all signs of an offensive of this scale.

Vaishali was under siege.

There was consternation in Vaishali. The enemy was at the gate, and the Lichchavis struggled to keep them at bay. Caught unprepared, they were left scrambling for a solution. It was uncertain how long the Lichchavi soldiers would be able to fend off the Magadh forces.

While the Vajji Confederacy was under tremendous pressure to hold off the Magadh army, Bimbisar and his soldiers were in an upbeat mood. They had planned well and knew that victory was close at hand.

The grounds just beyond the imposing gate were alive with activity. The Magadh soldiers sharpened their swords and went about their daily routine, confident they would storm the city gates. It had been three months since they left Magadh, so they were eager to return home.

In these three months, they had made remarkable headway. Vaishali took great pride in its impenetrable defences. The formidable fortification was protected on three sides by walls that seemed impossible to breach. Watchtowers punctuated the walls at regular intervals, with soldiers keeping vigil for any potential intruders. The fourth side of the city had a natural barrier of dense forests and mountains. Yet, the Magadh army was now chipping away at their defences. They intended to knock down the gates and breach the walls. The prospect of looting the legendary coffers of the Lichchavi capital fuelled their efforts.

Reports from Magadh's spies kept coming in, showing worsening conditions and scarce resources in the city. The king was informed about the despair that cast a shadow over the meetings at the Vaishali sabhagriha. It was a good sign for Bimbisar and his army. He was poised for the last thrust. It was easy enough to batter down the massive gate by using war elephants who had been brought across the mighty Ganga. Once they battered down the gate, he didn't visualize any hurdles in storming the city. All that mattered was to find an auspicious day and time for the final assault.

In the Magadh camp, the royal astrologer drew up charts to predict an auspicious day for the attack.

Meanwhile, a spy from Vaishali received information about the date of the impending attack. He swiftly delivered the news to his master, who then passed it on to the senapati. When the distressing news was delivered to the king, his face turned pale as he grasped the seriousness of the situation.

King Chetak, the leader of the Lichchavi Confederacy, called his parishad to prevent a battle with the Magadh king. Nobody, especially the ministers, desired a large-scale war that would devastate the economy and result in a significant loss of life. Anxiety swept through the Vaishali sabhagriha as the parishad gathered to discuss the matter.

'Gentlemen, we are here this evening to discuss the challenges faced by our republic,' the mahamantri began. 'According to our information, Bimbisar is just outside the fortification with a vast army. This time, the Magadh king is prepared for a long siege.' Taking in the stunned expressions in the sabhagriha, he felt the weight of the news he was about to share. 'The Magadh army has set up a large camp in a huge quadrangle, a mile or so away from the riverbank.'

'What is the level of our readiness?' King Chetak came straight to the point.

The senapati cleared his throat and spread out his hands in

a gesture of helplessness. 'Maharaj, the Magadh soldiers have strategically positioned themselves in ideal ambush locations. Our troops are ill-prepared to handle an attack of this magnitude.'

'How and when did they cross the river?' asked a minister. 'And why was the movement not noticed by our guards or spies?'

'What steps are you planning to take against the enemy?' asked another minister.

'Amatya, there is a large presence of heavily armed soldiers right outside the gate.' With unwavering honesty, the senapati admitted, 'I don't know how long we can fend them off.'

As his words echoed through the sabhagriha, the ministers spoke agitatedly, filling the room with a cacophony of voices seeking a solution.

'We will defend the city as long as possible,' assured the senapati. 'I'll lead the soldiers personally,' he declared. 'The united might of our clan chiefs is likely to work to our advantage.'

'…and what happens if you can't hold the enemy at the gate, and Bimbisar's army enters the city?'

The senapati stood in silence, unable to respond satisfactorily to the king's question. Unlike many ministers in the sabhagriha, he recognized the uselessness of making grandiose statements.

'Based on your uncertainty about being able to fend off the attack, what would you suggest as an alternative plan?' King Chetak asked, deeply concerned.

Worried voices filled the sabhagriha as the ministers grappled with the looming threat of a crushing defeat. Optimism and bluster faded as reality dawned.

Was there a way to avoid war? Could they bribe Bimbisar with Vaishali's treasures? Should they send an envoy with a peace offer? Ideas flew fast and furious; everyone gave their suggestions.

'May I offer a humble suggestion?' The rajguru, who had

remained quiet all this time, finally spoke up. All eyes turned towards him.

'What is your suggestion, Amatya?' the king asked gently. He had immense faith in the rajguru's abilities. He was a wise man who had served the Vajji Confederacy for a long time, and had lived through many political upheavals.

'It may be wise to follow King Prasenajit's strategy,' said the rajguru.

His idea took a few moments to sink in, and then he saw a few greybeards whispering among themselves. The king appeared interested too.

'Are you suggesting we should present one of our princesses as a bride to the Magadh king?' asked King Chetak.

'Yes, Maharaj! The Kosala king made a strategic decision to prevent violence and chaos. He arranged a marriage between his sister and Bimbisar. It was a wise movement. Now he has a formidable ally, someone he can rely on and trust,' the rajguru replied.

King Chetak stroke his beard thoughtfully as he considered the suggestion. 'It is a prudent idea, but who should we offer as a bride to Bimbisar?' he asked.

The rajguru's eyes met the king's, his voice full of conviction as he said, 'Princess Chellana would be an ideal choice.'

The weight of the decision pressed on the king's shoulders; he hesitated before taking any action. Chellana was his favourite daughter. More significantly, she was a woman who possessed a fierce determination, a wild nature, and a mind of her own. King Chetak dreaded her reaction if he proposed her as a bride to Bimbisar. As a proud Lichchavi, she saw the Magadh king as nothing less than an adversary.

'I do not think Chellana is an ideal choice,' said the king, his voice tinged with scepticism. 'There are many other princesses in the kingdom. I'm sure they would be happy to marry the mighty Magadh king.'

His words were greeted with silence in the sabhagriha. Despite their desire to propose their daughters in marriage, the clan chiefs of the Vajji Confederacy hesitated to say so before the king.

With keen interest, the mahamatya observed the expressions on the faces of the clan chiefs. An astute man, his intuition allowed him to grasp their thoughts with ease. He cleared his throat and started speaking, 'Pardon me for saying this, Maharaj, but I don't think the Magadh king will settle for anyone other than your daughter.'

King Chetak knew the mahamatya was right in assuming that Bimbisar, known for his pride, would take great offence if he was offered a clan chief's daughter in marriage.

'It remains to be seen whether the Magadh king will agree to our proposal,' the mahamatya remarked. 'If he has arrived with the intention of conquering Vaishali, he might reject the offer to marry a Lichchavi princess.'

'That may be true, but we have to take a chance,' said the rajguru.

'The rajguru is right, Maharaj. We must spare no effort to stop the war,' said the mahamatya.

His words found favour with the parishad members. They all spoke in unison, their voices echoing through the hall, 'Let us follow the rajguru's suggestion, Maharaj.'

'There is no time to lose,' opined the senapati. 'The Magadh army is chipping away at our defence, even as we speak. Let's make haste, Maharaj.'

The senapati's voice was soon accompanied by a chorus of others. King Chetak raised his hand to silence them. 'I'll do everything possible to prevent bloodshed,' he promised.

# 15

# A Peace Offering

Dawn approached the riverbanks gently, enveloping the shimmering waters in an unsettling silence. The buzz of activities shattered the stillness in the enemy camp. Bursting with energy, the soldiers shrugged off their inertia and began readying themselves for the battle that was scheduled to begin shortly. Buckles were secured, and swords and weapons were meticulously polished.

Bimbisar emerged from the royal tent in his majestic war garments, his piercing gaze sweeping across the rows of tents.

The Magadh commanders and soldiers stood in perfect formation, their uniforms crisp and swords shining. The sound of their swords clinking softly filled the air as they eagerly waited for the king's command to destroy the Vaishali gates and start their assault on the city.

The sound of Bimbisar's booming voice resonated in the air as he declared, 'The Magadh flag will soon fly high on the ramparts of Vaishali. This battle is important for everyone. We have been enduring the attacks of the Lichchavi raiders for a considerable period. They are relentless in their looting, taking our crops, cattle and treasures without hesitation. The villagers living on the borders are the most affected. It is our responsibility to hold the Lichchavis accountable for their assaults.'

He paused briefly before continuing, 'We will make them pay for their aggression, no matter the cost.'

'Magadh Maharaj Bimbisar ki jai!' the commanders shouted.

The multitude of soldiers joined in, their voices creating a powerful effect.

It was a pleasant day. The sky stretched like a magnificent blue canopy, decorated with swirling clouds, while the Magadh troops made final preparations for their imminent attack. Bimbisar surveyed the ramparts, observing the Lichchavi soldiers standing resolute with their bows drawn, ready to release a barrage of arrows at the approaching Magadh troops.

Suddenly, there was a commotion. The senapati rushed towards Bimbisar and urgently announced, 'Maharaj, the gate has been opened by the Lichchavis!'

'Strange!' remarked Bimbisar. His eyebrows arched, he continued, 'Are they inviting us with open arms, or luring us into a snare?'

The Magadh soldiers watched as King Chetak's chariot rode out of the gate, its golden embellishments glimmering in the sun. A white flag gently fluttered in the wind.

'Has he decided to call for a truce?' asked Bimbisar sarcastically. 'Good sense seems to have finally prevailed.'

'Our soldiers are ready for a battle, Maharaj…'

'Wait!' Bimbisar held up his hand. Turning to the senapati, he ordered, 'We will not take any hasty steps. Let's see what King Chetak has to say.'

King Chetak had disembarked from his chariot and at that moment, was making his way towards Bimbisar. Accompanying him were his wise and trusted advisor, the rajguru, and the Vaishali mahamatya. The Magadh soldiers cleared the path for the three as Bimbisar patiently waited for them to draw close.

The Lichchavi king respectfully folded his hands and greeted the Magadh king. Startled by the sight, Bimbisar too automatically folded his hands.

'Magadh Samrat, I'm so delighted to see you here. You have

saved my weary bones from journeying to Magadh,' said King Chetak affectionately.

'Were you thinking of visiting us, Lichchavi Naresh?' Bimbisar was taken aback by the Lichchavi king's words. Using his astute mind, he meticulously reviewed the information given by the Magadh spies. There was no indication that the Lichchavi king intended to visit Magadh.

'How else would a doting father escape his responsibilities? It was to seek my child's happiness that I wanted to go to Magadh.'

The king's mysterious words left Bimbisar bewildered. 'I do not understand,' he said.

'Ah, my excitement makes me babble incessantly, without a moment's pause. Please allow me to clarify the situation. Since my daughter, Princess Chellana, is now of marriageable age, it is my responsibility to find a suitable partner for her and there is no one more befitting than you. Maharaj, I humbly request you to regard her as a suitable bride.' The Lichchavi king looked imploringly at Bimbisar.

Bimbisar was taken aback by the unexpected turn of events. Unfazed by the imminent attack, the old king carried on the conversation about his daughter's wedding as if nothing was amiss. It was impossible for Bimbisar not to be impressed by King Chetak's astute strategies. Clever and sly, the wily old fox had successfully outdone the strategies of Magadh. Bimbisar had heard of Princess Chellana's beauty, which was said to be as captivating as her wilful ways. The Magadh spies had taken great care to provide the Rajmata with a thorough account of the princess's qualities and flaws. The Rajmata had been thinking about the idea of arranging her son's marriage with Chellana. The princess intrigued Bimbisar. With his penchant for challenges, he was determined to meet her.

Meanwhile, the Vaishali rajguru and the mahamatya stepped

forward to join their king. The bonhomie that followed was absolutely unexpected. 'Magadh Samrat, this is not the right place to discuss delicate matters. You are an honoured guest and the royal palace is waiting to be graced by you. I came here the moment I learnt of your arrival,' said King Chetak.

Watching the situation unfold, Vassakar, who had joined Bimbisar by now, looked apprehensive. 'Maharaj, please be cautious and do not fall for their cunning strategies. I have a feeling they are up to something,' he said softly, expressing concern.

The Magadh king was determined to not be deceived by the Lichchavis. 'Do not worry, mahamatya,' he assured Vassakar, his voice brimming with confidence.

Turning to King Chetak, Bimbisar said, 'That is a splendid suggestion, Lichchavi Naresh. I agree this is not the right place to discuss delicate matters. What do you suggest I do with my soldiers?'

Bimbisar's unexpected question caught King Chetak off guard, leaving him flustered as he struggled to find a suitable response.

'It is a matter of trust, Maharaj,' he finally replied. 'It will not be prudent for the entire Magadh army to march into Vaishali. The people of Vaishali might easily mistake their entry for an invasion and the consequences could be undesirable.'

'That's impossible.' Vassakar's temper flared up in response to the suggestion. He exclaimed, 'How can you possibly expect our king to come to your palace with no protection? Would you do the same if the situation was reversed?'

Meanwhile, the Magadh troops were growing increasingly uneasy. The Lichchavi king was trying to stop the Magadh king from attacking. They saw it as an attempt to rob them of the victory and the rewards they had been promised.

Clearing his throat, the Vaishali mahamatya joined the conversation. 'May I humbly suggest that they remain in their camps for the moment? We will make all arrangements for their food and entertainment. The Magadh mahamatya and your commanders are welcome to the Vajji capital.'

'We could discuss the matter in my tent,' offered Bimbisar.

The Vaishali king and his minister exchanged meaningful glances. 'We have no hesitation in doing that,' said King Chetak. 'I'm disappointed that you have no faith in our offer,' he said, looking hurt. 'Believe me when I say that my invitation to you is completely sincere, with no hidden agenda whatsoever. I give you my word, you will be treated as an honoured guest.'

The old king's words landed squarely on the target. King Chetak was too wise to resort to treachery. Not heeding Vassakar's advice, Bimbisar responded gently, 'I have faith in your words, Lichchavi Naresh. I accept your invitation.'

The Magadh king entered the city with a magnificent display of bodyguards and commanders, captivating the onlookers as they journeyed towards the royal palace. The grand avenue to the royal palace was humming with murmurs of the intrigued residents, their gaze shifting anxiously as they attempted to decipher the sudden development.

Bimbisar and his group were guided to opulent chambers adorned with exquisite furniture that immediately caught their attention. A lavish banquet was organized to honour him, with extravagant entertainment for his enjoyment. An energetic buzz filled the air as the Lichchavi ministers and courtiers diligently attended to every detail, working to create a festive ambiance.

The grandeur of Vaishali made a powerful impression on the Magadh king and his ministers. The assembly hall of the Vajji Confederacy was lined with meticulously carved wooden pillars, each embellished with sculpted flowers, vines and peacocks, providing support to the ornate gilded ceiling. Exquisite paintings adorned the walls, and the expansive windows framed breathtaking views of the lively gardens.

King Chetak carefully supervised every detail to ensure his guest's comfort. 'Maharaj, if you agree to the marriage proposal,' he said, folding his hands, 'I'll approach the royal astrologer to determine an auspicious date and we will begin the wedding preparations.'

'I would like to meet your daughter before you arrange for a wedding,' said Bimbisar. 'It is important to know if she has given her consent for this marriage.'

The Magadh king's condition put King Chetak in a quandary. Knowing how stubborn Chellana was, he had not informed his daughter about the proposal. However, he couldn't decline Bimbisar's request.

'It's a wise decision, Maharaj. I'll ensure that Chellana meets you in person,' replied King Chetak.

The thought of facing his daughter made him cringe, knowing that she would surely rebel against the decision. Chellana's deep affection for Vaishali motivated him to appeal to her loyalty. The flickering diyas cast eerie shadows on the walls, hinting at the obstacles and sacrifices awaiting the kingdom.

The news of her arranged marriage with the Magadh king ignited a fury within Princess Chellana. Frustrated and fuming, she paced back and forth in her chamber.

King Chetak, exhausted and apprehensive, stepped into Chellana's chamber. He had successfully averted a war, but felt uneasy about the upcoming meeting with his daughter.

Anger welled up inside her at the sight of her father. 'How could you do this to me?' she cried, as he tried to pacify her. 'So you want me to tie the knot with someone I consider an enemy? How could you even think that?'

'Chellana, come sit next to me,' her father said, patting the empty seat next to him. 'Let us have a sensible conversation about this.'

'There's nothing to discuss,' retorted his daughter, as she resumed pacing.

'I'm an old man and your pacing is making me anxious, my dear. A meaningful conversation can resolve any issue in life. You are the one I love the most of all my children,' King Chetak continued gently. 'Had you given the matter some thought, you would have realized there must be a strong reason for my decision to get your married to Bimbisar.'

'But why me? Why not my sister?'

'You are the more beautiful and wise one, my dear. Bimbisar is a powerful king who can have the pick of women, and his mother is a shrewd lady. They may not have accepted my offer for your sister. The Magadh army is at our gate and they can burst upon the city at any moment. Our ministers felt that a matrimonial alliance, like the one offered by the Kosala king, could prevent bloodshed. I had to go with their suggestion to buy peace for the kingdom.'

'Is it not possible to defeat the arrogant scoundrel from Magadh?' Chellana raged. 'We have an unparalleled force of skilled warriors and experienced commanders who can launch a powerful counterattack.'

'Not this time. Bimbisar's timing is perfect. He has caught us on the backfoot. We can't retaliate because of our current circumstances. As a patriot, I'm calling upon you to make a sacrifice for your country,' King Chetak appealed. 'To be fair to him, Bimbisar is a handsome and powerful monarch. I'm sure you will be happy as his queen.'

'He already has a queen and a score of mistresses,' retorted Chellana scornfully.

King Chetak made his last move. 'Alright! You win. All I want is for you to meet him once. Make him go back to Magadh and you will not have to marry him.'

As Chellana's anger subsided, there was an air of resignation about her, hinting at the tough decision she would have to make. While dressing for the evening, Chellana resolved to find an escape from the situation with minimal consequences.

Princess Chellana shared Bimbisar's love for a challenge. Resolutely, she made her way to the royal garden where she was to meet the Magadh king, aiming to persuade him to go back to Magadh without a wedding.

Vaishali had never witnessed such a significant assignation before. The princesses had no control over the arranged alliances between kingdoms, making them mere pawns in the game of politics. Nor did the kings bother to seek their consent. That Bimbisar had thought her consent important made Chellana see him in a different light, but she was still not ready to marry him.

The approaching dusk turned the sky into a mesmerizing spectacle, with colours splashed across the horizon as if painted by the heavens themselves. The trees swayed to the sweet melodies of chirping birds, silencing everything else. A gentle breeze caressed her skin as the evening air carried a fragrant scent. Nature whispered all around her.

The royal garden was Chellana's sanctuary, a place of natural splendour that always made her heart leap with joy. Fountains adorned the place, their gentle splashes creating a soothing melody. Rows of vibrant flowers and plants lined the narrow, twisting walkways, creating a stunning contrast of hues. In the middle of the garden was a calm pond that reflected the beauty of the surrounding garden in all its glory. The lanterns hanging from trees cast a gentle glow that elevated the tranquil mood.

Bimbisar was taking a leisurely walk in the garden when

he spotted the princess entering through a beautifully adorned archway. He stopped in his tracks, staring at the lady in the distance. The sight of two princesses, not just one, caught him off guard. As the shorter one hurriedly tried to catch up, the taller princess marched towards him with determination.

'Pranam, Magadh Samrat!' the taller princess greeted him stiffly.

Bimbisar looked at the lady standing in front of him. A yellow kanchuki covered her shapely bust and a white silk antariya was wrapped around her hips. An orange uttariya was casually draped across her shoulders. Instead of wearing bulky jewellery, she had adorned her bun with a delicate string of flowers. Without a doubt, he knew it was Chellana.

'Pranam, Devi Chellana,' he said.

'That is a smart guess,' the princess smiled, and the atmosphere seemed to brighten.

'I didn't expect you to bring a companion, Devi,' Bimbisar remarked, his eyes taking in the shy young woman standing behind Chellana.

'This is my younger sister, Kalyani,' Chellana pushed her blushing sister forward.

'Pranam, Magadh Samrat!' Kalyani said softly, her words barely audible, while a shy smile played on her lips. In contrast to her older sister's self-assured stance, she stood awkwardly, almost as if she was attempting to blend into the background. Her delicate manner and soothing voice were a perfect embodiment of femininity.

'Pranam, Devi!' Bimbisar flashed a warm smile at the younger princess, attempting to put her at ease. 'I'm filled with gratitude to have the company of not one, but two princesses this evening.'

Chellana's words were quick and business-like as she addressed Bimbisar, 'I'll come straight to the point, Samrat.'

'Don't you think it is a good idea to settle in before we talk?' he smiled, gesturing towards a bench in a secluded alcove nestled among shrubs and tall trees, providing some privacy.

Kalyani expressed her gratitude with a smile, while Chellana appeared to be in a rush. She was eager to free herself from the weight of her thoughts.

'Do you agree that a war benefits neither the attacker nor the defender?' she asked brusquely. 'Wars result in needless bloodshed and cause unimaginable suffering.'

'I do not agree with the first part of your statement,' countered Bimbisar. 'Although the loser gains nothing, the victor of the battle undoubtedly reaps benefits. Also, it is the weaker party that suffers more harm, not the stronger one.'

Chellana changed her strategy. This time round, she attempted to compliment him by saying, 'I've heard great things about you. As a mighty and compassionate ruler, you have the power to avoid disastrous consequences.'

'And how can I accomplish that?' There was an amused smile on the Magadh king's lips as he watched the Lichchavi princess. She was as fiery as he had expected.

'You could go back to Magadh.'

'I could, but I'll not. I have come here with a purpose, Devi, and I will not go back empty-handed.' Bimbisar was enjoying the sparring session.

'And your purpose is to wed me?' Chellana countered.

'Absolutely not, Devi. That was never my intention. Your father put forth the idea of the marriage, intending to bring peace to Vaishali.'

'Alright! If marriage is what will save Vaishali, why don't you marry Kalyani? She is feminine and timid, and I'm the exact opposite. I enjoy horse riding, sword fighting, hunting and martial arts. Kalyani will make a better queen for Magadh.

Besides, she is open to the idea, while I'm not,' Chellana argued, while Kalyani shrank into the background.

'Give me a few more points and I may consider the alternative offer,' said Bimbisar. The conversation was getting more and more interesting.

'You are too old for me,' declared Chellana, as her eyes swept over his body. Her appraisal was bold and frank. When their eyes met, she couldn't help but be captivated by his strikingly handsome features and the unmistakable aura of power that seemed to radiate from him. 'You must be close to thirty or thirty-one, and I'm barely seventeen. That is almost half your age.'

'You are a little off the mark. I'm forty,' he laughed, his eyes twinkling with mischief. The princess had no idea that he was far from forty. 'If your rejection is solely based on age, it is important to consider that the age difference between Kalyani and me is much greater.'

'Don't you have enough queens and concubines that you want to marry me too?' Chellana made a last attempt. She had exhausted all her justifications and turned to Kalyani in search of convincing points. The sister's blushing face made it obvious that she had a crush on the Magadh king.

'I have just one queen and no concubine at the moment,' Bimbisar replied. There was a mischievous glint in his eyes as he said, 'Keep the ideas flowing, Devi. I may reconsider my decision to marry you if you can come up with some more convincing arguments.'

'Would you be open to at least considering my suggestion?' Chellana pleaded in desperation.

'Do not worry, Devi, I will let your father know about my decision. Thank you for meeting me and offering the alternatives for me to consider.' Bimbisar folded his hands, his gaze fixed on Chellana.

'Thank you, Magadh Samrat!' Chellana's response came out as a soft murmur. She felt defeated. Her confidence and pride shattered, she left empty-handed.

Kalyani conveyed her thanks in a faint voice, as she followed her sister out of the royal garden.

# 16

# A Reluctant Bride

After carefully studying the alignment of stars and planets, the royal astrologer declared an auspicious day for the wedding. The announcement resulted in a flurry of activities as everyone scrambled to get things done.

Excitement and anticipation filled the royal palace, as every corner bustled with preparations for the marriage. Magadh and Vaishali's union was of utmost importance, so they went to great lengths to make it truly unforgettable. Although there wasn't much time for preparations, the guest list was quite long. Among the attendees were royalties, settlers, merchants and many relatives.

Performers of all kinds, including musicians, buskers, magicians and ganikas, travelled from far and wide to exhibit their abilities and earn quick money. Culinary experts from distant lands came together to craft a range of delightful dishes for the wedding guests. Merchants brought extraordinary and expensive madira for connoisseurs.

Throughout the city, houses were decorated with flowers, buntings and flags. New clothes and jewellery were bought for the occasion. The atmosphere in Vaishali was one of pure joy. King Chetak was resolute in his efforts to leave a lasting impression on the king of Magadh.

While everyone else was celebrating, the bride wore a gloomy, despondent expression. Even the most soothing words couldn't cheer her up. Despite the best efforts by her sisters, friends and maids, she was reluctant to get dressed for the occasion.

'You are about to marry the most eligible king in the neighbourhood. Not only is he the most powerful king,' her friends reminded her, 'but he is also incredibly handsome.'

'I hate him,' she muttered through gritted teeth.

'In that case, think of it as a sacrifice for your kingdom,' advised her mother. 'When we first got married, I did not love your father, but over time I grew to care for him.'

Frustrated by the futility of explaining her point of view, the bride reluctantly went through the motions. She waited patiently for the right moment to seek her revenge, confident that it would present itself later.

Even though the wedding was planned in a short time, it turned out to be a magnificent affair. Initially hesitant, Bimbisar was pleasantly surprised by the extravagant treatment he received from King Chetak. The fact that he had successfully established an important alliance with Vaishali and managed to avert a battle brought him immense happiness.

The seventeen-year-old bride looked stunning in a red silk antariya skilfully woven by the artisans of Kashi. In addition, a delicate uttariya with elaborate golden embroidery rested gracefully on her shoulders. Her hair was elegantly braided, with golden threads adding a touch of luxury while a fragrant jasmine garland enhanced its beauty. An indulgent sandalwood scrub had transformed her skin, giving it a radiant glow that highlighted its honey-hued tone.

King Chetak went to great lengths to provide his beloved daughter with the finest in everything, not worrying about the expenses. The most exquisite jewellery was crafted by the local artisans. One by one, she was made to wear the bajubands, pearl satlari, jhumkas. An emerald-encrusted katibandh clasped her slim waist in a loving embrace. The heavy chandrahaar and chudamani had come from her mother's collection. Kohl lined her beautiful eyes. A unique ointment made from ripe pomegranate gave her lips a rich red hue, while the essence of parijat petals gave her pale cheeks a subtle blush. Her eyelids were touched up with a dash of gold, adding a subtle glow to her overall look. The scent of exotic essence exuded from her clothes.

She stole a glance at the man seated beside her under the flower-festooned canopy. He was dressed in a maroon silk antariya embroidered in gold. The rippling muscles of his arms were highlighted by armlets crafted in pearls and gold. A stunning ruby-encrusted filigreed necklace adorned his broad chest. His hair, arranged in the Gandhara style, was thick and glossy, complemented by a jewelled medallion that added a touch of sophistication.

Her scrutiny let no detail go unnoticed. The thick-lashed dark eyes, sharp nose, chiselled jaw and curved lips, all caught her attention. It was hard to not notice his impressive muscular frame and broad shoulders. Her bias and the partially dark garden had stopped her from realizing how attractive he was.

The unexpected whisper from Bimbisar caught Princess Chellana off guard, 'Are you satisfied?'

He found it impossible not to be entertained as he observed the stunning bride. In response, she shot him a fierce, mutinous glare. Quietly he declared, 'I don't know about you, but I feel I got a good deal.'

The celebration ended with a lively procession that meandered through the beautifully decorated streets of Vaishali. Onlookers lined up the streets, cheering for the newly married couple as their chariot passed by.

The celebrations continued from Vaishali to Rajgriha. It was late evening when the procession reached the Magadh capital. That day, the city had outdone itself to welcome the bride. There was music, dance, fireworks and jubilation everywhere.

The royal palace was beautifully decorated to welcome the king and his bride. Fragrant flowers adorned the exquisitely carved pillars, while silk and brocade draped the arches. The marble floors were covered in silk carpets, and the palace shimmered with countless lamps.

Amidst the chanting of holy verses, the Rajmata stepped forward to receive her son and his bride. She had taken a personal interest in the festivities and decorations. The reception was followed by more feasting and merry-making. Late into the night, the worn-out couple finally retreated to their bridal chamber.

The Rajmata was overjoyed. The powerful kingdoms of Kosala and Vajji Confederacy helped Magadh achieve peace and prosperity. What made it truly remarkable was that the process remained untainted by bloodshed.

What the Rajmata had not foreseen was Chellana's wilfulness. Before long, she proved to be a handful for both the Rajmata and Bimbisar. Recklessness and immaturity were clear in the behaviour of the seventeen-year-old queen. While in Magadh, she stayed confined with her childhood friend, Mugdha, and refrained from mingling with the women of the royal palace. They chatted for hours, went horse riding, hunted in the forest, and enjoyed the luxuries offered by the palace.

Fuelled by her desire for revenge, Chellana resolutely rejected the king's advances and refused to consummate their marriage. Although initially he ignored it, but when it occurred again during his second visit to her chamber, he confronted her, 'You are my wife, and I can enforce your compliance.'

'I understand that you have the power to make me sleep with you,' she replied, unfazed by his threat. 'But my heart will never belong to you.'

He gave her a disdainful look before storming out of the chamber. After that evening, Bimbisar completely ignored the petulant and immature bride. Rather, he spent each night with Queen Kosala, revelling in her profound affection for him. Gossip swiftly circulated among the palace inhabitants. Some rumours were shockingly cruel. The gossip eventually reached Chellana's friend, Mugdha, who relayed it faithfully to the young queen. Soon, the Vaishali princess grew worried about Bimbisar's lack of interest in her.

The annual commemoration of Bimbisar's coronation was a significant event for Magadh. The event was a lavish spectacle, complete with intricate ceremonies, generous contributions, and a sumptuous banquet. Queen Kosala Devi and the Rajmata worked closely to plan and execute the event. In her efforts to make the preparations remarkable, she sent a message for the young queen to join in the planning.

'The king's coronation day holds no significance for me whatsoever. I'm not interested in being involved in the planning,' Chellana responded brusquely to the message.

The Rajmata's heart sank on learning about Chellana's response. She was surprised by the utter disregard for her order. She couldn't shake off the sense of outrage at what had transpired. 'It was an order, not a request. Not even the king refuses to honour my order,' she fumed. The dasi who had acted as the messenger stood silently with her head bowed down. She was fully aware of the consequences.

The Rajmata sent the message to her son, who assured her he would talk to Chellana. It was not a satisfying response. But she knew that the kingdom had many pressing concerns, and her son couldn't afford to be preoccupied with insignificant matters. The Rajmata had extensive experience dealing with various challenges in the palace, but this one was beyond her capabilities.

Frustrated by her inability to get through to the young queen, the Rajmata sought Queen Kosala Devi's help.

'Queen Chellana is a stubborn and ill-mannered woman, totally unsuitable to be Bimbisar's wife. She has no sense of decorum or duty,' the Rajmata raged. 'Her childish behaviour is starting to annoy me now. It is your task to convince Chellana to conduct herself in a manner befitting a Magadh queen.'

Chellana's blatant disregard for the customs of Magadh didn't go unnoticed by Kosala Devi. She had been the first one to welcome Bimbisar's young wife to the kingdom. Despite her best efforts to win over the young queen's love and trust, Chellana remained resistant to her gentle persuasion.

Uncertain of how the young queen would respond, Kosala Devi proceeded to Chellana's chamber.

'How are you doing, Chellana?' Kosala Devi asked her affectionately.

Despite her hostility towards most women in the royal palace, Chellana found herself inexplicably drawn to Kosala Devi. Although she initially intended to be rude, the senior queen's affectionate nature eventually melted her heart. The day after Chellana arrived in Magadh, Kosala Devi had hosted a private feast in her chamber, inviting only a select group of women. She had spread out all her jewellery before the young queen, inviting her to choose the pieces she fancied. It was a rare and generous gesture from the senior queen. Chellana, who rarely cared for jewellery, reluctantly picked out a few pieces at Kosala Devi's insistence.

Chellana felt touched when Kosala Devi showed kindness to her friend as well. Mugdha was surprised when the senior queen unexpectedly asked her to pick out a piece of jewellery for herself too. From that instant, Chellana and Mugdha were utterly enchanted by Kosala Devi's irresistible charisma.

'You didn't have to walk to my chamber,' Chellana respectfully greeted the senior queen. 'Why didn't you summon me instead?'

'I would not dream of doing that, Chellana,' Kosala Devi said with a gentle smile.

After ensuring that Kosala Devi was at ease, the young queen directed one of her attendants to bring a refreshing drink and a variety of exquisite delicacies for the senior queen.

Kosala Devi decided not to reveal the reason for her visit. Instead, she diverted the conversation to other subjects, such as the delightful milestones achieved by her little daughter. The two queens laughed and engaged in gossip about the happenings within the palace. The amusing anecdotes contributed to a lively atmosphere. Only after they had finished gossiping and Chellana was relaxed, did Kosala Devi finally get to the point.

'Have you chosen what you will wear for the coronation day celebrations?' Kosala Devi asked in a warm and friendly manner. 'I thought it would be a nice contrast if I wore pastel shades while you opted for more vibrant colours. I want everyone to notice your youthful beauty.'

'I'll not be joining the celebrations,' Chellana stated firmly.

Surprised by her decision, Kosala Devi replied, 'But Chellana, it is one of the most important days in the kingdom. Our presence is obligatory.'

'That may be true, but the celebrations will have to go on without me. I have plans to go hunting in the forest, hoping to catch some wild game.' Chellana noticed the worried expression on Kosala Devi's face and reached out to hold her hand. 'Do not worry, Didi. Your presence will make up for my absence. You are the senior queen anyway,' she said.

'We both are required to mark our presence, Chellana. There will be hundreds of guests from various kingdoms, including the ones from Vaishali. I think your father has also received an invitation. Your absence will be noticed and it will embarrass the king. He will take it as an insult.'

'I do not care,' announced Chellana petulantly. She fought back her tears. 'Do you know he has not visited my chamber in the past few months? The dasis have been gossiping about his disinterest. Is that not an insult too?'

Chellana's initial feeling of triumph had quickly turned into bitter disappointment when Bimbisar showed no interest in her. The more he disregarded her, the stronger her desire for him grew. Stripped of her pride, she desperately wanted him back in her bed. She had been dropping subtle hints through her friend, hoping to catch his attention at the grand banquet, but he remained unresponsive. She couldn't help but feel envious of the close relationship Kosala Devi had with the king.

Kosala Devi nodded in agreement, and said, 'Yes, it is definitely an insult. I'll ask him to visit you tonight. The king should spend time with you.'

'He has no time for me, Didi,' Chellana cried. 'It's my fault, of course. I didn't treat him well, and now it's too late.'

'It's never too late, Chellana. The king may appear tough, but beneath that exterior lies a gentle and kind heart. Why don't you try to catch his attention during the coronation day celebrations? He will be in a good mood and I'm sure he will respond favourably.'

Chellana nodded mutely. She decided to forgo her plans for the hunting expedition and devoted herself completely to the celebrations. First, she surprised the Rajmata by touching her feet and seeking her blessings. Then she proceeded to the sabhagriha, where the celebrations were about to begin.

Bimbisar couldn't believe his eyes when he saw her entering the royal sabhagriha, dressed in all her finery and beaming at him. With that moment as a turning point, the young queen set out on a mission to capture her husband's heart.

Kosala Devi felt a weight off her chest as things finally fell into place for her husband and his new queen.

The air was filled with the promise of change. As the new season began, the dasis observed Bimbisar's frequent visits to the chamber of the junior queen. A few months later, the news of the junior queen's impending motherhood didn't surprise the palace dwellers.

# 17

# Another Queen

Like his mother, Bimbisar noticed the difference in personalities between his two queens. Kosala's composed and wise disposition was in complete contrast to Chellana's volatile personality. He constantly had to balance between their distinct personalities to avoid offending either.

Bimbisar was aware that the Rajmata had always been fond of Kosala. Her fondness for the senior queen stemmed from the fact that she came from a powerful kingdom.

Chellana's rebellious behaviour annoyed the Rajmata; she would often express her frustrations to her son. 'A Magadh queen must behave with grace and dignity. She should not go on hunting expeditions without the right companions. It is even more necessary now that she is a mother. I know you have assigned the prince's care to Kosala, but she is not his natural mother.'

'Chellana has always been an independent-minded woman. She's a little wild perhaps,' Bimbisar said, trying to ease his mother's worries. 'But she will do nothing against the interest of the kingdom.'

'I think you are too lenient,' the Rajmata grumbled. 'Maybe you should send her back to Vaishali for some time. It would do her good. Also, King Chetak could spend some time with his grandson.'

Although he didn't entirely agree with his mother on the junior queen's recalcitrant nature, Bimbisar agreed that a change would be good for Chellana. Given her personality, he would need to proceed with caution. Chellana would immediately oppose the idea if she even suspected that he was sending her to Vaishali on his mother's advice.

Seeking Kosala's viewpoint, Bimbisar broached the subject with her. 'What is your opinion about the situation? Should I follow my mother's advice and send Chellana to her father's palace?'

Kosala was aware of the antagonism between the Rajmata and the junior queen. She proposed a solution that would allow the king to honour her mother's advice without upsetting Chellana. 'We could send a message to King Chetak congratulating him on his grandson's intelligence and then sit back and wait.'

'What do you think will happen if we send the message?' Bimbisar was confused by Kosala's suggestion.

'King Chetak would feel an intense desire to see his grandson. And he might ask you to send Chellana and Kunika to Vaishali.'

'That is a brilliant suggestion, Kosala. I knew I could rely on you to find a way.'

The message was quickly sent, and King Chetak promptly responded with generous gifts for Bimbisar and the royal family. Just as Kosala had foreseen, the king formally invited Chellana and his grandson to come to Vaishali.

At first, Chellana refused to leave for her father's kingdom. 'You are trying to send me away because your mother doesn't like me,' she said.

'Your father wants to spend time with Kunika, and as a grandfather, he has every right to do so. I cannot refuse him, Chellana,' Bimbisar tried to reason with her.

A few days later, Chellana and her son embarked on their journey to Vaishali. A sense of peace descended on the palace, and everyone heaved a sigh of relief. The Rajmata, who had been pushing for a union between the Madra king and Bimbisar, suggested that Bimbisar and Princess Kshema should get married. A day after Chellana's departure, the Rajmata sent a message to the Madra king without waiting for her son's approval. Recognizing the chance to improve his standing and achieve harmony in his realm, the Madra king willingly accepted her proposal.

With all the obstacles out of the way, the Rajmata went up to her son. 'The princess is exquisitely beautiful, I'm told,' she said. 'Her radiant golden complexion can light up the palace.'

'I agree the princess is exquisite, her radiance will bring a new sparkle to our palace, but mother, isn't the palace already shining brightly with two beautiful queens?' Bimbisar commented humorously. He was aware of his mother's brilliant strategies, so he sensed the meaning behind her words.

'Son, this alliance promises us not only a beautiful queen but also many advantages,' the Rajmata explained. 'The Madra kingdom's location on the Uttarapath grants us a valuable edge in that region. The Madra king's alliance will provide the support to repel the Huna invaders and facilitate the expansion of the Magadh Empire towards the north. Also, the Madra king is equally eager to better our relationship.'

Chellana's absence injected a sense of urgency into the plans. Expecting the junior queen's disapproval, the Rajmata worked tirelessly to complete the alliance details before Chellana got whiff of her plans. The messengers, adorned in royal colours, rode tirelessly between the two kingdoms, their saddlebags filled with important documents that needed to be sealed before the wedding.

The wedding preparations were in full swing when Chellana returned to Magadh. Her anger knew no bounds as she discovered Bimbisar had intentionally kept her uninformed. She learned about the wedding when her father, King Chetak, received an invitation to attend the celebrations. Consumed by fury, she promptly began her journey to Magadh.

'Is this why I was sent away from Magadh?' Chellana demanded as she stormed into Bimbisar's chamber. 'So your mother could arrange another wedding for you? Is this a conspiracy to undermine my position?'

'Chellana, try to stay calm.' Bimbisar placed his hand on her shoulder and guided her towards a seat. 'No one is trying to undermine your position. You will remain as important as you were. It is just a political alliance, nothing more.'

She raged and wept until she exhausted all her energy. 'It is a humiliation,' she said. 'I do not know how Queen Kosala accepts everything so calmly.'

'Kosala is a wise woman. She is aware of how a kingdom functions. Alliances are created for political benefits rather than emotional reasons,' Bimbisar replied. 'Understanding and accepting this would be easier if you were more mature.'

'I'll never accept such alliances,' Chellana said firmly. 'It is degrading to treat a woman as a commodity to be exchanged for political advantages.'

'Do not forget that our wedding too was arranged for political reasons,' he jogged her memory.

'And let us not forget, I strongly opposed the wedding. Sadly, circumstances compelled me to agree. It was emotional blackmail. I was told to sacrifice my happiness for the sake of the kingdom,' Chellana said bitterly.

'But we fell in love, didn't we?' Lifting her face by the chin, he asked gently. Her innocent confidence and stunning beauty never failed to astonish him whenever he saw her. Despite her efforts to appear confident, her vulnerability never failed to affect him. 'Neither kings nor princesses have the freedom to marry for love. The lavishness of a royal wedding conceals many political motives. For countless ages, this eternal cycle has been repeating itself, seemingly with no end.'

Chellana, overcome by his affectionate words, instinctively nuzzled her face against his chest. Being held by him brought her a sense of calm. She whispered, 'Promise me that nothing will alter our relationship.'

'Nothing will change between us, my dear queen, I promise.' Filled with intense passion, he led her towards the bed.

Princess Kshema arrived as the youngest of Bimbisar's queens, carrying a trove of treasures. Along with her came the commitment of a firm alliance with the Madra king that couldn't be undone. As soon as she set foot in the palace, it was transformed with a new surge of energy and joyous laughter. Her irresistible charm and youthful radiance made her the focal point of everyone's attention. Kshema's face captivated Bimbisar so much that he couldn't take his eyes off her. The king became so captivated by the youngest queen's charms that he temporarily forgot about everyone else. Upset by the change in him, Chellana went with her complaint to Kosala.

Chellana found Kosala in a sombre mood. She had just returned after visiting the Rajmata, who was bedridden. However, the senior queen was pleased to have Chellana's company.

Seated on Kosala's balcony, the two queens enjoyed the peaceful atmosphere of the evening and the music played by a dasi.

'I'm appalled by Kshema's arrogance. She may be beautiful, but that doesn't mean she can disrespect the senior queens. When it comes to beauty, she cannot hold a candle to Amrapali, Vaishali's famous nagarvadhu,' Chellana whined. She reached for a piece of fresh mango on the platter in front of her. It was her favourite fruit, and even the foulest of moods couldn't deter her from enjoying it. She wiped her lips and carried on, 'What is even more irritating is how she constantly boasts about the magnificence of her palace in Sagala, as if it is the most extraordinary palace in the world.'

A smile tugged at Kosala's lips as she recalled Chellana's rebellious attitude when she first arrived. Just like Kshema, the Vaishali princess was both proud and disrespectful. Maybe even more than Kshema. The junior queen's once wild spirit had been tamed by her experiences in Magadh, Kosala's gentle persuasion, and the responsibilities of motherhood, but occasionally, traces of it would show up.

'She is still very young and has a lot to learn,' Kosala observed softly as she handed Chellana another piece of mango. 'It is our responsibility as senior queens to educate her about the traditions and customs of Magadh.'

However, Chellana was not in the mood to relent. 'I agree Kshema is very young, but I'm astonished by the king's actions. Although he is not young anymore, he walks around looking completely besotted. It is not the first time he has gotten married.'

Kosala couldn't help but burst into laughter at Chellana's words. 'Let's be fair to Bimbisar. He is captivated by Kshema's dazzling beauty. I'm no longer young, while you still embody a sense of wildness and freedom. It is natural for him to be inclined towards the young wife,' she said.

'But it is several months since they were married. Is it not fair for him to divide his time equally between the three of us? For how much longer will he be attached to her uttariya?'

Chellana's rant was cut short by the unexpected entry of the very person they were discussing.

Followed by a dasi, Kshema glided gracefully into Kosala's chamber, her presence immediately filling the room with the fragrance of sandalwood. She looked regal in her elegant outfit, comprising a maroon silk antariya and a beautifully patterned brocade kanchuki. The delicate fabric of the uttariya gracefully draped over her shoulders was embellished with intricate golden embroidery. Her hair was braided and perfumed with a thick garland of parijat, while around her slim waist was an emerald-encrusted katibandh. Her beauty was absolutely breathtaking.

Kosala didn't hold Bimbisar responsible for being besotted with Kshema.

'Pranam, Devi,' Kshema folded her hands. 'May I join you for a while?'

'I'll be happy if you joined us,' Kosala got up and welcomed Kshema. Holding the young queen's hand, she guided her towards the balcony where Chellana was relaxing against a cushion.

Kshema settled comfortably among the luxurious cushions and gestured for the dasi to come closer. The dasi held a silver tray with an intricately carved jewellery box. After dismissing the dasi, Kshema opened the jewellery box with great care, unveiling a stunning chandrahaar and a pair of intricately crafted bajubunds.

Chellana's eyes brightened when she saw the stunning jewellery, but she pretended not to care and shifted her focus to the plate of mangoes.

'Thank you, Kshema,' Kosala said, as she placed the jewellery back in the box and smiled warmly at the youngest queen. 'But I cannot accept such lavish gifts. The thought behind the gifts means a lot more to me, and I genuinely appreciate it.'

'But…'

'Accept the gifts, sister,' Chellana cut into the conversation. Her voice dripping with sarcasm, she remarked, 'The Madra princess seems to have quite a selection of these pieces. Some she brought with her to Magadh, and some were gifted by the Magadh king.'

Chellana's sarcasm was not lost on Kshema. Her face turned

red as she admitted, 'I didn't realize you would be here. I should have brought your gifts too.'

'You have a lot to learn, Kshema…'

'Enough, Chellana,' Kosala interrupted, signalling with her raised hand to stop the discussion. 'We should be respectful towards one another. Let's not forget that we are the queens of Magadh.'

'Very well, I'll leave the two of you to exchange pleasantries. It's clear I'm not wanted here,' Chellana got up abruptly. Despite Kosala's attempts to stop her, she stormed out of the chamber.

Embarrassed by Chellana's immaturity, Kosala went back to the balcony, but by then the atmosphere was no longer enjoyable.

'I'm sorry for the unpleasantness caused by my arrival,' Kshema apologized. 'I shouldn't have barged into your chamber without following the proper protocol of sending a dasi for permission beforehand.'

'You don't have to apologize, and you don't need my permission to visit my chamber.'

Kshema left a little later, but only after Kosala had accepted the gifts. Despite the unpleasantness caused by Chellana, the incident brought Kshema closer to the senior queen.

Kosala accompanied Kshema to Chellana's chamber with equally extravagant gifts. Initially, the junior queen adamantly refused the gifts, but eventually Kosala pacified Chellana. Before the visit concluded, she successfully orchestrated a tenuous truce between the two queens. She considered it a major achievement to have gained the trust of Kshema.

The peaceful atmosphere of the palace was abruptly disrupted one night when a distressing report startled the people inside. The condition of the Rajmata had worsened, and her chances of survival were slim. Bimbisar and the three queens rushed to her chamber, where they discovered the royal vaidya tending to her with a herbal potion. He shook his head solemnly to express the utter hopelessness of the situation. Seated on one side, the purohit recited holy verses.

'Mother, it is me. Please open your eyes.' With a firm grip on his mother's hand, Bimbisar pleaded desperately.

The Rajmata's eyes fluttered momentarily as she appealed to him with her eyes. 'Abhay!' she whispered.

'What about Abhay?' asked Bimbisar urgently. 'Do you want me to summon him here?'

The Rajmata shook her head and mumbled something. Leaning forward, Bimbisar strained to catch her words. Then she mumbled incoherently, 'He is your son. Kadambini…'

The air grew still as Bimbisar grappled with the weight of the news. Within moments, the Rajmata grasped his hand and whispered something indistinctly. With a great deal of effort, he could grasp the word 'Kashyap...'

He noticed her hands growing colder as he held them. Filled with despair, he pleaded, 'I beg you, don't leave me.'

She stared at her son with a vacant look in her eyes before finally closing them and letting out the final sigh. As he sobbed over her lifeless body, he wondered what she had wished to convey.

Kosala sat on the far side of the bed and massaged the Rajmata's feet, hoping to restore some warmth to them. Tears flowed down her cheeks, uncontrollable, relentless.

The Rajmata's hand went limp in her son's hand as a gust of wind swept through the chamber. Bimbisar shook his mother gently, hoping for a reaction, but she lay still.

The vaidya examined her pulse. There was none. Gently, he guided her hands to rest on her chest.

The Rajmata had passed away. The uneasy calm in the chamber was shattered by the sound of wailing.

# 18

# Tragic Times

The death of Rajmata Hemavati created a void that was deeply felt by everyone. While the Rajmata was alive, her son never made important decisions without first seeking her advice. Bimbisar was overwhelmed by grief. The atmosphere in the royal palace was sombre. Within a short span of time, the king's once proud shoulders sagged under the weight of sorrow. His ambitions had been stoked by the Rajmata, who pushed him relentlessly from one victory to another. Her passing away had taken away his desire for victories.

With slumped shoulders and shaky hands, the king shuffled through the palace corridors where his mother once strolled. Shocked at her husband's plight, Queen Kosala, who loved the Rajmata, struggled to console Bimbisar. Her chamber became her sanctuary, and she emerged from it only to take part in the sacred funerary rites.

After his mother passed away, the king subsisted on meagre portions of food, just enough to keep himself from starving. No one except Kosala and Abhay had permission to enter his chamber. Abhay had always held a special place in his heart, but discovering that the boy was his son added a newfound warmth.

Setting aside her own grief, Kosala tried to comfort her husband, but he didn't respond to her efforts.

'She was the fulcrum of my existence,' he cried. 'Without her, I can't find the strength to carry on and live a normal life, Kosala.'

Kosala's voice was full of compassion as she acknowledged that.

'I understand, Maharaj. But the world does not stop spinning. You are a king. The future of this kingdom lies in your hands. You do not have the luxury of wallowing in grief.'

Bimbisar was unresponsive to all her statements. 'Leave me alone, Kosala,' he begged. 'There are many ministers in the kingdom. They will take care of everything.'

Kosala sought help from the remaining queens. Despite the kind attention and loving approach of Chellana and Kshema, Bimbisar couldn't shake off his dejection. The last words of his mother had left him confused. What had she wanted to say about his brother Kashyap? He spent many nights pacing the palace halls.

Meanwhile, the kingdom went through a period of immense suffering. Encouraged by Bimbisar's inertia, the rebels started regrouping.

Having waited for the perfect moment, Kashyap finally saw his chance to strike. Without his mother's presence to hold him back, he could now execute his plans unhesitatingly. He assembled a group of dissenters, and together they conspired to remove Bimbisar from power. Disgruntled ministers and courtiers who had been penalized for corruption were among the dissenters. The meeting also had a group of soldiers who felt they had been unfairly denied the promotion they deserved.

During the meeting at his forest hunting lodge, Kashyap promised to give them important portfolios for their support. There was ample supply of madira and food to appease the rebels. The lure of attractive portfolios made the offer from the king's brother even more appealing.

'Magadh's integrity is in danger because of our king. He can't function without the guidance of the Rajmata,' Kashyap bellowed arrogantly. 'If we don't act swiftly and remove Bimbisar, our adversaries will attack and we will lose our kingdom.'

'Bimbisar has to go,' echoed his supporters.

'It is important to win Vassakar over to our group if we want to achieve our goal,' suggested an old minister. 'He is cunning and adept at manipulating. The sly minister will prove to be an indispensable ally in our mission to gain power.'

Everyone nodded in agreement. Vassakar's power and abilities were well known to all the citizens of Magadh. Kashyap, however, was reluctant to include him in his group. Aware of the minister's ambitions and deceitfulness, he dreaded that the minister would betray him at the first opportunity.

'It may be difficult to enlist Vassakar's support,' Kashyap expressed his opinion. 'He is too loyal to Bimbisar.' What he didn't tell his supporters was Vassakar hated him, and considered him a snake in the grass.

'Every man has a price,' said a minister. 'All we have to do is dangle the right bait. All we have to do is to find the price.'

'Any indiscretion at this stage could prove lethal to our plans, so let us not jeopardize the effort. We will have to do without him till we have the king out of our path,' Kashyap cautioned the minister. 'Vassakar will come around when the kingdom is in my hands. He is an ambitious man who will go any length to gain an upper hand in most matters.'

The meeting ended with a decision to explore ways to enlist some of the most important ministers in the kingdom. This would further undermine Bimbisar's power over his kingdom.

'Brothers, we will meet again after a week,' Kashyap announced. 'Meanwhile, I hope to bring more ministers into our fold soon. By next month, God willing, we will oust Bimbisar from the throne and you will have a new king.'

Standing proudly in front of the gathering, he could already feel the heaviness of the crown on his head.

The hunting lodge resounded with the chant, 'Oust Bimbisar! Oust Bimbisar!'

Little did they know that one of Vassakar's spies had penetrated Kashyap's group of rebels. After receiving intelligence that Kashyap was secretly plotting with some disgruntled ministers to harm the king, he put a spy on the job of investigating the matter. Not only had the spy infiltrated the intricate web of conspiracy, but he had also meticulously collected the identities of every traitor involved.

Without wasting time, the spy conveyed the details of their plans to Vassakar.

Vassakar was horrified. He knew Kashyap had been attempting to exert influence over Kunika and several ministers, but he had not expected the traitor to begin his nefarious activities so soon after the Rajmata's death. Nor did he expect Kashyap's success in recruiting so many people in his plot to overthrow the king.

Bimbisar was still mourning, and had no intention of granting audience to any of his ministers. Fearing the situation would worsen, Vassakar reached out to the former rajpurohit for help.

'There are disturbing developments in the kingdom. My intelligence sources have informed me that Kashyap and his supporters are plotting an uprising against the king. Any delay in dealing with them could lead to disastrous results. You have been his trusted advisor for a long time. Please help the king understand the consequences of his absence from the court. He may listen to you,' said Vassakar.

The rajpurohit had been a trusted advisor to King Bhattiya and the Rajmata before taking on that role for their son. He regarded Bimbisar as his child and was concerned about his well-being. The old priest could take a few liberties, which were denied to other ministers.

On realizing the urgency of the matter, the rajpurohit immediately made his way to Bimbisar's chamber.

'I understand your loss, Maharaj,' the rajpurohit said, his greying eyebrows furrowing with empathy. 'The entire kingdom is grieving the Rajmata's death, but a king can't afford to continue grieving for long. Your enemies are mobilizing themselves. The Rajmata would have wanted you to attend to the matters of the kingdom.'

When the rajpurohit failed to motivate Bimbisar, he told him the truth, 'Maharaj, your brother Kashyap is conspiring against you. There is an urgent need to restrain him.'

The words had an immediate impact on the king. He recalled the final words his father uttered before passing away: 'Beware of Kashyap!' The Rajmata had also uttered the traitor's name on her deathbed.

Bimbisar stood up, roaring like a tiger. 'I'll resolve this matter once and for all.' Seizing a sword, he rushed out before the rajpurohit could stop him.

Without delay, the king summoned the court. Bimbisar didn't want any of the traitors to escape, so he summoned the security chief and handed him the list of traitors given by Vassakar.

The ministers were delighted to see the king in the court. There were many pending matters, and Bimbisar quickly dealt with them. Apart from the chief minister, security minister and rajpurohit, no one else was given information about the traitors.

While the king attended to pressing matters in the court, the security chief apprehended and swiftly executed the traitors following a brief trial. All that remained was the decision on the quantum of punishment to be awarded to Kashyap. The security chief held the treacherous brother in the dungeon until his punishment was decided by Bimbisar.

'I can't have my brother's blood on my hands,' Bimbisar confessed to Kosala later in the day. The thought of punishing Kashyap filled him with distress. 'The battle for succession took the life of my oldest brother, leaving me with just one brother. How can I order his death?'

The problem was complex, but it needed to be resolved. Even though Kosala could always come up with the perfect solution, she was now in a dilemma.

'Maharaj, you must follow the raj dharma. Death is the only punishment for traitors. Your brother will strike back if you pardon him. It will establish a negative precedent, leading all traitors to seek clemency.'

'You are right, Kosala. I must follow the raj dharma. I'll seek the advice of the mahamatya and the rajpurohit before deciding on Kashyap's punishment.'

The mahamatya and the rajpurohit repeated Kosala's words. The king couldn't pardon traitors. Bimbisar, however, showed mercy by allowing Kashyap to choose how he wanted to die.

'I would like to die like a prince,' declared Kashyap, putting the king in a quandary.

It was easy for the wise mahamatya to resolve the matter. The kingdom's finest warrior was ordered to take on Kashyap in a sword fight. The news left Kashyap terrified. He knew he would meet an inglorious end at the hands of his opponent in the duel.

'I would rather die without bloodshed,' he told the prison guards. 'I would rather die by consuming poison.'

That evening, he was given a potent poison to ensure a quick death. But the villain had one last trick up his sleeves. He knew Bimbisar wouldn't want a scandal, so he would try to keep his execution a secret from the Magadh citizens.

'I'm very fond of my nephew Kunika,' Kashyap conveyed his last wish to the prison in-charge. 'I want to bless him before I die.'

Kashyap's last desire was communicated to Bimbisar, who saw nothing wrong in permitting his son to visit the prisoner.

Kunika had little respect for his uncle, who he thought was too pompous and deceitful. It came as a surprise to him that his uncle wanted to meet him.

The malicious man held no affection for his nephew, yet he was keen on poisoning his mind before his death. Kashyap had seen the cruel streak in Kunika when the boy was just seven years old. Kunika and his friends bound a young servant boy to a tree covered with red ants. Despite the poor boy screaming in pain, the prince laughed and refused to set him free.

When Kashyap spotted Kunika approaching, the uncle eagerly extended his hands through the prison bars to his nephew. In a voice filled with honeyed sweetness, he said, 'My dear nephew. I was dying to see you one last time.'

'What is it you want?' Kunika looked down his nose at the grovelling man. 'Let me warn you. I can do nothing for you, nor appeal for your release.'

'I want nothing from you, dear nephew. I just wanted to hold you in my arms one last time.'

'Sorry! I can't oblige you,' said the prince curtly. 'I don't like being hugged. Anything else?'

'Your father is...' Kashyap said coaxingly, but the prince interrupted him mid-sentence.

'You deserve every bit of your punishment. In my father's place, I would have executed you a long time back. You are nothing but a snake. Traitors have no place in this kingdom.' Kunika turned on his heels and began walking away.

'Your father is to blame for the death of his older brother, and now he is determined to have me executed. He is a murderer!' Kashyap shouted. His gamble did not pay off. Kunika refused to bite the bait.

Kashyap was aware of his nephew's greed for the crown, and he had hoped to exploit it. He also knew the prince was jealous of Abhay. 'You will not be able to sit on the throne until your back is bent with age. Your father will cling to his throne until his last breath,' shouted Kashyap. Frustrated with Kunika's response, the traitor added, 'Did you know your father loves Abhay more than you?'

'Don't waste your breath, uncle. I wish you a peaceful death,' Kunika sniggered as he strode away from the prison.

Infuriated by his failure to incite the nephew against the king, Kashyap vented his anger by repeatedly banging his head against the prison bars, the sound echoing through the empty corridors. No one stopped him. No one cared. That evening, he died an inglorious death. Alone and embittered.

# 19

# The Wayward Son

The kingdom experienced a series of transformations following the Rajmata's passing. Bimbisar appointed Queen Kosala Devi as the Rajmata to fill the void created by his mother's death. Kosala was reluctant to accept the position, but the king insisted on it. She was wise and mature, and he trusted her capabilities. He also revealed to her that Abhay was his son. Kosala's surprise was short-lived as she swiftly came to terms with the truth.

Kosala was fond of the illegitimate son of her husband. She had witnessed his transformation from a friendly boy to a sociable teenager, and finally to a confident and skilled young man who wielded a sword with ease and possessed a fine understanding of warfare. The total opposite, Kunika was rebellious and irreverent right from childhood. He showed no respect for anyone, not even his own father. His unruly behaviour worsened as he grew into a teenager.

Through his consistent display of patience, respect and kindness, Abhay acquired a strong reputation and enjoyed goodwill within the palace. The Rajmata fulfilled her promise, devoting herself to his education and paying careful attention to his progress. In contrast, Kunika earned a negative reputation, evoking animosity in all those with whom he crossed paths. Drunk with power, he swaggered along the palace corridors, his arrogance and cynicism apparent to all.

On Kosala's insistence, Bimbisar appointed Abhay as one of

his army commanders. Her confidence in the young man was fully justified. Within a short span of time, Abhay gained the love and loyalty of his soldiers.

Royal heads never lie easy. Secrets abounded within the palace, with webs of intrigue and plots lurking behind every pillar. Add to that assassins, traitors, informers and spies hiding in every nook and cranny. Like the earlier Rajmata, Kosala too had to stay abreast of the whispers and murmurs in the kingdom. It helped her pick up subtle cues and hints of trouble brewing before any untoward incident actually occurred.

When Kosala became Rajmata, she inherited a complex network of palace spies from Queen Hemavati. Within a couple of years, she learned the art of employing spies with great efficiency. Kosala depended heavily on Abhay for many crucial and covert assignments. So impressed was she by his ability to keep secrets and his trustworthiness that she chose him to lead her spy network. No one except the king had knowledge of this.

Spies seldom deliver good news. The bulk of the intelligence gained from them was about evil plots, malicious rumours, and pernicious intrigues. Kosala experienced a similar situation. Kunika's behaviour was one of her primary worries. As his foster mother, she believed it was her responsibility to watch over his welfare and assist him in making wise choices. However, he has been quite a handful since he turned three. The boy consistently displayed a rebellious temperament. Kosala was surprised to discover his cruel side.

Kosala had received reports about Kunika's wrongdoings, which exposed his troubling transformation from a jealous and violent child to an insecure and merciless young adult. The scales fell from her eyes as the truth emerged.

When he was eight years old, he came close to causing the death of his half-brother because of an angry outburst. At ten, he won a duel against his rival through deceit. By the time he turned thirteen, he had already developed a tendency to gamble.

At the tender age of fourteen, he sneaked into a brothel and tasted the pleasures of illicit love, and just a year later, at fifteen, he found himself entangled with a corrupt group of people.

Although Kosala had tried to warn Chellana, she displayed a complete lack of interest in her son's reckless behaviour. Bimbisar's decision to entrust his son to Kosala had deeply bothered the junior queen, and she didn't hesitate to show her displeasure.

'Aren't you able to handle him, Rajmata?' she snarled. 'The king has assigned his upbringing to you. Why seek my help now?'

Fearful of what he would do next, Kosala called for Abhay and instructed him to compile a comprehensive report on Kunika's activities.

One morning, Kosala was supervising the garden near the temple when she saw Abhay striding toward her. He had grown from an awkward teenager to a strapping and handsome young man. She marvelled at the confidence with which the young man carried himself.

'Pranam, Rajmata,' said the young commander. 'I'm sorry to bring you disturbing news.'

'What is it, Abhay?' she asked, her heart pounding with fear at what he was about to reveal.

'It's about Kunika,' Abhay looked abashed. Even though he didn't know of his father's identity, Kosala had a gut feeling that he knew who it might be. The uncanny resemblance between the king and Abhay was unmistakable. 'Rajmata, I have great affection for Kunika and I strongly dislike gathering intelligence about him. I'm troubled by what I have learned and feel obligated to alert you about his behaviour.'

She knew of his evil company, gambling, and whoring. What could be worse than his lust for the throne. *What had Kunika done this time?* Kosala wondered. Although most courtiers addressed him as Yuvraj Ajatashatru, she continued to think of him as Kunika, as did Bimbisar and Abhay.

'Don't hesitate, Abhay. Give me the details. Regardless of how unpleasant these may be.'

'Well, we already know of his intense dislike for the Buddha. This time, he has colluded with some misguided companions to burn down several huts within a Buddhist sangha.'

Shocked by the news, Kosala sank into a bench. A feeling of disappointment overwhelmed her on hearing of Kunika's brutality. The prince displayed a clear tendency towards cruelty in both his thoughts and actions.

'Rajmata, there is even graver news,' Abhay said gently. He was aware of the deep affection Kosala had for Kunika. 'Kunika has come under the influence of the Buddha's cousin, who has been conspiring against the king. I heard Kunika has been bragging about seizing the throne soon.'

'This can't be true,' Kosala clutched at her heart and moaned.

'Unfortunately, it is the truth. It is crucial that we put an end to the conspiracy soon, else the outcome will be grave.'

'Thank you, Abhay,' Kosala mumbled, grasping his hand. He smiled reassuringly, 'Don't worry, Rajmata. As long as I'm alive, I'll not let any harm come to the king.'

Then he turned on his heels and left her alone with her thoughts.

Kosala, unable to believe that Kunika was scheming to seize the throne, assigned the responsibility of uncovering the truth to a trusted spy. He simply repeated exactly what Abhay had reported.

Kosala could no longer ignore the warnings. Failing to stop Kunika could have disastrous consequences. Finally, one evening, Kosala walked down the guarded corridor to her husband's room.

It had been a strenuous day for Bimbisar. News had reached him that the Lichchavis were planning to raid a mine located near the border of Magadh. The day had been a whirlwind of meetings and strategizing with ministers. Vassakar was tasked with gathering information related to the Lichchavi pilfering at the mine. Then, there were reports of unrest in a village, and the security minister was tasked with ensuring a peaceful resolution of the matter.

Rajmata Kosala Devi entered Bimbisar's room at the exact moment he was lifting his glass of madira.

'Ah, I was hoping to have a word with you. There's something important I need to talk to you about. Come here, Kosala,' he patted the seat next to him.

'I'll go first, Maharaj,' she said. 'I can't put off what I want to discuss any longer.'

'Alright, let's start by discussing your point.'

In a nutshell, Kosala detailed everything she had discovered about Kunika. She had tried to warn Bimbisar about the behaviour of his wayward son in the past too, but blinded with love, he had refused to accept the truth.

'We can't allow this matter to get out of hand. I'll summon the Yuvraj and ask him to explain.' An irate Bimbisar stood up to summon the guards, but Kosala stopped him.

'Let's not be hasty, Maharaj. We have to plan our actions carefully to avoid any negative consequences,' she said.

Bimbisar's anger subsided as suddenly as it had erupted. His shoulders drooped in defeat as he sat down heavily. 'Where did I go wrong, Kosala? Did I fail in guiding my son?'

'Please don't blame yourself, Maharaj. It is as much my fault as yours. We both have failed in our duties.' With tears welling up in her eyes, she gazed at her husband. 'Let's think of the way forward. What strikes me most is his overpowering ambition to become king.'

'Why is he not satisfied? Have I not made him the governor of Anga? Not just that, I also declared him my heir. Is he prepared to take my life in his pursuit of the throne?'

Kosala felt a sharp pang in her heart when she saw the pained expression on Bimbisar's face. 'Maharaj, the prince is impatient. He doesn't understand the sacrifices and struggles that have to be made for a throne.'

'I have no one else to blame for my negligence. You have consistently alerted me to Kunika's nefarious activities, but I disregarded them, attributing them to his youthful vigour and impulsive temperament.'

Bimbisar's sadness prevented Kosala from revealing Kunika's persecution of Buddhist monks.

The kingdom was in a state of turmoil that exceeded Bimbisar's understanding. Most of the problems resulted from his son's actions. With Kunika's encouragement, there was a sharp rise in incidents of religious persecution. His hostility towards the Buddhists was fast growing.

Kosala tried to discuss the issue with Chellana, but she seemed indifferent to Kunika's behaviour. The Buddha's influence was the sole factor that made Queen Chellana react. The widespread acceptance of the Buddha's teachings in Magadh, which led many individuals to embrace Buddhism, rankled the junior queen.

Chellana, who was Mahavira's cousin, was deeply committed to practising his teachings. Once she became Bimbisar's wife, she wholeheartedly dedicated herself to persuading him to adopt Jainism. With an open and liberal mindset, he was receptive to positive thoughts and ideas from all sources. The king had given the people in his kingdom complete freedom to worship as they pleased.

Chellana, however, was concerned about Bimbisar's fascination with the Buddha and his teachings. The Buddha's sermons always had a powerful impact on him, and now he was becoming deeply interested in his teachings.

Rajmata Kosala Devi was a devout follower of Buddhism, and she would regularly attend the Buddha's sermons whenever he visited Magadh. Bimbisar often accompanied her on those occasions. When the Buddha was journeying from Griddhakuta to Vaishali at the request of his followers, the king repaired the entire stretch of road from Rajgriha up to the riverbank. He built resthouses along the route and had the Buddha's path strewn with flowers. Bimbisar accompanied the Buddha to the boats. Deeply resentful, Chellana stood helplessly on the sidelines, unable to intervene or halt her husband's actions.

The situation became even more overwhelming when Kshema, the third queen of Bimbisar, came under the influence of the Buddha and decided to convert to Buddhism. She also became a dedicated follower of the Buddha. Chellana opposed the king's growing fascination with the Buddha. She disregarded her son's persecution of Buddhist monks. From time to time, accompanied by a group of misguided friends, he would launch sudden attacks on the monks and their followers. Soon, there was a growing rift in the royal family due to the two religions.

One evening, while Bimbisar and Rajmata Kosala were sitting together and discussing the arrangements for the Buddha's upcoming visit to Rajgriha, Queen Chellana walked into the chamber and sat down beside the king.

'Maharaj, you will not be here when the Buddha arrives. I have planned a hunting expedition for the two of us for a couple of days,' she told the king. 'The thick forest near Pataligram is an ideal location for hunting.'

'I appreciate your concern, but I can't accompany you on the hunt,' said Bimbisar, gently patting Chellana's hand.

'Why is that, Maharaj? It has been a long time since we went hunting,' Chellana pouted.

'Haven't you heard the Buddha is returning to Rajgriha after his travels? I would like to welcome him when he arrives. Kosala and Kshema will also be there. Why don't you join us?' The king asked Chellana. 'Why don't you postpone the plans for the hunting trip? We can all go after the Buddha has retired to his hermitage in Griddhakuta.'

'That's not possible!' Chellana replied indignantly. 'I have already issued instructions for all the arrangements along the route.'

'In that case, I suggest you go ahead with your plans,' Bimbisar suggested calmly. 'Take Kunika with you. He loves hunting.'

'I may do that. Anyway, he has no love for the Buddha,' Chellana quipped sarcastically.

'I can't quite understand why you bear such resentment towards the Buddha,' Bimbsar asked his queen.

'Are you aware of what is happening around you?' Chellana countered. 'His followers are violating the Jain religious structures.'

Fuming, she went on, 'Buddhist monks, who are supposed to exemplify tolerance and peace through their vow of simplicity and renunciation, are now placing pressure on Jains to convert to Buddhism.'

Chellana's outburst took the king by surprise. 'That's impossible. Every person in my kingdom has the right to practise the religion of their choice freely.'

'Although you have allowed people to practise their preferred religion freely, the current circumstances prove otherwise. Don't you believe me, my king?' Chellana challenged Bimbisar.

'I don't question what you're saying, but it's hard for me to believe that such things are occurring in Magadh.'

'Your Majesty, I think the matter can be resolved by ordering a thorough investigation,' Kosala interjected, having listened silently to Chellana's remarks. 'We can't allow such a thing to happen in Magadh.'

'You are right, Kosala, but the Buddha has never imposed his thoughts on anyone,' the king put forth his argument. 'His teachings impart a sense of peace, which is why people choose to follow him. Buddhism is not a violent religion.'

'So why are his followers demolishing Jain temples and erecting Buddhist stupas instead?' asked Chellana.

Seizing the moment, Kosala intervened. 'Dear sister, I think that Kunika's shocking behaviour reflects your perspective.'

'What has he done now?' asked Bimbisar. His unease grew as his two queens brought to light the oppression faced by different religions. It was inconceivable that this could be happening in his kingdom. He had always shown an open-mindedness and admiration for both religions.

'Kunika has been displaying intense animosity towards Buddhist monks. He has orchestrated the deliberate destruction of Buddhist monasteries. He also conspired to deface and demolish multiple stupas and viharas with his misguided followers. No doubt, his actions were driven by his belief that Buddhists had desecrated Jain temples. Maharaj, it is of utmost importance that you discourage him from engaging in such actions,' Kosala pleaded.

The realization that his son was sabotaging the harmony he had painstakingly built in his kingdom filled Bimbisar with profound sadness. How could Magadh's citizens find harmony when conflicting beliefs were tearing his own family apart? He decided it was time to speak to the Buddha and plead with him to use his influence over his followers.

'I'll order an investigation into the matter, and those

responsible for damaging any religious building, whether or not it's my son, shall face the consequences.' Bimbisar made it a point to highlight the last part of his statement.

'Meanwhile, I request you to persuade Kunika to put an end to his destructive activities. He will one day become the ruler of Magadh, but his subjects will always remember his misconduct. We must make sure that doesn't happen.'

With his son's misdeeds weighing heavily on his conscience, the king shuffled out of the room, his shoulders slumped. Kunika appeared determined to destroy all that he had painstakingly built up.

# 20

# A Meeting with the Vaishali Nagarvadhu

Winter brought a sense of tranquillity ushering in a string of celebrations. At first, the intense rains of Shravan and Bhadrapada gave way to sporadic light showers in Ashwin, and eventually, the cooler month of Kartik arrived. As the rainy season ended, a pleasant cool breeze whispered through the kingdom, announcing the onset of winter and the commencement of joyful celebrations.

The air hummed with enthusiasm and cheer, providing a refreshing break from the imminent wave of tasks. The strength of the sunlight waned with each passing day, and the nights grew progressively longer. A delicate chill hung in the air, giving a preview of the approaching winter months.

Burdened with the son's misdeeds, Bimbisar wanted to escape somewhere to recoup. He wished to flee from the palace's tangled webs of intrigue for a while. It had to be somewhere away from Magadh. But where could he go?

A sudden thought crossed his mind. He would go to Vaishali.

Bimbisar's interest was aroused after hearing about the Vaishali nagarvadhu. The annual poetry competition in Magadh marked the beginning of his curiosity. Poets from distant locations flocked to the event, enticed by the abundant prizes and recognition. Among the attendees was a poet who had come from Vaishali. His name was Damodar. The young poet captivated the audience with his mesmerizing voice, and mellifluous compositions that praised the ethereal charm of Amrapali.

Completely engrossed, the king leaned forward, fascinated by the captivating details of the nagarvadhu. The judges were impressed by the poet's extraordinary talent and immediately declared him the undisputed champion of the competition. Bursting with curiosity, Bimbisar eagerly desired to learn more about the enchanting woman. After the competition ended, he bombarded Damodar with questions about Amrapali.

'Does the beauty of the Vaishali nagarvadhu really rival that of the apsaras?' Bimbisar asked the young poet.

'Yes, Maharaj,' Damodar humbly replied, bowing before the Magadh king. 'Trying to describe the immense beauty of Devi Amrapali is an impossible task. She is the most beautiful woman in Jambudweepa. Her slender waist, sculpted hips, and proud bust create an epitome of perfection. Her complexion and skin are as smooth as the purest marble, and her enchanting smile has the power to captivate even the most resilient hearts. Kings, nobles and merchants willingly empty their coffers for a fleeting moment in her company, while bards compose songs praising her unparalleled beauty.'

With a dreamy look in his eyes, Damodar passionately listed all her admirable qualities. 'Watching her dance, one is transported to a celestial realm, where graceful apsaras glide through the air, and her veena playing surpasses all others in the kingdom.'

As Damodar painted a picture of her beauty, Bimbisar found himself increasingly fascinated by the Vaishali nagarvadhu. The Magadh court had many beautiful rajnartakis, but the descriptions of Amrapali's beauty captivated his heart. He wanted her as a rajnartaki of Magadh.

As a ruler, Bimbisar spent a considerable amount of time

carefully handpicking talented individuals to serve in his court. Ananda, known as the Sur Samrat, possessed a voice that could deeply influence the surrounding atmosphere. Chandrasena, known as the Nritya Samragni, had an unparalleled talent for dancing. The nearby kingdoms coveted Mahagovinda for his extraordinary skills in architecture and engineering. Kumbaghosaka, the treasurer, effortlessly managed the treasury, demonstrating his exceptional talent for mental calculations as he smoothly handled a lengthy series of figures. Both Kingshuk, the poet, and Jivaka, the physician, were sought after by rulers of the neighbouring kingdoms.

Jivaka, an exceptional doctor, spent seven years studying medicine at the prestigious university of Takshila. After Dhruvakriti's death, Jivaka had taken over the duties of the royal vaidya. The king as well as every individual in the kingdom took immense pride in these exceptional men.

Bimbisar wished to appoint Amrapali to his royal court. As soon as he learnt about Amrapali, the Vaishali nagarvadhu, with her mesmerizing beauty and extraordinary talents, he wasted no time in sending a messenger to offer her a prestigious position in the Magadh court. The proud woman refused to see the envoy. Instead, she sent a scornful message through her dasi: 'Tell your king to conquer Vaishali. If he wins, I'll go to the Magadh court.'

Overwhelmed with anger at the rejection of his offer, Bimbisar decided he would either win her over with his charm or forcibly bring her to the Magadh court.

*How dare she refuse my offer?* Even powerful kings thought twice before insulting him. He let out a roar and slammed his fist on the wall. Unable to sleep, he wandered restlessly in his room. *Despite my willingness to give her any amount of money, she rejects my offer. Should persuasion fail, I'll conquer Vaishali and return with her in shackles. But is she worth a war? I must make a trip to Vaishali to confirm if she is as beautiful as everyone claims.*

With every passing day, Bimbisar's fascination for Amrapali intensified. He wanted her more than ever. Once the Magadh king resolved to do something, nothing could stop him. After considering all possibilities, he decided to travel to Vaishali in disguise.

His unexpected plan to travel to Vaishali surprised the queens and the mahamatya. Anticipating objections, Bimbisar chose not to reveal his true motive for the visit.

'Maharaj, what draws you to visit Vaishali?' asked Vassakar. An intuitive man, he had noticed the king's restlessness since the poetry competition.

'I'm keen on having a one-on-one meeting with Dhana Samant,' the king responded. 'It's a confidential issue, so I can't disclose the details.'

There were dozens of Magadh spies operating in the Vajji Confederacy. Disguised as traders and labourers, several men went about their tasks, while several women spies donned the garb of ganikas. Magadh's main spy in Vaishali, Dhana Samant, was in charge of the group of spies.

Dhana Samant operated as a prosperous cloth merchant in Vaishali. In just eight years, he had built up a strong reputation and developed valuable connections with influential people in the city. He lived in a lavish residence in the affluent area of the city, where he hosted extravagant parties that were attended by the elite. He gained unrestricted entry into the royal palace because of his seemingly harmless demeanour, and he even provided garments for the queen. His ample girth, charming smile, and smooth talk were the ideal cover for his effective spy operations in Vaishali.

It was highly unusual for the king to go to Vaishali and have a rendezvous with a spy. Bimbisar's excuse was unconvincing.

'You don't have to go, Maharaj,' Vassakar objected, his voice full of concern. 'We can send our chief of security to interact with Dhana Samant.'

The relationship between Magadh and the Vajji Confederacy had deteriorated in recent years. One reason for the tense relationship between Magadh and the Vajji Confederacy was the mining of precious minerals. The uneasy truce between the two kingdoms was close to snapping and the situation had become so serious that Bimbisar was considering attacking Vaishali.

'Why don't we go together?' asked Queen Chellana. 'I can arrange a royal invitation for our visit to Vaishali. You are King Chetak's son-in-law. Why would you choose to hide your identity when you have the option to be welcomed as a respected guest?'

'She is right, Maharaj,' said Queen Kosala, lending her support to the argument. 'It is dangerous to explore Vaishali without revealing your identity. It is easy for the citizens of Vaishali to identify you in a crowd. No matter how well you disguise yourself, the spies have a knack of uncovering identities. As soon as the spies report to the king, suspicions will be raised, and your intentions will be called into question.'

Bimbisar remained resolute in his decision, regardless of what anyone said. He selected Devavrata as his companion for the journey to Vaishali.

Devavrata, a warrior of great skill, was famous for his exceptional mastery of weapons and his ability to deliver persuasive speeches. Bimbisar could always count on the young commander. Devavrata was not only good-looking, he was also a discreet and optimistic man. His exceptional sense of humour made him a delightful companion.

Assuming identities as perfume traders from Avanti, the two men made their way to Vaishali. Bimbisar took on the identity of Indrajeet Varma, while Devavrata played the role of his dedicated assistant.

Armed with intelligence that Amrapali regularly visited the Amravana in the evening, they stealthily entered the mango orchard. The royal gardener had found the baby under a mango tree in the orchard, so she was named Amrapali. Once she was chosen as the nagarvadhu, the king gifted the orchard to her. The mango tree had occupied a special place in Amrapali's heart from a young age, and she found immense happiness in taking refuge under its shade. It made her feel calm and at peace.

A magical aura enveloped the orchard as the sun's last rays danced upon it. The sky put on a stunning show, its colours constantly changing in an enthralling display of beauty. The westward clouds glowed with a fiery orange-red hue in the warm sunlight, while the eastern clouds remained a medley of cool blue and indigo. As twilight descended, the forest transformed into a tapestry of colours. In that light, the woman appeared as though someone had sculpted her with utmost precision.

The white silk antariya was securely tied below her navel, while a transparent embroidered uttariya hung loosely over her shoulders, her hair flowing down in a cascade. She looked as if she had wandered in from another realm.

Completely unaware of her surroundings, Amrapali remained lost in her thoughts as the two men watched her. Concealed behind a tree, they were a short distance from her. Both men were tall and powerfully built. One of them, with an air of maturity, possessed a captivating handsomeness. An impressive moustache added to his majestic aura. With his crimson silk dhoti and fine uttariya, he appeared to be a wealthy setthi. He wore a beautifully crafted jewel on his turban, embellished with sparkling emeralds and pearls, which enhanced his opulent bearing.

The person he was with was younger. 'There she is,' the companion whispered. 'She is known as the epitome of beauty in Jambudweepa.'

'She is truly ethereal. I have not seen anyone as beautiful as her,' said the older man. The beautiful woman sitting under the large mango tree captivated him.

'Now that you have seen her, it is in our best interest to leave this place before the guards catch us,' warned the young man.

'Wait! Let me stay for a while. My eyes are reluctant to stray from her face.'

The ecstasy was easily recognizable in the older man's dark-brown eyes. The companion sighed resignedly and sat down under the tree. 'Let me know when you are ready to leave,' he said.

'Not in this lifetime,' said the other man. 'I want to whisk her away with me to Magadh,' he whispered.

Suddenly, he noticed a reptile crawling out of a hole by the mango tree, and making its way quickly towards the woman. In a flash, he charged at the woman. Drawing his sword, he skilfully severed the black snake near the woman's ankle, saving her from harm.

He was a bit late. The venomous snake had already bitten the woman, leaving her in excruciating pain.

The poison took effect, causing her to lose consciousness and her body to go limp. Two marks on her skin showed where the snake had bitten her. Taking off his uttariya, he wrapped it tightly around her ankle. With a bejewelled dagger hidden in the folds of his clothes, he deftly made an incision on the afflicted area. Then he began sucking out the poison and spitting it out, one mouthful at a time.

In a matter of seconds, he had deftly extracted the poison from Amrapali's body, inadvertently absorbing it into his bloodstream. With a sudden loud thud, he collapsed to the ground, while Amrapali regained consciousness and looked around in confusion.

'Arya!' shouted the younger man, his voice reflecting a sense of urgency. He shook Amrapali vigorously, hoping to jolt her out of her stunned condition. 'Devi, while attempting to save your life, my friend unintentionally consumed a dangerous quantity of poison. We have to get him to a vaidya immediately.'

His words spurred the dazed Amrapali into action. The man who had rescued her was now struggling to survive. 'My chariot is standing outside the orchard. Carry him to it and we will drive to my home,' she urged. 'I know a good vaidya.'

The young man quickly lifted up his ailing friend and carried him to the chariot. Immediately thereafter, they raced away at breakneck speed. When they arrived at her palace, Amrapali summoned her vaidya, who was known to be one of the most skilled vaidyas in the city.

The vaidya examined the patient and concluded that there was a significant level of venom in his body. In villages, snakebites were frequent, especially during the monsoon season, and he had developed expertise in treating such incidents. 'Your quick action has saved his life. A few more minutes and he would have died,' he declared after examining the patient.

'We must make sure he survives. I owe him my life,' Amrapali said, her voice filled with gratitude. 'I would have died if he had not been in Amravana today.'

Amrapali looked anxiously at the stranger as he lay on the bed.

An hour later, having administered his treatment, the vaidya gave instructions on the dosage of the various herbs. 'The asavas and other medicines must be given on time.'

'Please don't worry, Arya. I'll be here to look after him,' said the younger man.

'He will survive,' the vaidya reassured Amrapali as she saw him to the door. 'The medicinal herbs will heal and expedite his recovery. However, it is of utmost importance that he gets full rest for the next two days. Thereafter he will be out of danger.'

Devavrata and Amrapali took turns to nurse the patient. Despite a restless night's sleep, Bimbisar woke up the next day bursting with energy, making it difficult to restrain him in bed. He longed to stretch his legs and explore Amrapali's palace. Despite his companion's urgings, he stubbornly refused to stay in bed.

That morning, when Amrapali walked into the chamber, she heard the stranger scolding his companion. 'I'm not an invalid, Deva,' he said. 'I'll not lie on the bed for another moment.'

'Don't behave like a child, Arya. You will do as you are told,' she said sternly. 'The vaidya has instructed that you remain in bed for two days. He will examine you later today to decide if you can walk around.'

A gentle rapping on the door announced Amrapali's dasi. She entered the room with a tray of herbal medicines and a glass of freshly squeezed fruit juice.

'Now let me help you up, so you can have the medicine and the juice,' said the nagarvadhu gently.

Devavrata was taken aback as he observed the powerful effect that Amrapali's words had on his master. Not only did he let her assist him in getting up, but he also agreed to her request to take the medicine and juice. Placing him back on the bed, she settled down next to him.

'Why don't you freshen up, Deva?' she said. 'You have been up all night. I'll take care of him while you have breakfast and rest for a while.'

'You have been very kind to us, Devi,' said Bimbisar after his companion had left the room. 'But we must leave now. I can't take advantage of your kindness.'

'Shhhh!' Amrapali placed a finger on her lips. She gently pressed her cool hand against his forehead and whispered, 'Say nothing, just lie down and shut your eyes. Relax!'

Her hands had a magical effect. He closed his eyes and soon he was fast asleep. When he woke up, Amrapali was gone and Devavrata was sitting by his bedside. The day was almost over. 'Where is Amrapali?' he asked.

'She worked her magic on you and went away,' chuckled Devavrata. 'Do you know how long you have slept?'

'Has it been very long? I feel absolutely refreshed.'

'Arya, you slept through the entire morning and afternoon. Meanwhile, the vaidya arrived and assessed your condition. He seemed pleased with your progress, and has declared you out of danger,' said Devavrata.

'In that case, I should be allowed to leave the bed,' declared Bimbisar.

Amrapali entered the room holding a silver plate filled with food, and said, 'Not yet, Arya.'

The sun's rays streamed through the window, casting a golden glow on her face, making it even more radiant. She looked more beautiful than he could remember; his throat turned dry. 'Not until you have finished everything on this plate,' she said firmly, placing the platter on a low table near the bed.

'You can't expect me to eat all that, Devi,' Bimbisar protested, inwardly pleased at being admonished by her. This was a novel experience for him. It had been ages since a woman had bullied him. He looked at the bowls filled with gruel, meats, vegetables and yoghurt, and said, 'This is far too much food for one person.'

'Sshhh! Just eat!' She placed a finger on her lips. 'I'll be left with no option but to feed you if you refuse to help yourself.' Her eyes danced with mirth as she playfully threatened. 'This is what the vaidya ordered, and you will have to finish everything if you want to leave the bed.'

'You are a mercenary, Devi. A beautiful one at that. How can I disobey you?' He eagerly tucked into his meal, aware of her watchful eyes. He felt surprised by how ravenous he was.

Amrapali's gaze roamed all over the man in front of her, capturing every intricate aspect of his rugged face. His flawlessly carved, royal appearance made him undeniably attractive. He emanated a strong sense of masculinity with his broad chest, muscular physique, and a square, determined chin which was enhanced by a stylish beard. His well-defined eyebrows and prominent forehead enhanced his commanding presence. She couldn't help but notice the thick, wavy black hair and the captivating amber eyes. However, the cruel twist of his thin lips was in sharp contrast to his otherwise composed appearance.

'I'm puzzled, Arya,' she said, raising an eyebrow in confusion.

'What's puzzling you, Devi? he asked, pushing away the almost empty platter.

'The way you dress and carry yourself suggests you are someone of significance. It seems odd to me that you are travelling without a horse, carriage, or attendants.'

Bimbisar hesitated momentarily. Even though he and Devavrata had practised their fake personas extensively, he found it difficult to lie to her. Staring out of the window, he said, 'Your assumption is not correct, Devi. I'm an ordinary person, with no claim to importance.'

'I could be incorrect, but it seems you are a person of importance,' she remarked curiously, her gaze focused on the valuable jewel on his turban. 'But I'm sure you have a name and a vocation,' she remarked.

'I apologize, Devi. I should have made my introduction much earlier.' Although he detested being dishonest with her, he had no alternative. He coughed and continued with his false story. 'Well, my name is Indrajeet Varma, and I make a living as a perfume trader,' he explained. Even though Avanti is my base, my business ventures extend beyond its limits, to destinations like

Gandhar and beyond. While it might sound like I'm bragging, my perfumes are selling in far-off locations such as Misr and Basra.'

With each lie he told, his discomfort intensified, adding to the weight on his conscience. But telling her the truth could be dangerous.

'Do you travel a lot?' she asked, curious to know more about him. The idea of travelling to far-off lands filled her mind with images of exotic places and vibrant cultures. 'It must be fascinating to travel to unknown places and meet new people. You are a fortunate man, Arya. I long to travel, but I'm bound to this place.'

'Yes Devi, traders have to travel. While it may seem exciting initially, it can become tedious after a while. I want to stay in one place.'

'So let's exchange places, Arya,' she laughed. 'You take my place here and I'll take your business to various places.'

'Imagine me dancing in this palace,' he echoed her laughter. Worried about being exposed, Bimbisar avoided discussing business further and changed the topic of conversation. 'Your palace is beautiful. I can see the garden from my bed, and it seems so peaceful.'

'The garden, with its flowers and greenery, is my favourite place here. My father was a gardener, and from him I learned a lot about trees and flowers,' she said proudly. 'I have an extensive collection of exotic plants.'

'You are very fortunate to have the time to tend to your garden and do the things you love,' he sighed. 'My life offers very little time to spend on things I want to do.'

'I wonder if anyone is happy with what they have. When it comes to time, I don't have as much free time as I would like. My entire existence is centred around music, dance practice, and keeping my patrons entertained. It's not as pleasant as it might seem. But let's not discuss my life. Your life intrigues me, and I want to know more about it. May I ask you what are the things you would like to do if you had the time?' she urged him to disclose his wishes.

'I would like to play the veena, and paint,' he replied with a wistful look in his eyes.

'You play the veena?' Amrapali asked. 'I love playing the veena. There is a gazebo in the garden where I practise music every morning.'

'Why don't you take me for a stroll through your garden?' Bimbisar asked. 'I would love to see the gazebo too.'

'Don't be impatient, Arya,' she rebuked him gently. The vaidya is the deciding authority. Once he gives the go-ahead, you are free to explore whatever you want.'

The patient's recovery brought immense delight to the vaidya that evening. 'Arya has a robust and healthy constitution,' he said to Devavrata and Amrapali. 'This has helped in his speedy recovery. He can go for morning and evening strolls, but I don't want him to push himself too hard.'

Deva and Amrapali promised the vaidya that they would ensure Bimbisar only took gentle walks.

# 21

# A Torrid Romance

Bimbisar went from leisurely strolls in the garden to playing the veena in the gazebo and enjoying long walks and conversations with Amrapali.

With each passing day, their relationship grew stronger and more meaningful. Amrapali's attention shifted from her patrons, her priority now being the man she affectionately called Indra.

She wondered why she was so strongly drawn to him. She admitted to her best friend that she knew very little about Indra. 'All I know is that he has a family and lives far away in Avanti. He can make no promises and I have nothing to look forward to. Despite everything, his irresistible pull makes me want to sprint into his loving arms.'

So strong was Bimbisar's grip on her that no amount of persuasion could convince her to leave his side. He described to her the vast trade routes that extended well beyond the Uttarpath and Dakshinapath, bustling with merchants and caravans. Through his vivid descriptions of sailing to far-off places, he painted a captivating picture of storms unleashing colossal waves that battered ships, and enormous sea creatures lurking in the deep, ready to attack. He recounted to her the perilous journeys he undertook, traversing dense forests, and fending off ruthless bandits who were hell-bent on robbing him. His accounts were like a meticulously woven tapestry, brimming with details that he had gathered from the stories he heard in his formative years.

Bimbisar animatedly recounted his incredible journeys to

exotic destinations like Swarnabhumi and Misr. The intricate stories captivated the unsuspecting Amrapali, much like a spider's web ensnares its prey. His words evoked images of exotic places where gems the size of a hen's egg were traded, jewels and diamonds shone in the absence of light, deep red rubies and corals created a mysterious allure, fragrant incense intoxicated the senses, and sheer fabric draped the body like a whisper. His description painted the picture of a mesmerizing journey through the awe-inspiring mountains of Simhaladweepa, where he discovered breathtaking blue sapphires and vibrant rubies from Brahmadesh. He told her about the enchanting pearls found in the seas of Chin, the extraordinary madira produced in Misr and Gandhar, and the impressive horses hailing from Kambhoja.

Amrapali's patrons grew increasingly frustrated as she spent more and more time with Bimbisar. They accused her of neglecting her obligations as a nagarvadhu and threatened to complain to the king. But she didn't care.

As the sun rose, the gazebo came alive with the melodic strains of music, as he played the veena, captivating her and inspiring her to dance. She closed her eyes, inhaling the scents of citrus fruits and flowers in the garden. Everything felt new and wonderful.

As expected, it happened one evening. Amrapali and Bimbisar couldn't resist their feelings and fell in love, completely oblivious to their surroundings. They were consumed by an intense passion that made time meaningless.

There was no sign of any commitment or hint about what might happen next. The only thing that mattered was the present, to be treasured and embraced completely.

Bimbisar felt a sense of liberation as he let go of self-control and embraced the present. As he experienced the overwhelming force of love, he forgot about his royal obligations. He forgot his motive for coming to Vaishali. Nothing mattered except love.

It had been a week since he arrived in Vaishali. Bimbisar moved into Amrapali's chamber to be with her all the time. Devavrata watched the events unfold from the sidelines with growing unease. Dhana Samant, the Magadh spy, had warned him to be careful. There was much talk about Amrapali's lover, and the king's spies were actively gathering information.

Amrapali's favourite place in the palace was the terrace, which was meticulously designed to cultivate a tranquil ambiance. In the sweltering summer nights, she found relief on the terrace, where she could lie down beneath the sparkling stars, enjoying the invigorating night air.

Unaware of the foreboding events, the lovers enjoyed themselves on Amrapali's terrace. It was a night of pure enchantment. A gentle radiance enveloped the couple as the moon emerged from behind a layer of clouds. The air was filled with the gentle and captivating scent of flowers in bloom. The fragrant vines created a barrier, providing them a secluded space to relax together.

Bimbisar's passion was set ablaze by the irresistible atmosphere. This was the first time he had ever felt such a strong arousal. The woman's irresistible charm ignited a powerful, primal desire within him. He could no longer contain the overwhelming desire he had for her. Amrapali mirrored his eagerness. She felt intense passion and longing for a man she barely knew.

They inched closer to one another without uttering a word, the silence between them growing more intimate. The longing to leave behind his past as the mighty ruler of Magadh consumed Bimbisar. Kings had no freedom to love. He had no interest in being involved in the plotting and intricacies that came with the throne. He wanted to forget that he was a pretender who had arrived in Vaishali on a mission. There was nothing he longed for more than to spend time with the person he loved.

Amrapali wanted to forget that she was the nagarvadhu, whose duties lay in entertaining any man who could pay her price. She wanted to erase the memory of the predatory glances of her patrons. All she wanted was to put the unpleasant parts of her life behind her and be with her lover.

Her skilled and eager fingers explored his body, igniting a fiery passion, seeking, searching and urging. Their heavy breathing filled the air, as his feverish breath intertwined with hers. Tremors ran through Bimbisar's body as he pressed against her yielding form, gasping with fervour.

He wished for the night to never end. She yearned for their love to endure forever. With each successive wave, their passion surged higher, like a tumultuous sea. The climax, when it finally happened, was absolutely perfect.

A flood of powerful emotions carried away Amrapali. A smile of satisfaction remained on her lips. She propped herself up with her elbow and looked lovingly at the man lying next to her. She knew she had given him more than just her body. He now held her heart in his hands. Was it an expression of gratitude? Was this a repayment for saving her life? Absolutely not. She felt more than just grateful. She was teetering on the edge of a passionate, unrestrained love.

Side by side, they lay together, their limbs tangled. Completely content. With a deep sigh, she closed her eyes. They both knew that their lives had altered irreversibly. A significant shift had occurred that evening.

'It's so peaceful here.' Closing her eyes, she breathed in the fragrances of citrus fruits and flowers on the serene terrace. 'One can easily forget the worries when surrounded by so much beauty,' she said.

With a cup of madira in hand, Bimbisar found himself in a peaceful state of mind. The tranquil environment awakened something deep within him. He could no longer continue deceiving Amrapali. Not after the intimate moments they had enjoyed for the past few days. He strongly desired to reveal his true identity.

With urgency in his voice, he said, 'Pali, I need to tell you something important.'

Her eyes lit up as she asked, 'Is it another story, Arya?'

'No, this is about…' At that very moment, a soft knock on the door interrupted their conversation. 'Pali, please ignore it,' he urged.

'I hate to be interrupted,' she said, reluctantly rising from her seat to open the door, 'but it might be something important.'

Amrapali found Devavrata standing at the door. He wanted to have a word with Bimbisar.

'He is busy,' she said, but he insisted the matter was of great importance and couldn't wait.

Despite being annoyed, Bimbisar noticed the distress on his companion's face and promptly guided Devavrata into the chamber. Amrapali tactfully excused herself and left the chamber to allow them to continue their conversation.

'We must leave this place immediately,' said Devavrata. 'I have received an urgent message from Dhana Samant. Vaishali's spies have found out who you are and are heading to Devi Amrapali's palace. We must reach his place without delay. He is making the arrangements for our return to Magadh.'

'But…' Bimbisar protested.

'There is no room for hesitation, Maharaj. We must leave without delay,' Devavrata insisted.

'I have to tell…'

'I'm sorry, Maharaj, but we can't trust Devi Amrapali with our secret. Her intense love for her country might lead her to allow the soldiers to arrest us. It is crucial to not take any chances.'

Bimbisar shook his head vigorously and said to Devavrata, 'I can't escape like a thief. I'm a king, and I must behave like one. Devi Amrapali has the right to know the truth.'

'Maharaj, sometimes even a king needs to adjust their actions to fit the situation,' Devavrata insisted. 'Wisdom demands it. You are a king, no doubt, but you must think of Magadh at this moment.'

Devavrata realized that the king's deep love for Amrapali made it impossible for him to address the problem logically.

He dropped to his knees and made a heartfelt plea to his king. 'I beg you to consider, Maharaj. Both your father and you have made many sacrifices for Magadh. Will Magadh or Devi Amrapali gain any advantage from your arrest, humiliation, or death? It is best if we leave quietly before the Vaishali soldiers arrive.'

Bimbisar realized the truth in Deva's words. It would be foolish to waste any more time. In the past few years, he had destroyed his relationship with Vaishali. The people of Vaishali would want him to be punished for his attack on the city. The memory of his father's humiliation in Anga quickly appeared in his mind, creating a whirlwind of emotions. He decided that he wouldn't let the Vaishali soldiers humiliate him. The future generations of Magadh would never forgive him for making a reckless decision when wisdom was needed.

Devavrata was right. His obligations as a king were of utmost importance. He couldn't allow his heart to rule his head. He needed to handle this situation wisely. 'All right, Deva, let's slip away right now,' he said sadly.

Swiftly and silently, they discarded their silks and jewels and donned homespun peasant clothes. They melted away into the night, departing from Amrapali's palace as silently as they had arrived.

Dhana Samant had arranged for a rundown cart to pick up the two men from the rear lanes of the palace. Unaware of the importance of the two poorly dressed individuals, the cart driver waited patiently under a tree. Emerging silently from the shadows, they stepped onto the rickety cart, which started moving abruptly.

The chief spy anxiously awaited their arrival at his mansion. 'Pranam, Maharaj,' he greeted Bimbisar. 'I apologize for the inconvenient vehicle, but it was necessary to be inconspicuous.

'You are a wise man, Samant,' remarked the Magadh monarch, dusting off the straw from his clothes. 'It was a safe choice, since no one would expect a king to travel in such a manner.'

'I have made sure that your dinner is prepared and everything is ready for your trip to Rajgriha. By now, the soldiers would have made it to Devi Amrapali's palace. Once they realize you are not present, they will swiftly proceed to my mansion. Maharaj, we must hurry as time is running out.'

'You have done an outstanding job by giving us a timely warning, Samant. Time is precious,' Bimbisar emphasized. 'I'd rather not squander it on a meal. I'm ready to leave for Rajgriha.'

'I can't allow you to leave without having something to eat. Just give me a moment, Maharaj, while I bring you some fruits for the journey,' Dhana Samant humbly folded his hands in plea.

Dhana Samant returned with a basket of fruits, and said, 'Everything is ready, Maharaj. I have arranged for a boat and two reliable individuals to accompany you on your journey to Magadh.'

'You are an efficient and loyal man, Samant. I'm fortunate to have you in Vaishali. I shall soon return to this city as a victorious ruler.'

'I shall await that day, Maharaj.'

Bimbisar, along with Devavrata and two men appointed

by Dhana Samant, departed from Vaishali. Thanks to Samant's meticulous planning, Bimbisar could escape safely.

Despite the uneventful journey back to Rajgriha, Bimbisar couldn't shake off the profound feeling of loss as he distanced himself from Vaishali. Overcome with guilt, he couldn't help but think of the woman he had deceived. He had betrayed her confidence.

Back in Vaishali, Amrapali, who had been sleeping in her palace, woke up and stretched her limbs. She felt an overwhelming tiredness in her body following the passionate night with her lover.

At the break of dawn, the world awakened to the sounds of birds chirping and leaves rustling. A gentle breeze filled the air, playfully tantalizing her senses with the soft scent of flowers touched by dew. Amrapali's garden was like heaven on earth.

A surge of happiness left her with an inexplicable feeling of contentment. Light as the wind, she felt herself floating with the clouds. All traces of darkness had vanished, replaced by warmth and light from her loving heart.

While Bimbisar spoke with Devavrata, she drifted off to sleep, confident that he would join her once their discussion ended. But the space next to her was still empty. Where was Indrajeet?

She wandered through the palace looking for her lover, but he was nowhere to be found. Indrajeet and Devavrata had vanished without a trace. Despite everything appearing unchanged, an eerie shift in the atmosphere made her feel uneasy.

Shocked, she discovered that the soldiers had raided the palace while she was asleep. Despite searching the entire palace, they refused to reveal why they were looking for Indrajeet and his companion. Her closeness to the Vaishali king had prevented them from searching her bedroom.

# 22

# Disturbing Developments in Rajgriha

Worn out and emotionally drained, Bimbisar journeyed towards the capital as the first light of dawn illuminated the city. To avoid the crowds of morning vendors and bathers, he purposely diverted from the busy path and followed a secluded and meandering trail to his palace. All he wanted was to escape to his chamber, where he could give in to the whirlwind of his thoughts and give up his body to a peaceful sleep.

The news of Bimbisar's trip to Vaishali was only known by a few individuals in Magadh. His ministers were not curious about his absence, since they were aware of his frequent travels throughout his kingdom. The moment he stepped into the palace, Vassakar hurriedly made his way to greet him. Although the king was naturally perceptive, he was too preoccupied with thoughts of the Vaishali nagarvadhu to notice the mahamatya's unusual nervousness that morning.

'Pranam, Maharaj!' Vassakar folded his hands in greeting, avoiding the king's eyes. The wily man felt a sense of relief when he realized Bimbisar was not as attentive as usual. 'I hope the journey was fruitful,' he added.

The mahamatya had instructed his spies in Vaishali to keep a close watch on both Bimbisar and Devavrata, ensuring that he had full information about every detail of the king's relationship with Amrapali. Vassakar lived through several tense moments, especially when he found out that the security chief of Vaishali had doubts about the two strangers residing in the nagarvadhu's palace. He had breathed a sigh of relief when the king finally left Vaishali without incident.

During Bimbisar's brief absence, there was a series of unsettling incidents in Rajgriha. Vassakar was hesitant to bring up the matter with the king because it was associated with Ajatashatru's stubbornness. He knew about the king's blind love for his son and his complete unwillingness to acknowledge anything against the prince. The mahamatya was also waiting for the right time to strike the king.

A few months back, Bimbisar had pulled him up publicly in the court for crossing the line, and accused him of prying into his personal affairs. He had also heard rumours that the king was planning to replace him with another minister. There were many things he could overlook, but he couldn't overlook public humiliation. Nor could he tolerate demotion. It had taken him many years to reach where he now stood. Hadn't he made enormous sacrifices for Magadh's supremacy? He had no friends, and no family. He lived frugally and worked harder than anyone in the kingdom, but the king seemed to have forgotten all that. He couldn't allow Bimbisar to get away with his arrogance and ingratitude.

Yuvraj's misdeeds were known to him, but he would use them for his benefit. He had gathered many interesting bits of information over the years, and intended to use them when the time was ripe.

'I hope everything is fine, mahamatya,' Bimbisar said, his voice laced with exhaustion.

'Yes, Maharaj,' replied Vassakar. 'There's nothing that can't wait until you have rested.'

The mahamatya knew it was important to address the

unpleasant subject quickly to prevent any potential issues, but he was looking for the right moment to bring it up. Why stir the hornet's nest prematurely?

The king walked towards his chamber and said, 'Well, then I'll discuss the pending matter with you later.'

Queen Kosala Devi approached Bimbisar only after he had rested and had lunch. She presented him with a paan from a beautifully crafted silver paan daan, and they retreated to the balcony of his private chamber. Only Kosala could make a paan to his liking, with the perfect blend of herbs, and she always gave him one after lunch.

'Maharaj, has the mahamatya mentioned anything about Devadatta?' she asked casually.

'Devadatta? No, he hasn't mentioned him.' Bimbisar lounged on the plush silk cushion, exuding an air of nonchalance. 'Is he the trouble-causing cousin of the Buddha?' Bimbisar asked, somewhat curious.

'Yes, Maharaj. Devadatta's influence on Kunika has led them down a path of destructive acts. I need to tell you this urgently so that you can warn the prince.'

'Kunika is a hot-headed young man, and young men will behave inexplicably sometimes.' True to form, Bimbisar reacted like a loving parent. 'He is immature and gullible too.'

'Hot-headed and immature young men don't try to kill the Buddha at the behest of his jealous cousin,' Kosala sounded annoyed.

'What are you saying, Kosala?' Bimbisar sat up in alarm. 'Has my son tried to kill the Buddha?' He couldn't believe his ears. Kunika held a deep disdain for the Buddha, much like his mother Chellana, and adamantly rejected the Enlightened One's teachings. But Bimbisar couldn't imagine his son being involved in any conspiracy to kill the Buddha.

'That is exactly what I'm saying, Maharaj.' Kosala's annoyance was obvious. She loved the prince as much as her children, but she was not blind to his faults. Since he was young, Kunika consistently showed a lack of concern for others, frequently resorting to violent and impulsive actions. His father's excessive love and indulgence had completely spoilt him; he had no sense of responsibility or discipline. She was surprised by Bimbisar's ability to ignore his son's wrongdoings.

'Devadatta has been plotting relentlessly to overthrow the Buddha and take charge of his sangha. Initially, he threw a massive boulder from the peak of Griddhakuta while the Buddha was descending a slope. Thankfully, the Enlightened One had a miraculous escape and suffered only a minor injury to his toe.'

The king found it hard to accept that someone could stoop so low. He shook his head in disbelief.

Kosala took a moment to catch her breath before resuming. 'Despite a couple of failed attempts, Devadatta remained determined to kill the Buddha. He bribed an elephant handler to feed toddy to Nalagiri.'

'Nalagiri, the rogue elephant, known to be so wild that only one keeper could control it?' Bimbisar's eyebrows arched in horror.

'Yes, it's the same elephant. Can you imagine its reactions when drunk on toddy? In a frenzy, the intoxicated elephant charged down the Buddha's path, trumpeting loudly. The Buddha's followers urged him to alter his path, but he refused to do so. Much to everyone's surprise, the furious elephant calmed down as soon as the Buddha touched it.'

'I'm relieved to hear that the Buddha is unharmed,' Bimbisar heaved a sigh of relief.

'There is more to the story, Maharaj. When Devadatta's strategies didn't yield results, he reached out to Kunika for support,' Kosala continued. 'Kunika agreed to collaborate with the wicked cousin. When you were not in Magadh, he provided Devadatta with a group of highly skilled royal archers to attack the Buddha. Devadatta planned to kill them all after the Buddha's assassination, so they would not live to tell anyone about the plot.'

'What?' Bimbisar exclaimed angrily. 'How could our son commit such a heinous act?'

'There's no need to worry, Maharaj. The Buddha survived the assassination attempt. Captivated by his aura, the archers fell at his feet and pleaded for his mercy. Devadatta's plot failed, once again.'

'I'm relieved to hear that,' said Bimbisar, who had been holding his breath. 'But I'll speak to Kunika and insist that he puts an end to his friendship with Devadatta.'

'It will not be easy, Maharaj,' Kosala said, her voice filled with sadness. 'Our son is completely in the grip of the evil man. Devadatta continues to poison his mind.'

Bimbisar couldn't stop thinking about Kosala's words even after she had left his chamber. The truth finally sank in; a wave of sadness washed over him. The son, who he had hoped would become the future ruler of Magadh, was now on a dangerous path. *I must consult the Buddha for guidance.*

That evening, Bimbisar summoned Kunika to his chamber. Disregarding the king's order, the prince swaggered into his father's chamber late at night.

The sheer audacity of his son's behaviour infuriated the king. 'Why were you delayed?' he shouted angrily.

'I was preoccupied,' said Kunika. 'Is it a matter of importance?'

'If it wasn't important, would I bother wasting my time on you?' Bimbisar replied sharply. 'I have received disturbing reports about your misconduct. Can you explain your actions?'

'Are you talking about my collaboration with Devadatta?' he

enquired arrogantly. 'I find it unnecessary to justify my actions,' he declared firmly. 'Is there anything else?'

Kunika turned to go.

'Wait! I haven't given you permission to leave!' Bimbisar's words resounded loudly in the chamber. 'I demand an explanation, and you will give me one.'

'I don't think so,' said the prince, strutting out of the room.

Bimbisar was too shocked to react. The prince was completely out of control. He had no choice but to take immediate action. Wasting no time, he quickly summoned Vassakar.

'I want you to arrange for Ajatashatru's immediate departure from Magadh,' he ordered the moment the mahamatya appeared. 'He has lingered on in Magadh for too long. He must leave for Anga tomorrow morning.'

'But Maharaj...'

'No buts. It's an order,' Bimbisar roared. His spies had reported many instances of the mahamatya's indiscretions, revealing a pattern of questionable behaviour. The king had been patiently waiting to remove the mahamatya and had already chosen someone else to take the position. He decided to do so as soon as he got back from Vaishali.

'It shall be as you desire, Maharaj,' said the mahamatya, bowing out of the king's presence. The weight of his humiliation in a crowded court gnawed Vassakar's mind. He was a patient man, who hoarded all his frustrations and insults carefully, and waited for the right momen to strike.

For many months, the mahamatya had nursed a deep-seated resentment towards Bimbisar, which fuelled his desire for vendetta. Having waited eagerly, he finally saw his chance to execute his strategy against the king. This was the perfect moment, and he could feel adrenaline coursing through his veins as he prepared to make his move. The wily man quickly devised a plan.

# 23

# Amrapali's Son

Dealing with Ajatashatru's shortcomings and the disloyalty of a trusted noble in his court kept Bimbisar busy for the next few months. The king kept Ajatashatru occupied with the matters at Anga, which put an end to Devadatta's plots. Seasons changed. The harsh winter months transitioned into the pleasant ones of Vasant. Nature blossomed with newfound energy. Dormant plants sprung back to life, with fresh seedlings emerging, while hibernating animals woke up.

It was time for the harvest celebrations, but he had no time for festivities. Finally, an astute management of the circumstances brought about peace in Magadh.

Spring brought many joys. The hills turned green, flowers bloomed, and the weather became pleasant.

There was rejoicing among lovers, but sadness for those who had parted ways. Even though Bimbisar had returned from Vaishali some time ago, he couldn't forget the memories of his time with Amrapali. Even as years went by, his listlessness didn't diminish. A strange inertia overcame him. It left him feeling empty, with no motivation or drive to push forward. The weight of the kingdom and its endless obligations left him drained. The once-fulfilling process of meting out justice in the court became a burden for him.

Rajmata Kosala Devi sensed her husband's restlessness. She wondered about the cause of his distraction.

Reports of unexpected violence on Magadh's southern border

shook Bimbisar out of his languor. Despite his strong longing to be with Amrapali, Bimbisar's responsibilities as a ruler required his complete focus, leaving him exhausted and unable to satisfy his longings. The kingdom came first. Amrapali would have to wait. Yet again, he toughened his heart, allowing his mind to govern his actions.

Once the situation calmed down, he couldn't resist the urge to set off on a trip to Vaishali and disclose his true identity to the nagarvadhu. Bimbisar was aware that there would never be an ideal time for the mission. It had to be now or never.

It was while Bimbisar was planning to travel to Vaishali that Devavrata requested an audience with the king. The young warrior had proven himself to be an efficient companion during their last trip to Vaishali, and the king had granted him some privileges.

The timing couldn't have been better, as the king's intention to take the young man to Vaishali aligned flawlessly with the situation.

'Pranam, Maharaj!' Devavrata joined his hands in a humble gesture.

'What a coincidence! I was just planning to summon you,' Bimbisar greeted the young man with a smile.

'Maharaj, I have brought you some good news,' said Devavrata.

'What is it, Deva? Have you become a father?' Bimbisar asked playfully. The trip to Vaishali had forged a connection between the ruler and the warrior.

Devavrata blushed and replied hesitantly, 'Maharaj, I can't claim the title of a father just yet. I thought you might be interested to know Devi Amrapali has given birth to a son.'

The news was so overwhelming that Bimbisar, who had been pacing the room, immediately sank in a chair. He was certain the child was his. Bursting with joy, he desired to share the news with everyone. Prudence assumed control once he grasped the potential impact on Ajatashatru. The competition could heighten the prince's insecurity, causing him to conspire against the baby. It would be better to bring both Amrapali and the child to Rajgriha and then make a public announcement.

'How did you learn of this news?' Bimbisar asked.

'My brother-in-law is a high-ranking intelligence officer in the security department. He has to go to Vaishali frequently for intelligence gathering. Last night, he visited us and shared some news, Maharaj. Of course, he is not aware of our trip to Vaishali.'

'Whom does your brother-in-law report to?'

'To the chief intelligence officer. Lately, however, the mahamatya has been taking an interest in Devi Amrapali and has requested my brother-in-law to provide regular updates about her.'

'Has he given this news to the mahamatya?'

'Yes, Maharaj! The mahamatya received this news yesterday. Since I was not in Rajgriha, I couldn't bring you the news earlier.'

'It doesn't matter. You deserve a reward for the news, Deva,' said the king. Taking the precious necklace off his neck, he handed it to the young warrior.

'You are very kind, Maharaj,' Devavrata folded his hands in gratitude.

'Devi Amrapali and her son are no longer safe in Vaishali, so we must bring them to Magadh. We must leave for Vaishali immediately. Wait for me at the main ghat at dawn tomorrow.'

'I'll be there, Maharaj.' The loyal soldier bowed respectfully and left.

After dismissing Devavrata, Bimbisar began planning his journey. Just like earlier, he had to travel incognito to Vaishali. But first, he had to deal with Vassakar. Why was he taking so much interest in Amrapali? What was his motive? *I must find out why he didn't give me the news. Amrapali and the baby's safety is at stake if the mahamatya shares the news with Ajatashatru.*

Bimbisar promptly called for the mahamatya. His anger grew more intense as each minute went by. It seemed like an endless wait until the mahamatya finally arrived.

Vassakar was breathless. He bowed his head respectfully and said, 'My humble apologies, Maharaj. An important matter delayed me, and I couldn't come immediately.'

'You have a lot of urgent matters vying for your attention. Some of them are more important than your king,' Bimbisar's voice cut through the air sharply.

'Please forgive me, Maharaj. You are the most important person to me,' Vassakar's voice took on a wheedling tone.

'Is your urgent work related to the Vaishali nagarvadhu by any chance?' Bimbisar gnashed his teeth in anger.

'The nagarvadhu? No, Maharaj. It has nothing to do with her,' the mahamatya lied smoothly.

'Are you sure, Vassakar?' The king hardly ever used the brahmin's name, saving it for times when he was extremely angry. 'According to my sources, you have been taking a lot of interest in Devi Amrapali.'

'That's not true, Maharaj.' The mahamatya's face appeared flushed. 'Someone is trying to poison your mind against me.'

Switching gears, Bimbisar enquired, 'How is everything in Anga? Can Ajatashatru handle things by himself?'

'Yes, Maharaj!'

'The prince has successfully quelled the rebellion, but there are still factions operating in the forests. They might regroup and launch a surprise attack on the prince at an ideal time.' Vassakar's mind struggled to make sense of Bimbisar's eccentric dialogue. *Why had the king switched the conversation from Vaishali to Anga?*

'I want you to leave for Anga, immediately,' Bimbisar commanded. 'Ajatashatru needs a wise advisor.'

'But...'

'No buts, Vassakar. Ajatashatru needs you in Anga. I want you on your way to Anga within the next hour.'

There was nothing the mahamatya could do or say. The king's decision was final. He wanted Vassakar out of Magadh quickly to ensure he could create no mischief. The crafty mahamatya knew the reasons for his dismissal. He knew the king was eager to meet the nagarvadhu. Without his presence, Bimbisar's plans would proceed smoothly. The king's mission was a dangerous one. It could lead to death if they recognized him at Vaishali.

'It shall be as per your command, Maharaj.' The mahamatya lowered his eyes to conceal his joy. He deliberately misrepresented the news regarding the turmoil in Anga. The discontent among the Anga generals was constant, and it would persist. Vassakar's goal was to find a chance to devise a strategy and dethrone Bimbisar.

The mahamatya disapproved of Bimbisar's infatuation with a courtesan. He strongly believed that the Magadh throne required a young and courageous person, and Ajatashatru was the ideal choice. Vassakar had plans to make him the ruler. For some time, he had been looking for the perfect opportunity to train the prince for his upcoming role as king. The hot-headed Yuvraj was a putty in his hands. He would be the perfect puppet king. A torrent of intense thoughts swirled through his mind as he left the palace.

A worried Bimbisar paced his chamber restlessly. Vassakar's treachery weighed heavily on his mind. He couldn't shake off the nagging feeling that the mahamatya was plotting something, but his priority was getting Amrapali and his son safely to Magadh.

On an impulse, he called for Rajmata Kosala Devi. She was

the only one he could trust. He wanted to tell her the truth about his relationship with Amrapali.

'Kosala, I'm leaving for Vaishali to bring back my son,' he sprang the surprise on her as soon as she entered his chamber.

'Your son?' Kosala wore a puzzled expression. 'In Vaishali?'

Recalling the king's visit to Vaishali, she realized what he meant. Her spies had intercepted rumours about Bimbisar's visit to Devi Amrapali and promptly relayed the information to her. She had dismissed them as mere gossip, but now she realized they were true.

'Is it the nagarvadhu's son?' Kosala sounded resigned.

Bimbisar nodded his head, 'Yes, Kosala.' He looked away, unable to meet the penetrating gaze of his queen. Not only did he deceive his three queens, but he had also played with the emotions of the woman he professed to love.

'Maharaj...'

'Say nothing, Kosala. Please don't burden me with any more guilt. I have made countless mistakes, and this is just another one to add to the list. Little did I realize that my visit to Vaishali would have such a lasting impact on my life, all because I fell head over heels for Amrapali.' Tenderly, the king took hold of Kosala's hand, his eyes pleading while acknowledging her unwavering support and wise counsel. 'I want to ensure that my son gets the recognition he deserves in Magadh.'

'You must do the right thing. Why should an innocent child suffer because of the actions of two adults?' Kosala turned her face away to hide her bitterness. Ever since she married Bimbisar, she had constantly accepted whatever came her way. She had to navigate the customs of Magadh, and the Rajmata expected her to obey her orders. Without seeking her consent, Bimbisar placed the burden of raising Chellana's son on her. Despite their difficulty, she had faced each transition uncomplainingly, with a positive attitude. Yet, years of emotional turmoil had taken a toll on her. The weight of Bimbisar's troubles had become too much for her to bear. 'It is only fair that your son is given the place he deserves,' she said wearily.

'As always, you are right. I must go to Vaishali to bring Amrapali and our son to Magadh.'

'There is nothing else to be done, Maharaj. It is your responsibility to make amends for what you have done.'

As Kosala walked out of the king's chamber, her footsteps grew increasingly heavy. She didn't know how long she could continue to hold Bimbisar's hand.

# 24

# A Journey Gone Wrong

The journey to Vaishali was a difficult one, with obstacles at every turn. The mild, unseasonal rainfall that began at night gathered momentum by the time Bimbisar and Devavrata met at the riverbank. It gradually turned into a torrential downpour as Devavrata began navigating the boat.

The water level in the river rose steadily, resulting in a significant swell. While navigating the tumultuous waters of the Gandak, they noticed a small leak in the hull. Water trickled steadily into the boat. Bimbisar swiftly began to scoop out the water while Devavrata struggled to seal the hole. As they sailed deeper into the water, the hole grew bigger, causing water to rush in at an alarming rate. The boat that Devavrata had purchased from a fisherman was proving to be ill-suited for the journey.

Although the king didn't believe in omens, he couldn't shake off a feeling of uneasiness as they struggled to stabilize the boat. Despite his inner voice urging him to retreat, he forged ahead, fighting the waves in the sinking boat. Having already crossed more than half the river, there was no alternative but to press on.

Devavrata shouted to make himself heard over the noise of the water. 'The boat is sinking too fast, Maharaj. We can't make it to the other side.'

Bimbisar shouted back, 'We will have to swim to the other side. Jump into the water, now.'

Devavrata was taken aback when he saw the king suddenly

plunging into the water. 'Wait, Maharaj!' he shouted and leapt into the water after him.

In a matter of moments, the forceful riptide trapped them. Despite his swimming prowess, Bimbisar was overwhelmed by the powerful force of the current. As he struggled against the current, his energy rapidly depleting, he gave up on the idea of reaching Vaishali.

Broken branches and floating debris slowed down the king's progress. In addition, battling the crashing waves required him to double his effort. There was no alternative but to continue pushing ahead. He tried to catch hold of a log that was floating in the water, but it slipped away. It was pointless to continue fighting the powerful current.

Fate intervened. Suddenly, he remembered the valuable advice his father had given him. 'Never swim directly towards the shore when faced with a strong current. Swim diagonally instead,' he had instructed. 'And stop swimming against the current.' His father's words echoed loudly in his ears. Bimbisar felt a rush of energy as he put into practice the lessons he had been taught.

'To float on your back, align your feet downstream and keep your head positioned upstream. By doing this, you will minimize the risk of head injuries. Your legs and feet will withstand any damage caused by rocks and debris. Keep your feet flexed and sticking out of the water, while keeping your head above the water level. Synchronize your breath with the downstream current to prevent swallowing excess water. Once you have passed the riptide, turn over and swim diagonally towards the shore with the flow of the current.'

The strategy proved effective. Bimbisar discovered that he could effortlessly navigate his body through the turbulent waters.

Delight filled Bimbisar's heart as he observed Devavrata flawlessly imitating his every action. Despite the arduousness of the task, they moved forward, their muscles aching and their breaths rasping as they finally reached the opposite bank. All they longed for was a moment of respite on the bank.

The king looked at his muddy clothes. His hair was covered in dirt, and his uttariya had been carried off by the river. Unfortunately, the dagger tucked in his waistband had also disappeared. The rain had whittled down to a gentle drizzle, and the river was gradually settling into a peaceful flow.

'Don't look so downcast,' the king said, trying to lift his companion's spirits. 'Look at the bright side, Deva. There is no need for any disguise. No one can recognize us now.' Despite the gravity of the situation, the two of them burst out laughing.

Much to their dismay, they discovered that they had landed miles away from their destination. It would take them hours of walking to reach the remote ghat they had selected for landing. They were starving, dirty, and completely exhausted, which made the long walk seem impossible. The sun beat down on them, intensifying the musty atmosphere.

A lush forested area next to the riverbank caught Devavrata's attention. The presence of trees meant a chance of finding some fruits. His eyes sparkled with hope as he caught sight of the forest. Silently, they entered the woods together. After a while, they lay down under a tree, feeling sleepy from the sun's warmth and a satisfying meal of figs and wild berries. The pleasant breeze lulled them into a peaceful slumber.

As the sun sank below the horizon, the king woke up from his sleep. He dusted off his clothes and woke up Devavrata, and they resumed their journey to their destination. They continued their journey as night descended, catching glimpses of small hamlets nestled amidst vast expanses of paddy and barley fields.

While Bimbisar made his way to Amrapali's palace, Vassakar engaged in his deceptive plots in Anga. Over the past few days, he had been manipulating Ajatashatru by narrating stories about Bimbisar's romance with the nagarvadhu. As a result, the prince's anger towards his father grew even stronger. Finally, one morning, Vassakar revealed his trump card.

His eyes gleaming with malice, he said, 'Maharaj has gone to Vaishali to bring Amrapali and her son to Magadh.'

The news came as a shock to Ajatashatru. 'What is his motive for bringing a courtesan to Magadh?' he asked.

'The Maharaj has been besotted with Amrapali.' Vassakar's eyes gleamed with delight as he watched Ajatashatru's face flush with anger. 'A few months back, he ventured to Vaishali in secret, where he delighted in the company of the courtesan for a couple of weeks. The outcome of this was the birth of a son. Now, he plans to marry the courtesan and announce the son as his heir.'

'Impossible!' Ajatashatru rose from his seat and bellowed thunderously, 'How can he marry a courtesan and tarnish the repute of the Magadh throne? She is nothing but a prostitute. How can the king be sure that the son is truly his? As long as I'm alive, I'll not allow such a thing to happen.'

'You are right, Yuvraj. I tried to dissuade him from going to Vaishali,' said Vassakar. His heart swelled with happiness as he beheld the successful outcome of his deceit.

'Apart from the reasons you pointed out, the threat of the Maharaj being killed is exceedingly high. Things have not been smooth between Magadh and Vaishali,' Vassakar added more fuel to the fire.

'Do you think I live in a bubble?' With his patience wearing thin, the prince snapped, 'I have spies in both kingdoms, and I'm well aware of all that transpires.' He was irritated by Vassakar's habit of speaking indirectly. 'Come to the point, mahamatya.'

'The Vaishali spies will soon find out that the Magadh king is in their city, and they will quickly inform their superiors. The arrest of our Maharaj will signify a great triumph for the Vaishali king.'

Amused, Ajatashatru reflected, 'Wouldn't that be wonderful? My path to the Magadh throne will be clear if that happens.'

'Please keep your voice down, Yuvraj,' Vassakar cautioned, glancing around the chamber. 'Be careful, for walls have ears. There are many loyal courtiers of the Maharaj here.'

'Just name them and I'll have them killed. This is my domain, and my word is law here.'

'The right timing for any action is key to achieving success. Don't be hasty, Yuvraj.' Vassakar soothed the restless prince. 'I'm here in Anga to help you ascend the throne at the right time, but now is not the time.' Vassakar waited patiently as Ajatashatru took a few sips of madira and settled into his chair. 'Right now, I'm worried about the Maharaj's life.'

'Nonsense! Knowingly, he stepped into a dangerous territory, so it is only fair that he faces the consequences.'

'Yuvraj, Magadh's honour is at stake. We can't allow any harm to come your father's way.'

After taking a sip of madira, Ajatashatru asked, 'What do you propose we do?' He had observed Vassakar's strategies and admired his shrewdness. He understood the advantages of having the mahamatya by his side. 'Do you want me to rush after my father and rescue him from the prostitute's house?'

'Something along those lines, Yuvraj. I want you to gather your soldiers and swiftly advance towards Vaishali. Meanwhile, I have already alerted the Magadh army commanders about the imminent threat to the Maharaj. We will join forces with the Magadh army, and together we will unleash a fierce assault on the Lichchavi capital. Vaishali is an indomitable fortress, thanks to its three robust walls and watchtowers. Entering the city by breaking through the gate will not be easy and will demand a lot of effort. I have instructed my spies to keep a close watch on the situation and promptly notify us of any changes.'

True to form, the mahamatya had come up with an excellent plan. The prince's eyes lit up as he enthusiastically proclaimed, 'Incredible! You have a brilliant mind!'

Despite appearing to be a simple strategy to save the Magadh king, its repercussions were far-reaching. If Ajatashatru's army won the battle against Vaishali and rescued the king, they would receive praise for their victory. The prince's commitment and bravery would make him highly respected in Magadh. If they couldn't save Bimbisar, Ajatashatru would ascend the throne. Either way, the prince would come out on top. The subjects would enthusiastically praise his actions, and the army commanders would reconsider their views on the prince.

It was an incredible opportunity that Ajatashatru couldn't pass up. Defeating Vaishali would not only grant him the crown but also allow him to show his bravery in combat. Despite participating in several battles alongside his father, he never received praise for the victories. That was only showered on the king.

'We have no time to lose, Yuvraj,' urged the mahamatya. 'The Magadh chief commanders, along with their soldiers, would have already started their journey to Vaishali. I'm leaving immediately to join the Magadh army.'

On his way to the door, he paused and turned. In a voice filled with urgency, he said, 'Yuvraj, you must set out with your army immediately. The success of our plan relies on you reaching Vaishali before the Magadh army attacks.'

'I'll arrive well ahead of you,' assured the prince.

As Ajatashatru set off with his army from Anga, Bimbisar and his companion undertook a quiet and cautious passage through the Lichchavi region. Taking great care not to draw attention, they moved at a slow pace towards the city. Even though they were exhausted and covered in dirt, they pressed on. With determination, they navigated the arduous hills and dense forests, ultimately arriving at the bountiful plains sustained by the nearby river. Along their journey, they came across charming little villages with just a handful of simple houses.

Mistaking them for beggars and travellers, the villagers offered them whatever food they could afford. In the absence of hospitable villagers, Bimbisar and Devavrata opted to gather fruits from trees and consume whatever they found. They stumbled upon streams that quenched their thirst and washed away their fatigue.

Vaishali was still a significant distance away. They slept during daylight hours and only moved under the cloak of night to avoid detection. Even though it took them longer, they decided on the safer option. Taking occasional breaks to rest, they continued walking for two days. The risk of detection and death heightened with each passing minute in the enemy's domain. Bimbisar never expected to be so far off course from where he had originally planned to be.

He had no idea that the armies of Magadh and Anga had already reached Vaishali's gates. Thanks to his vision, Magadh had a highly effective and nimble army, ready for war at an instant's notice.

With the sun vanishing beneath the horizon, the tired soldiers assembled to listen to the Yuvraj. They had to take a long and exhausting detour due to the river's elevated water levels. Ajatashatru delivered a rousing speech that infused them with energy.

His voice, full of determination, echoed powerfully through the crowd, commanding attention. 'My dear brothers, we are here today to liberate our king from the clutches of the Vaishali soldiers. Let's show them how brave we are, so they never dare to underestimate the might of the Magadh kingdom.'

The combined might of the Anga and Magadh soldiers responded to his call to action with a resounding battle cry, 'Long live the king!'

Before him stood the king's best warriors, renowned for their unmatched skills in warfare and unwavering loyalty. There were the commanders with exceptional prowess in battle strategy. Bimbisar commanded the unwavering allegiance of both the warriors and their commanders.

When Bimbisar set off for Vaishali, the shrewd mahamatya slyly circulated false reports among the commanders of the king being held captive. He knew they looked down on Ajatashatru's limited knowledge of military tactics and had little respect for the impulsive prince.

The Magadh commanders came together under Ajatashatru's leadership solely because of Vassakar's warning about the imminent threat to Bimbisar.

Unitedly, the commanders of Magadh and Anga pledged to rescue their king. 'You must follow the orders of the Yuvraj,' Vassakar told them. 'He is the future king of Magadh.' In the face of the crisis, they promised to remain loyal to Ajatashatru and fight until the bitter end.

After a discussion with the prince, the Magadh and Anga commanders declared their plan to break the gates at dawn the following day.

Wasting no time, the soldiers swiftly set up camp and were promptly tasked with their responsibilities. The Magadh camp was soon filled with the sounds of swords being sharpened for the impending battle. The soldiers ignited fires to prepare their food. When the lights went out, the soldiers fell asleep while sentries kept watch. With the dawn of a new day, they knew that they would have yet another opportunity to show their loyalty. They were prepared to stake their lives to rescue their king.

# 25

# A Confession and an Ultimatum

As night descended, the city of Vaishali embraced tranquillity. The stillness was palpable, with no sign of any movement or breeze. Amrapali anxiously paced back and forth in her chamber, carefully watching over her sleeping son. The news of enemy soldiers camping outside the gates of Vaishali had reached her ears, and she could feel a knot tightening in her stomach. As long as she ensured her son's safety, she had no concern for herself.

She walked to the terrace and looked out at the garden in the moonlight. The view triggered a flood of memories in her mind. Amrapali was filled with nostalgia as she recalled the delightful evenings spent with Indrajeet in the gazebo. She wondered why he had disappeared, leaving no trace or explanation behind. Where was he now? Would he ever come back? Did he know of his son's birth?

She longed for his warm laughter and embrace.

The quiet of the night was interrupted by a soft rustling noise, as if someone was walking carefully. Suddenly, a shadow appeared near the terrace and momentarily blocked her view of the garden. A second figure joined the first, and there were two shadowy figures under her terrace.

Amrapali looked around, her senses becoming more alert. Were they patrolling guards or thieves? Recent floods had taken a toll on the city. Hunger compelled people to resort to crime. They wandered through the city, committing theft. Over the past few weeks, there had been numerous cases of robbery. Just as she was about to call for help, she saw the dishevelled man in tattered clothes standing below the balcony. As soon as she saw the crooked smile and shimmering eyes, a feeling of familiarity engulfed her.

It seemed too good to be true. Perhaps her thoughts about Indrajeet were making her mind play tricks on her. She let out a strangled scream and stumbled backwards, her heart pounding in her chest. Amrapali dashed towards the door, eager to discover if it was truly Indrajeet.

Their paths crossed as they reached the entrance to her chamber. With tears of joy streaming down her face, she eagerly ran into his open arms, crying out, 'Oh Indrajeet! You are back at last.'

'Hush, sweetheart! I'm here.'

'Why did you take so long?' she exclaimed, unwilling to leave his embrace. 'I had resigned myself to the idea that you would never return to Vaishali.'

'Don't cry, Pali, I'm here to take you with me.' There was urgency in his voice as he said, 'We have to leave quickly before anyone sees us.'

'Why should we leave?' she asked petulantly. 'You have just arrived, and now you want us to leave. I don't understand...'

'Please, Pali,' he said, his voice filled with desperation. 'Try to understand. We don't have much time. Both Deva and I'll face death if we are found.'

'I don't understand. Where exactly are we heading and why is it not possible for us to leave later?' she persisted, clinging to him.

'We can't waste time here. My life is in danger.'

'You are safe in my palace,' she said. 'No one will dare to lay a hand on you. I'll protect you with my life.'

'Vaishali's army is currently on the hunt for me. Pali, do you have no idea who I am?' He gently turned her face towards him, forcing her to meet his gaze. 'I'm Bimbisar, the ruler of Magadh.'

'You must be joking, Indra. Bimbisar is an evil person, and you are so gentle. Magadh king, indeed!' Amrapali suddenly erupted into giggles, her nerves getting the better of her. Events were unfolding at such a rapid pace that she struggled to keep up.

'It's true.'

'Wait, are you saying you're not Indrajeet?' Her face paled as she took in the weight of his words.

'That is what I'm saying. When I realized you hated the king of Magadh, I had no choice but to fabricate my identity. I never expected to fall in love with you.'

'This can't be happening,' she whispered in an unsteady voice as she slowly backed away from him. He reached out to hold her, but she flinched away from his touch as if his hands were on fire. 'Stay away!' she screamed. Anger flickered in her eyes as she accused him, 'You tricked and misled me.'

Shame filled his eyes as he looked at her. Her revulsion was justified. He had ruined her life.

'Come with me, Pali,' he pleaded. 'I'll make you the queen of Magadh. Our son will be a prince.'

Amprapali said vehemently, 'He is not your son; he is mine. Mine alone. You have no right over him.'

Her face contorted with anger as she took slow, deliberate steps away from him.

'Our son needs a father. He is a prince. Denying him his rights would be unjust, Pali.' Bimbisar dropped to his knees. His voice trembled as he implored her, 'Come with me to Magadh.'

'I'll call for the guards if you don't leave immediately,' she declared firmly. She clenched her fists, her nails digging into her palms as she fought to maintain control. 'I'll never allow you to take my son.'

'Don't you love me anymore?' Bimbisar asked. Taking a step

towards her, he gently grasped her arm. 'Look into my eyes and say that you don't love me.'

Amrapali attempted to control her feelings. The closeness between them made her weak. To yield to her emotions would be akin to betraying Vaishali. She didn't want to summon the guards because she knew they would kill him. Despite everything, she still loved him. She couldn't bring herself to be the cause of his death.

'I loved Indrajeet, not Bimbisar,' her voice was barely above a whisper. 'Leave now, before I completely lose control,' she warned Bimbisar.

'I know you love me, otherwise you would have summoned the guards.' His voice was a gentle caress. A shudder travelled along her spine, causing her to close her eyes.

'Yes, I love you. But my love for Vaishali runs even deeper,' she replied. 'Becoming a queen holds no appeal for me, and I have no intention of raising my son as a Magadh prince. But I want you to prove your love for me.'

'I'll do anything to prove my love for you, Pali.'

'I want you to withdraw your troops and return to Magadh before the crack of dawn.'

'Magadh troops? I didn't come with troops.'

'Stop pretending. If you didn't bring the troops, then who did?'

'I intend to find out,' he promised. 'But I'll not leave without you.'

For a moment, she felt an irresistible longing to flee with him, to leave everything behind. Amrapali was tempted to raise her son like a prince, but her loyalty to Vaishali prevented her from agreeing to flee to Magadh. 'That can never happen. I'll kill our son and then myself if you don't leave now. That is my promise to you.'

He froze at her threat.

'You can't do that,' he moaned, the sound of defeat clear in his voice. The strong desire to see his son had driven him to undertake the perilous journey. Unlike his other children, Amrapali's son was conceived purely out of love. Bimbisar experienced a profound affection for the child. 'What sort of mother would speak about taking the life of her child?' He locked his desperate gaze with hers, and begged, 'Please, don't be so cruel, Pali.'

'My mind is made, and it can't be swayed,' she declared firmly. 'Your lust for power has resulted in many deaths. Two more will not matter. Leave now, Arya.'

He flinched at her words. 'It shall be as you say. I'll leave now,' Bimbisar whispered almost inaudibly before walking away.

Bimbisar and Devavrata stealthily crept out of Amrapali's opulent palace and embarked on their perilous journey towards the secluded ghat. The decision made by Amrapali weighed heavily on the king's mind. He had lost not just the woman he loved, but also the son he wanted. Sensing the burden in the king's heart, Devavrata held back from speaking. The darkness of the night shrouded their movements as they made their way along the riverbank until they reached the Magadh camp outside the Vaishali gates.

The guards at the camp noticed two unkempt individuals approaching and quickly raised an alarm. One of them ran to inform the Magadh army commander, and he rushed out of his tent to confront the two men.

With a steely gaze, the Magadh army commander confronted the two vagrants, and then recognition dawned on him. He was flabbergasted to see Bimbisar standing before him. Vassakar had informed them that the Lichchavis had imprisoned the king.

The commander humbly bowed his head and brought his hands together in greeting, 'Pranam, Maharaj'.

The camp was abuzz with the news, and the soldiers quickly assembled before Bimbisar. Where had the king disappeared, and why was he in such a condition? Those questions would come later. For now, everyone was glad to see him safe. The air was filled with their jubilant shouts of 'Long live Magadh Samrat!'

Vassakar, the expert strategist, quickly joined the soldiers in expressing his delight. He understood it was beneficial to align his interests with Bimbisar's. For the moment, at least.

The boisterous cheering from the Magadh soldiers roused Ajatashatru just before midnight. After securing his sword to his belt, the prince stepped out of his tent. He was surprised to see his father standing in front of the soldiers.

Bimbisar's regal aura remained unaffected by his torn, filthy garments and his tangled hair. His posture and smile exuded confidence and poise. Ajatashatru wondered what it took to earn such unwavering loyalty from his soldiers. He wondered if he could ever command such respect from them.

Vassakar stood next to the king, with a sycophantic smile. Ajatashatru was filled with rage. Bimbisar's sudden appearance had defeated his meticulously crafted strategies, and shattered his dreams of achieving greatness. He cursed his father.

Bimbisar thanked the mahamatya and his son for their concern. 'I'm impressed by the mahamatya's efficiency. He brought not just the troops from Magadh, but also bolstered the army by including the troops from Anga. However, there is no need for a battle.'

The crowd erupted in even louder cheers in response to the king's words. He raised a hand to calm the soldiers, and continued, 'I'm pleased with your preparation and enthusiasm. As a token of appreciation, I hereby approve an additional payment to be included in your salary this month. We will march back to Magadh at first light.'

The soldiers burst into cheers once again as soon as the Magadh king finished speaking. They were glad to go back home without engaging in battle. Besides, they would receive an extra payment. Joy filled the air, yet Ajatashatru seemed unhappy.

Meanwhile, the Vaishali sabhagriha was abuzz with the voices of Vaishali's ministers who had gathered for an emergency meeting. Despite the late hour, the looming danger of an attack had prompted King Chetak to summon them for a meeting. The king couldn't help but notice the exhaustion clearly evident on the faces of his ministers.

'Gentlemen, the Magadh army is at our gate,' the chief minister announced. 'The crisis was believed to be caused by rumours of the Magadh king's imprisonment.'

'That's utter nonsense!' declared the intelligence head. 'When and how could we have imprisoned Bimbisar? As far as I know, he has come nowhere near Vaishali.'

Several ministers nodded their heads. No one had heard of Bimbisar's arrival. 'Given the recent conflict over the ore mines near the border, I highly doubt he would be foolish enough to venture into our kingdom,' said the finance minister.

'Maharaj, I received a couple of reports from our spies last year. The reports show that the Magadh king had spent some time with the nagarvadhu,' the intelligence head informed the king.

'I don't believe your report!' responded a minister. 'Devi Amrapali is a loyal citizen of Vaishali. She will never entertain Bimbisar.'

For a few moments, there was a hushed silence in the assembly, broken only by the murmurs of ministers whispering among themselves.

'Maharaj, according to our spies, the king of Magadh is not in Rajgriha or anywhere in the kingdom. His whereabouts are a mystery to everyone. All efforts to trace him have failed. I suspect

Vassakar is behind all this. According to my reports, he has been in disfavour for quite some time, and he has been consistently urging the Yuvraj to revolt against the king,' said the Vaishali rajguru, wiping off the beads of perspiration on his forehead.

The rajguru had been unwell, but the crisis had compelled him to come back to the sabhagriha for the discussion. He was past eighty, but King Chetak, who relied heavily on him for guidance, refused to relieve him of his duties.

'We must avoid a battle at all costs,' said King Chetak. 'The recent floods have devastated the kingdom, and a war at this time will only bring further devastation.'

'We should call Ajatashatru and Vassakar to discuss a truce and find a peaceful resolution,' suggested the senapati, but the rajguru shook his head.

'Ajatashatru is a stubborn young man with a closed mind. It will be difficult to reason with him. Besides, he will bring Vassakar for the discussion, and Vassakar will never agree to a truce,' he said. 'Based on my understanding, he intends to orchestrate Ajatashatru's ascension to the throne of Magadh. That will allow him to play the role of a puppeteer. The man's ambition knows no bounds, and he will let nothing stand in the way of his plans.' The rajguru coughed, showing signs of fatigue and illness.

'You don't seem to be in good health. Please go home and rest. Have no fear, we will find a resolution to this predicament,' King Chetak reassured the rajguru.

The rajguru raised his hand and said, 'Thank you for your concern, Maharaj. How can I relax knowing the enemy is at our doorstep?' Catching his breath, he continued, 'Our best bet is to find the Magadh king as soon as possible. We must send out our spies to search for him in Vaishali. Our first target should be the nagarvadhu's palace,' he declared. 'If indeed Bimbisar is in love with Amrapali, he will visit her, regardless of the obstacles.'

'But Rajguru, what if the Magadh king is not in Vaishali at all?' asked the senapati. 'If that be the case, how do we stop Ajatashatru from attacking us?

'We must take a chance. Vassakar would not have arrived with the elite soldiers if he had doubts about Bimbisar's presence in Vaishali,' replied the rajguru. 'Let's not waste time. King Chetak can go to Ajatashatru and invite him for a talk, while you send the spies to search for Bimbisar.'

The senapati dispatched his spies to search the nagarvadhu's palace, while King Chetak set out with his chief minister to meet Ajatashatru.

It was a night full of surprises. The guards at the Magadh camp were surprised when they saw the gate of Vaishali opening and, the next minute, they witnessed King Chetak racing towards them in his chariot. Was he coming for a battle, they wondered. As soon as the mahamatya was informed, he rushed out of his tent. The fluttering white flag on the chariot immediately caught his attention, and he heaved a sigh of relief.

Thereafter, things unfolded rapidly. Bimbisar, who had bathed and changed, now looked impressive in his regal finery. He greeted King Chetak with great warmth.

'Greetings, Vaishali Naresh,' the Magadh king extended his greetings. King Chetak was his father-in-law, and it was only fitting that he be treated with respect. 'What brings you to our camp at this hour?'

The Vaishali chief minister stood in complete shock, unable to comprehend what he had just heard. He had been ready to put forth his arguments against a battle, but there was no sign of one.

Displaying no astonishment, King Chetak calmly responded to Bimbisar's greetings. His astuteness allowed him to handle any situation that cropped up. It takes two to play the game. He was resolute in not allowing his son-in-law to outsmart him. 'I heard that you were camping at the gate of Vaishali, so I thought it would be more comfortable for you to stay in the palace for as long as you desire.' King Chetak extended a warm invitation to Bimbisar. There was no sign of anxiety on his face.

Ajatashatru couldn't believe his eyes when he saw the two kings laughing and joking. There was no sign of any hostility between them.

Vassakar, who was watching him, remarked, 'Yuvraj, your father is a true master of the art of diplomacy. Our king understands better than anyone else that diplomacy is more desirable than engaging in battles.'

The prince had many lessons to learn. His training for the crown had just begun.

# 26

# Murmurs of Dissent

A series of disappointments and heartaches marked the season. Bimbisar was devastated by the unsuccessful outcome of his mission. He couldn't stop thinking about Amrapali, and his heart ached for a glimpse of his son. She had denied him the right to see or hold the baby. Yet, the king had no choice but to set aside his personal grief and prioritize his kingdom.

The failure of Vassakar's plans left Ajatashatru fuming. It was clear to Bimbisar that his son harboured bitterness towards him. There was an unspoken tension in the air whenever they encountered each other. Suspicions lurked in the king's mind about Vassakar and his son hatching a fresh conspiracy. The king had a strong feeling that the simultaneous arrival of troops from Magadh and Anga in Vaishali was not a mere coincidence. Vassakar was up to no good, he realized. His malicious intentions needed to be thwarted before they could cause any further harm.

Little did Bimbisar know that a grand conspiracy was already unfolding, masterminded by the mahamatya who was intent on ensuring its success. Methodically and persistently, the mahamatya chipped away at Bimbisar's credibility. He planted seeds of doubt about the king's mental state and circulated vicious rumours about his obsession with the nagarvadhu. It took him some effort to destroy Bimbisar's reputation among the nobles of Magadh, but his plans had started working.

After his return from Vaishali, Bimbisar commanded both Vassakar and Ajatashatru to go back to Anga. Devadatta, who had been waiting for an opportune moment, immediately made his way to Anga to join them, and the three of them began plotting Bimbisar's downfall.

Meanwhile, Bimbisar called for Abhay and shared his concerns with the young man.

'I have an important mission for you,' Bimbisar told Abhay. 'Right now, Magadh is a hub of intrigue and secrets. My enemies are relentlessly plotting and scheming to sabotage my every move. They have successfully convinced some ministers to switch their allegiances. I have lost track of who can be trusted and who can't. You are the only person I trust, so I'm counting on you to gather information about Vassakar's plot.'

'I assure you, Maharaj, I'll bring back all the news,' Abhay promised the king. 'Vassakar will never harm you as long as I'm alive.'

Abhay's sincerity touched Bimbisar; tears welled up in his eyes. He fought the urge to reveal his true identity—he was the young man's father—but that would have to wait for the right time. The king contemplated the possibility of disinheriting Ajatashatru and designating Abhay as his successor. He would make a better king. But that too would have to wait until he regained a firm grip on his kingdom.

'Maharaj, please bless me so that I can come back victorious,' Abhay respectfully bowed down and touched the king's feet.

Bimbisar tried to control his emotions as he gently placed his hand on the young man's head and said softly, 'May you be victorious.'

'I'll return soon,' promised Abhay as he rushed out of the king's chamber.

Suddenly, Bimbisar had a premonition, and his mind was flooded with a vivid, unsettling image. His heart pounded in his chest, and beads of sweat formed on his forehead. The feeling that he had sent the young man to his death left him reeling. *I have to stop him immediately.*

He rushed out only to realize that the young man had already ridden away from the palace. The king beckoned his best warriors and ordered them to chase after Abhay.

The next day, Bimbisar received the heartbreaking news of Abhay's death. Abhay and a soldier had been ambushed and killed by bandits in the forest while travelling to Anga. The soldiers sent by the king had reached too late. Bimbisar was overcome with remorse and grief at the devastating news. He held himself responsible for the death of his beloved son.

It was Vasumitra, a loyal minister of many years, who broke another unsettling news to Bimbisar. Vasumitra's request for a private audience surprised the king. He knew the minister was visiting his family in the village.

It was early evening when the king found time to meet the minister. Bimbisar was surprised to note that Vasumitra looked anxious.

'Pranam, Maharaj. I'm sorry, but it was important for me to have a confidential conversation with you.' The minister bowed down before the king.

'What brings you here this evening, Amatya?' Bimbisar greeted the old minister. 'I hope it is not another request to leave the court.'

'Maharaj, I won't ask for retirement as it is a critical moment for the kingdom.'

Bimbisar's eyebrows shot up in surprise. 'Your mysterious words have piqued my curiosity, Amatya. Am I missing something?'

Vasumitra's words were filled with urgency. 'Maharaj, I have stumbled upon some unsettling information.' The deep creases on the minister's forehead reflected his worries. 'I thought it best to report it to you so you could take immediate action. I have been informed that it was not bandits but Ajatashatru's soldiers who killed Abhay.'

Shocked at this news, Bimbisar slumped into his chair. 'What are you saying, Amatya?' he mumbled after a few minutes. 'Why would Ajatashatru kill Abhay? As far as I know, Abhay had never harmed him.'

'Ajatashatru felt envious of Abhay's popularity and influence in Magadh and other regions. He was aware of your affection for Abhay and his loyalty towards you. Unfortunately, Abhay's proximity to you was the reason for his death.'

Bimbisar was speechless. First Amrapali refused to let him see his son, and now Abhay—he had lost the two sons he valued.

'Powerful people are working against you, Maharaj. My life will be at risk if anyone discovers I have conveyed this news to you,' Vasumitra continued.

'You need not fear, Amatya,' Bimbisar reassured the loyal man. As the old minister spoke, his words stirred up a sense of unease in Bimbisar. 'Your life is safe here. You may share the matter with no fear.'

'Rumours about you too have been circulating among the nobles in the court. According to them, you have grown disinterested in the kingdom and have been spending time with a courtesan from Vaishali. They also speak of a son with Amrapali.'

Every word uttered by Vasumitra made Bimbisar grit his teeth and his face turn red with rage. Bimbisar's suspicions about Vassakar were now confirmed. He knew that the mahamatya was the mastermind behind these rumours.

'Maharaj, they argue that Magadh requires a youthful and energetic ruler, suggesting that you are too old to rule.' A visibly embarrassed Vasumitra cleared his throat to regain his composure.

'Don't hold back, Amatya. Tell me everything,' Bimbisar urged.

'The nobles are divided in their opinion, with conflicting points of view creating a rift among them. Secret meetings are being held to influence each other. Many nobles have switched loyalties and are now demanding for Ajatashatru to be crowned.'

'Have you any information about the mastermind behind the conspiracy?' Bimbisar demanded angrily.

Vasumitra shook his head. 'I have my suspicions, but I can't be sure.' He had been unwaveringly loyal to the king, and the recent developments had filled him with sorrow. 'I think it is all Vassakar's mischief. He has been conspiring with Devadatta and Ajatashatru to spread these rumours about you.'

'You are right, Amatya. I had suspected his motives, but now I'm certain he intends to cause me harm. But why? He was a nobody when he arrived in Rajgriha. I believed in him and appointed him to the highest position in the cabinet.' Bimbisar's disappointment was writ large on his face.

'Vassakar is an ambitious man, Maharaj. He is not content with being your mahamatya. His desire for greater control and authority can be fulfilled only by placing Ajatashatru on the throne. It is widely known that he has been mentoring the prince and stoking his ambition to claim the throne.'

'Doesn't he understand the prince is inexperienced and prone to making hasty decisions? He is unfit to rule Magadh at the moment. Placing him in power right now will not be good for the kingdom.'

'That is what the mahamatya wants. Ajatashatru's incompetence will empower him to become the de facto ruler of Magadh.'

'As long as I'm alive, I'll never allow that to happen,' Bimbisar thundered.

The king's words shook the frail and aged minister. 'That

is precisely what I fear, Maharaj. They will eliminate you without hesitation to clear all obstacles in their path. Please be careful.'

Once Vasumitra departed from the king's chamber, Bimbisar's mind was filled with conflicting emotions for his son. Each person who was close to him was being eliminated, one after another. Ajatashatru and Vassakar were slowly tightening the noose around his neck. He quickly made his way to Rajmata Kosala Devi's chamber.

'What should I do, Kosala? My very own son desires to rebel against me, and that worm Vassakar is encouraging him.' He paced up and down the chamber agitatedly.

'I have never trusted that man,' said Kosala. 'There's something about his behaviour that seems too slick and calculated to be real.'

'That's true, but I must act swiftly before things get out of hand.'

'It would be best to consult the Buddha on this matter,' she advised. 'I have been informed that he has arrived at his sangha in Griddhakuta.'

Her suggestion pleased the king. He firmly believed that the Buddha would steer him in the right direction.

After a night of tossing about in his bed, Bimbisar made his way to Griddhakuta at the crack of dawn. As soon as the Buddha saw the dark circles around the king's eyes, he knew that a storm of emotions had been brewing within him.

Bimbisar fell at the Buddha's feet and pleaded for his guidance.

'What causes your restlessness, Rajan?' the Buddha asked after the king had settled near his feet.

'My restlessness stems from the threat my son poses, O Buddha.'

'Does he pose a danger to your life?'

'He wants the throne, but he won't hesitate to murder me if I oppose.'

'Are you troubled by the fear of losing your throne, or is it the fear for your life that is bothering you?'

'I'm afraid of both,' the king admitted to the Buddha.

The Buddha said gently, 'When you detach yourself from the throne, Rajan, you will see how everything falls into place. It is your attachment that is causing you grief.' He continued speaking softly, 'The prince is eager to take up the responsibilities that come with the crown. It would be prudent for you to step down before any disaster strikes.'

'I would gladly make way for Ajatashatru, if only I believed in his competence to rule. I'm not sure he will make a good and just king,' Bimbisar told the Buddha.

'Why do you feel your son is not mature enough to rule Magadh?' the Buddha asked gently. 'Did your father not crown you at fifteen? Your father trusted your ability. You should not doubt your son's ability either. He is much older than fifteen. Governing Anga has provided him valuable experience as well.'

The king prostrated himself before the Enlightened One and said, 'Thank you for leading me out of the dark labyrinth. My obsession with the throne had clouded my judgement completely, but you have shown me the light. I'll follow your advice and relinquish my crown.'

Bimbisar's peaceful expression caught the attention of Rajmata Kosala Devi as he came back to the palace. All signs of anxiety and restlessness had disappeared. He shared the Buddha's guidance with her, and they both agreed that crowning Ajatashatru as ruler of Magadh would be the best option.

'We can retire to the hunting lodge nestled on the outskirts of the city. We can live a peaceful life there.' There was urgency in her voice as she spoke.

'After meeting the Buddha, I realize I have been tightly gripping a fluttering butterfly. It never belonged to me from the very beginning. My father passed the throne down to me, and now it is my son's turn to receive it. It is time to let go of all attachments and embrace the new chapter ahead.'

'Let's not wait any longer, Maharaj,' said Kosala. 'Reach out to Ajatashatru and hand over the crown to him. Do this before he creates any more mischief.'

Bimbisar sent a missive summoning Ajatashatru and Vassakar urgently to Magadh. Ajatashatru wondered if his father had learned about the conspiracy to dethrone him. Eager to know what his father was planning, the prince hurried to the palace.

The next morning, in the court Bimbisar proclaimed his intention of relinquishing the crown to Ajatashatru.

'My father declared me king when I was fifteen years old. I have discharged the duties of the throne for a considerable time, and now it is my son's turn to take up the mantle,' said Bimbisar. The nobles were unprepared for the sudden declaration. Bimbisar noticed many of them fidgeting uncomfortably. They were the ones who had switched their allegiance, the king realized. Only a few ministers seemed saddened by the announcement. Bimbisar recognized that those were the trustworthy ones who would stick by him. Others, like Vasumitra, would retire from their duties.

Vassakar's intrigue ended in an anticlimax. The suddenness of Bimbisar's surrender caught him off guard, and he questioned the factors that influenced this unexpected decision. The prince, however, was elated to see his ambitions come to fruition.

From then on, Vassakar assumed control of everything. Bimbisar observed as the prince commanded the ministers and priests to expedite the coronation. 'There is no need for elaborate arrangements,' he ordered. His lack of grace and eagerness to be crowned king were obvious to all.

Bimbisar let out a sigh of relief. The sooner Ajatashatru sat on the throne, the better for everyone. He could retire to his hunting lodge in the forest.

The prince appeared resolute in his efforts to weaken Bimbisar's position. After the coronation ceremony ended, his initial command was to assign a series of small rooms for Bimbisar at the rear section of the palace, while he moved into the luxurious king's chamber.

The new regime was in a rush to eliminate all traces of Bimbisar's reign. Ajatashatru wasted no time in replacing Bimbisar's former ministers, while simultaneously promoting those who had been involved in the conspiracy. His actions in the childish game of one-upmanship came as no surprise, especially to his father. However, Bimbisar was surprised when Devadatta began visiting the palace frequently and spending long periods of time in Ajatashatru's chamber.

Bimbisar's edicts were reversed, and new rules came into force. The supporters of Ajatashatru designed new symbols for every newly built structure. A new flag was also created. It seemed as though Ajatashatru was determined to remove his father's name from the annals of history. There were rumours in the capital about Ajatashatru's brutal treatment of the king's loyal subjects. Bimbisar's devoted servants began living in fear. Soon, they began leaving Rajgriha.

A week after the coronation, Rajmata Kosala Devi visited Bimbisar's new chamber. The sun had set, leaving the rooms in darkness, but the servants had not lit the lamps. Bimbisar was sitting in the dark when she arrived.

'Why have the lamps not been lit?' she asked. 'Where are your servants?'

'I don't know. They have taken to disappearing without informing me,' replied her husband. He seemed to take things calmly. Bimbisar chose not to mention that he had to endure long waits for his meals to be brought to him, only to discover that they were inedible when they finally arrived.

Kosala promptly commanded her dasi to fetch the lamps and some food. Bimbisar noticed a sense of unease in her.

Despite being highly respected, Rajmata Kosala Devi's position had significantly deteriorated. Her status as Rajmata didn't prevent her instructions from being frequently disregarded. While she seemed calm on the surface, the reality of Bimbisar's predicament horrified her. This was not how the king's father deserved to be treated, she felt.

'We must leave the palace as soon as possible,' she said. Fear filled her eyes as she spoke in a hushed tone. 'I'm worried about your safety.'

'There is nothing to fear, Kosala,' Bimbisar hastened to calm the queen. 'Ajatashatru has got what he wanted. He doesn't care for us anymore.'

'No, Maharaj,' she responded. 'I have been informed otherwise. A faithful dasi has brought me disturbing news.' Kosala looked around fearfully, then dropped her voice to a whisper. 'Her husband, who is employed as Ajatashatru's servant, has asked her to warn us. We should get away immediately.'

Aware of her concerns, Bimbisar gently reached for her hand and said, 'Don't worry, Kosala. It is a matter of a few days. We will leave for the hunting lodge as soon as it is ready.'

'We should move out of this place immediately. Your safety is my first concern.' There was urgency in Kosala's voice.

'Very well. We shall leave at dawn tomorrow,' Bimbisar promised. He had absorbed some of Kosala's unease. His intuition was warning him about a potential danger. 'Have faith, Kosala, things will work out for the best. Tomorrow will be the beginning of a new life.'

The promised dawn didn't arrive. While Bimbisar was lost in thought about the unknown that lay ahead, two intruders wearing masks suddenly stormed into his chamber. Approaching his bed, they drew their swords and pounced on him. Before he could utter a word, they forcefully covered his mouth and blindfolded him.

Swiftly and forcefully, Bimbisar was dragged through the corridor, but no one intervened to help him. Where were his servants? Had they been bribed to remain silent? Had they perhaps been murdered? The kidnappers walked through the corridor without attempting to silence their footsteps. Sadness weighed him down when he discovered Ajatashatru was the one who had orchestrated his abduction.

# 27

# A Prisoner

The masked intruders pushed Bimbisar into a room. Immediately, he wrinkled his nose at the stench in the air. They took off Bimbisar's blindfold and walked away. The sound of the door being locked rang through the silence, sealing his fate with an irrevocable finality.

With a tired sigh, he rubbed his eyes and took in his surroundings. He felt a surge of despair. He was struck by the grim reality of the shadowy dungeon, with its dampness and oppressive atmosphere. Peering into the dimly lit cell, he noticed the hard wooden bed, its mattress worn and thin. Despite the damp air, he felt a chill go down his spine. His son had locked him away in the depths of the earth, where the darkness swallowed any hope of escape. There would be no tearful send-offs and no leave-taking from the loyal subjects. The dream of retiring to his hunting lodge would never come to fruition.

Poor Kosala! If only he had heeded her advice. Alas, even if they had retired to the lodge, Ajatashatru would have discovered them. They could have begged King Prasenajit to grant them asylum, as Kosala had suggested at first. Prasenajit was her brother, and she would have been safe in his kingdom, but pride prevented Bimbisar from begging for asylum. A wry smile twisted his lips.

Why was Ajatashatru so insecure? He had already been crowned king. What more did he want? The heavy door, fortified with sturdy bars and two armed guards patrolling outside, was a grim reminder of his status. Did Ajatashatru think he would escape from the dungeon? Bimbisar laughed deliriously.

'Can you fetch me some drinking water?' he asked the guards posted outside the door.

His son had chosen well. The guards were completely lacking in empathy. They looked scornfully at him and pointed to a clay pot near the bed. Bimbisar's gaze fell on it and the upturned clay cup on it. As he looked into the pot, he saw pieces of dirt floating in the cloudy water. Was he expected to drink that water?

Repulsed, he said to the guard, 'This water is unfit for drinking. Do you mind filling the pot with fresh water?

'Still feeling like a king?' the guards burst out laughing. 'What do you want? Water in a silver pot?'

'You are now a prisoner, just like the other criminals. You will eat and drink whatever is provided to you. There are no special privileges in the prison. Those are the orders.'

Deflated, Bimbisar lay down on his uncomfortable bed. It was difficult to determine whether it was morning or afternoon. Several hours passed, and he only realized it was morning when he noticed a fresh set of guards posted at the entrance to his cell. They served him a bowl of stale, tasteless gruel in a cracked clay bowl and replenished the water in the pot. The sight of the gruel disgusted him, so he chose to go hungry.

'I want to meet the king,' he demanded after a while.

The guards found his demand amusing. 'You must be joking? The king doesn't meet prisoners,' said one of them.

'Alright! Kindly pass on my message to your superior. I refuse to eat or drink anything until I meet the king.'

'In that case, be prepared to starve to death.'

Bimbisar stood by his decision. He refused to eat or drink anything. The prison supervisor showed up on the second day, but Bimbisar refused to meet him. Even though he was hungry, he remained determined not to eat until he saw his son. On the third day, the sound of footsteps broke the silence. In the dimly lit confines of his cell, Bimbisar caught sight of a person dressed in fine attire. It was Vassakar. Behind him stood a soldier with some food and water.

'Pranam, Maharaj!' greeted the mahamatya, who had been the main conspirator. 'Why are you starving yourself to death?'

Bimbisar's throat was dry and scratchy, making it difficult for the words to come out. All he managed was a groan.

'I realize that this place is not comfortable, and the food is of poor quality, but the king is determined to make it even worse.' Moving closer to Bimbisar's bed, Vassakar said, 'I'm the one who arranged for the gruel and water to be sent to you because I don't want to be responsible for your death.'

Bimbisar weakly motioned to Vassakar to leave.

'You want me to leave?' asked Vassakar. 'I'll leave as soon as you have the food and water. I wish you no harm, Maharaj,' the sarcasm in his voice didn't escape Bimbisar.

The soldier placed the bowl of fresh gruel and clean water before Bimbisar, but he refused to look at it.

'What is it you want?' Vassakar asked irritably. 'I came here because of my loyalty to you. Your son will never come to meet you, even if you starve to death.'

Bimbisar suddenly realized that he couldn't count on his son coming to see him. He would have to tell Vassakar whatever he wanted. He took a tiny gulp of water to hydrate his parched throat and emitted a strained, hoarse sound. 'The smallest favour he could grant me would be to let me decide where I want to be imprisoned.'

'I see no requirement for that,' replied Vassakar. 'One dungeon is as good as another. Why do you want a different one?'

'I want a cell from where I can gaze upon the Griddhakuta,' Bimbisar replied.

'Why so?'

'It will allow me to feel the aura of the Buddha, and that will provide me the strength to endure my hardships,' Bimbisar pleaded.

Something about the prisoner's attitude softened the usually cold-hearted mahamatya. It was pathetic to witness the decline of the once mighty king. Bimbisar had willingly accepted his imprisonment and refrained from blaming the treacherous Vassakar or his ungrateful son for his current situation. What was more surprising was the man's request. Rather than asking for improved comfort or food, he desired the privilege of beholding the Griddhakuta hills.

'I'll try to have your demand met, but please eat and drink whatever is provided to you,' requested Vassakar.

Bimbisar felt a peculiar sense of weightlessness when he heard the mahamatya's words. Despite its unappetizing taste, he consumed the gruel and broke his fast.

When the mahamatya reached Ajatashatru's chambers to discuss the matter, he was disappointed to find Devadatta there. The growing closeness between Devadatta and his protégé upset the mahamatya. Lately, the self-proclaimed monk had developed a habit of visiting the king's chambers. What made it even more disturbing was his manipulation of the naïve young man. As Devadatta's influence over the king grew stronger, Vassakar sensed his own control slipping. Although he preferred to not talk about Bimbisar's request in front of Devadatta, he had no choice but to do so when Ajatashatru brought it up.

'What was bothering the old man, mahamatya? Was he seeking an explanation for being imprisoned or was he demanding to be released?' Ajatashatru asked. 'I hope he isn't feeling uncomfortable in the dungeon.'

Devadatta laughed in response to the comment. With clenched fists, Vassakar controlled his anger and replied,

'Your father didn't ask for an explanation, nor did he demand to be freed.' Encouraged by the attention from Ajatashatru, Vassakar persisted, 'Maharaj, the dungeon is an extremely wretched and uncomfortable place. It is not befitting of a king in his old age.'

'You are forgetting something, Vassakar. My father is not a king anymore,' objected Ajatashatru. 'A deposed king is just a commoner.'

'I understand, Maharaj, but Magadh has never subjected even criminals to such deplorable conditions,' Vassakar replied bitterly.

'That's not for you to decide,' Ajatashatru retorted. 'I'm only interested in knowing why he wanted to meet me.'

'Your father has accepted his imprisonment. All he wants is a cell that overlooks the Griddhakuta hills.'

'So, he wants a room with a view?' Ajatashatru arched his eyebrows in surprise. 'Now, that's what I call a royal choice.'

'The Buddha lives in the Griddhakuta hills. Your father is convinced that looking at the hills will allow him to feel the aura of the Buddha, granting him the resilience to endure the punishment he is going through.'

'That's hilarious!' snorted Ajatashatru. 'Does he think that the nomad, who rarely stays in Griddhakuta, will rescue him from the dungeon?'

For the first time, Vassakar was overcome by self-doubt. Did he mistakenly mentor the wrong person? The qualities expected of a king included wisdom and benevolence. This man was unfit to be the ruler of Magadh. Ajatashatru displayed no compassion or understanding of justice whatsoever. Vassakar had committed an enormous blunder. He had been blinded by his pursuit of revenge and believed he had power over Ajatashatru, but the prince was now a puppet of Devadatta. Vassakar's overwhelming ambition had led him to harm the very person who was instrumental in his ascent to power. He was overcome with guilt.

'Granting him the request is the least we can do for the man who once ruled Magadh,' said Vassakar. 'Don't forget, he willingly gave up the crown for you. He had the power to imprison both of us, and we could have found ourselves stuck in the same dungeon where he is currently held.'

'You seem to have developed a sudden affection for him,' Ajatashatru said sharply. 'You were the one who plotted against him. Is your conscience burdened by guilt now?'

'Yes, I schemed to place you on the throne, but I have no desire for him to perish in a prison. I had received information from my spies that Bimbisar wanted to retire to the hunting lodge. We should have allowed him to do so. In what way does his death further our cause?'

Ajatashatru, having attentively listened to the mahamatya, seemed to agree with him. Just then, Devadatta, who had been listening as well, cut in.

'Fantastic!' Devadatta clapped his hands before Ajatashatru could speak. 'You have had a sudden change of heart. Listening to your words will make people think you are a saint and not a villain.'

'What do you mean?' Vassakar demanded angrily. 'I confess to having veered off course, but I'm now committed to making amends for my mistakes.'

'Do you intend to accomplish that by giving Bimbisar a room with a scenic view of the Griddhakuta hills?' Devadatta demanded. 'I advise you to not fall prey to the mahamatya's scheme, Maharaj. He is deceitful, and it is not wise to trust him anymore. Who knows what he has up his sleeve?'

'Please do not make derogatory remarks about my character,' Vassakar said icily.

The more time passed, the stronger Devadatta's ambition grew, and he would not stop until he had cast out the mahamatya from the royal circle. Turning to Ajatashatru, he asked, 'What is your decision, Maharaj?'

Ajatashatru seemed to vacillate for a few moments, and then he shrugged. 'There is no harm in granting his small wish, I think.'

Out of sheer frustration, Devadatta let out a sigh and slapped his forehead, attempting to reverse the situation, but Vassakar paid no attention and departed before Ajatashatru could change his mind. It was a minor victory, but a victory nevertheless. The mahamatya knew he had to come up with a strategy to outsmart Devadatta before things got worse. Unless he had control over Ajatashatru, his own life would be at risk.

A few hours later, Bimbisar was transferred to a new cell. The small barred window in the roughly hewn stone wall immediately caught Bimbisar's attention. He walked towards the window, which was set high on the wall. Looking outside through the window, he was moved to tears by the incredible view of the expansive scenery and the Griddhakuta hills. He clasped his hands together, shut his eyes, and prayed to the Buddha. The small action had a powerful impact, immediately filling him with a surge of vitality.

In Ajatashatru's chamber, Devadatta continued to argue against Bimbisar's transfer to a new cell.

'You are making a mistake,' he fumed. 'Your subjects will not accept you as king if your father is alive. You must get rid of him as soon as possible.'

Ajatashatru looked at Devadatta horrified. 'How can I kill my father? He has given me everything. This life. This kingdom. Everything. I'm sorry, but I can't kill him.'

'Don't tell me later that I didn't warn you,' Devadatta threatened. 'He was a king. He is a king and he will be a king till he dies. People will never accept you until he is dead.

Every person from Magadh will always remember him in their hearts. Only his death can erase that. Starve him to death.'

Devadatta's words had a significant influence on the young king. He paced back and forth in his chamber all night, struggling to decide. Before daybreak, he had made his choice. His father had to die.

# 28

# The Three Queens

**Kosala**

A nauseating smell overpowered the eldest queen the moment she stepped into the dark prison cell. Wrinkling her nose, she fought back the urge to gag. The stench of decay and death in the cramped prison cell assaulted her senses. Wooden boards completely sealed off the small window, leaving no room for light or fresh air to enter. In one corner, a solitary candle flickered, casting a dim and unsteady glow. The sound of mice scurrying about sent a shiver down her spine. Instinctively, she took a step back towards the barred entrance.

The man lying on the hard wooden bed was completely unrecognizable. Clad in a dirty antariya, he bore no resemblance to the fearless warrior who had won so many battles; the man who struck fear in the hearts of his enemies; the man who was capable of both immense compassion and unspeakable cruelty. It was hard for Kosala to accept the fact that Bimbisar, renowned for his handsome features and irresistible charm, was now reduced to a mere skeleton. This was the man who had captivated her heart with a mischievous sparkle in his eyes.

The sight of the man, with his pathetic bearing, messy grey hair, and sickly complexion, left Kosala speechless.

'Maharaj!' she whispered.

His eyes snapped open, and she could see the terror in them. In a voice trembling with emotion, he asked, 'Who is it?' He strained his eyes to look at her.

'I'm Kosala, Maharaj,' she rushed towards him and knelt before him. His hand shook as he extended it towards her. Kosala responded by gripping it with both her hands. Tears streamed down her cheeks as she stifled a sob.

'Kosala! Why have you come here?' he demanded.

'I have been trying to meet you, Maharaj,' Kosala's voice quivered with emotion. 'But Kunika refused to grant me permission to visit you.'

'Go away. I don't want you here.' He turned his back to her as his body convulsed with uncontrollable sobbing. His embarrassment was obvious. He felt disgusted at the idea of looking unkempt and vulnerable in front of his wife.

Kosala gently patted his shoulders and attempted to comfort him. Bimbisar hesitated briefly before turning towards her and exclaimed, 'How could he betray us in such a manner? How could my son, whom I have loved more than anything, behave towards me in such a way? Where did we go wrong, Kosala?'

Words failed Kosala. What could she say? Ajatashatru's actions had caused widespread anger throughout Magadh. His actions were being discussed not only in Magadh but also in the neighbouring kingdoms. Kings felt insecure about the fact that some day their heirs could behave like Ajatashatru. The news shocked Kosala's brother, Prasenajit. He offered to confront Ajatashatru in battle to free Bimbisar. Kosala declined the offer.

'You have done nothing wrong, Maharaj,' Kosala whispered. 'You have given him more love than any man can give his son. It is Kunika who has failed in his duty as a son.'

She couldn't shake off the bitter taste in her mouth. Resentment and anger flooded her. Even the king's worst enemy would not have subjected him to such ignominy. Dying on the battlefield was preferable to being imprisoned and tortured by one's own child.

'His cruelty knows no bounds. Once he learnt that I found solace in gazing at Griddhakuta, he immediately ordered the guards to seal the window,' Bimbisar struggled to speak as his voice faltered and his words got stuck in his throat.

What could she possibly say? Kosala was at a loss for words to comfort the distressed man. If only she could get him out of prison. She reached for the clay cup and filled it with water, only to discover that the water in the earthen ewer was unfit for drinking.

'Prahari!' Kosala called out. 'Get me some water.'

The air was filled with silence, uninterrupted by any reaction. 'Prahari!' she shouted.

This time, a guard peeped cautiously into the cell.

'I asked for water,' Kosala repeated.

The guard seemed to hesitate.

'Can't you hear me?' Kosala asked. 'God will not forgive you your sins. Even an enemy deserves clean drinking water. Have you forgotten that this is the man who provided you with a job, food and shelter?'

The guard hung his head in shame and said, 'Rajmata, please forgive me. We have been specifically told not to provide the prisoner with anything. I'll be in trouble if I help you.'

Casting a furtive glance, he fetched a cup of water from a container outside the cell and handed it to her. 'Please don't tell anyone about it, or I'll be in trouble.'

Kosala could well imagine. If someone could show such cruelty to their own father, it was unlikely that they would have any sympathy for a guard.

The water was clean and cool. She carefully brought the cup to Bimbisar's parched lips, and he slowly sipped from it, cherishing every small mouthful. Taking one last sip, he couldn't help exclaiming, 'I forgot how refreshing and soothing water could be!'

'Have you eaten anything, Maharaj?' With a cautious glance, Kosala reached into the depths of her uttariya and pulled out a banana.

In a matter of seconds, he consumed the fruit, peel and all. Shocked, Kosala realized the guards hadn't given him food for several days. Ajatashatru intended to starve his father to death.

Kosala couldn't hold back her tears any longer, and allowed herself to cry on Bimbisar's weak chest. This was the same chest, which had been her resting place on countless nights. It had offered solace during her darkest moments and given her love. It seemed like an eternity had gone by since those nights. So overwhelming was the darkness of despair that no glimmer of light could penetrate it.

For months, Kosala ran from pillar to post, trying to free Bimbisar. She had tried a multitude of approaches to sway Kunika—pleading, reprimanding, appealing to his rationality, shedding tears, and employing every trick she knew, but in vain. He remained completely unaffected by all her pleas.

Kosala had loved him more deeply than she had ever loved her child. She had spent countless nights singing to him, hoping to comfort him in his sickness and pain. He loved her so much that he affectionately called his mother 'Rani Ma' and referred to her as 'Ma'. She wondered what could have caused him to undergo such a drastic transformation. How did her Kunika—Ajatashatru—transform into a heartless monster without any concern for his own father? She could no longer think of him as her beloved son, Kunika.

Chellana and Kosala both tried desperately to convince him to let go of Bimbisar, but their attempts were unsuccessful. Out of desperation, Kosala sought the Buddha's counsel, only to find that he was not in Magadh. When she had exhausted all other options, Kosala reached out to Vajira, her niece, who was married to Ajatashatru. She thought he would refuse nothing to his beloved spouse, but she was mistaken. He warned Vajira to steer clear of the matter, which she ignored because Bimbisar held a special place in her heart.

'Kosala, will you do me a favour?' Bimbisar's voice broke through her reverie. 'Will you release me from this misery? I no longer wish to live.'

'Maharaj…' she protested.

'Hear me out before you say anything.' A sigh escaped his lips, as a shudder ran down his spine. 'Can you bring me some poison?'

'No…' Kosala let out a loud wail. 'I can't do that, Maharaj.'

'Can you do it for me, Kosala? Think of it as my last wish. Don't you want to release me from this agony?'

Kosala's body trembled as she sobbed uncontrollably. Unable to speak, she reached out her hand for him.

'Don't mourn my death, Kosala. I'll finally find release from the burden of suffering.'

Kosala's heart filled with sorrow as she lamented the countless acts of injustice that were heaped on her husband. Since childhood, he had carried the burden of high expectations and constantly striven to fulfil his mother's dream of expanding the kingdom. As a result, he had missed out on the experiences that should have defined his childhood and adolescence. Instead of chasing after girls and indulging in the carefree moments of youth, he committed his teenage years to confronting the trials of the kingdom. His son now ruled the kingdom Bimbisar had worked so hard to build, while he suffered in a filthy and gloomy prison cell, enduring endless torment.

As his first wife, Kosala had fulfilled the role of both a companion and a trusted confidante. They had tied the knot and begun their journey as a couple when he was only twenty-one.

Together, they had experienced the trials of life, weaving a tapestry of memories filled with laughter and tears. Bimbisar had relied on Kosala's maturity and frequently turned to her for advice. Their relationship had been unique and unlike any other. What they had built together went beyond the traditional concept of marriage.

Her company had always provided him with a sanctuary away from the complexities of politics, self-centredness, and hidden agendas.

'Will you do it, Kosala?' Bimbisar appealed.

'I can't do it, Maharaj,' Kosala wept. 'Please ask Chellana to carry out your wishes. She is much more intelligent and has a stronger willpower.'

'Chellana may be more intelligent, but I want you to be the one to do it. However, I hope to meet Chellana and Kshema before my life ends. Can you please arrange for them to come and see me today?'

'I'll convey your wishes to Chellana,' Kosala promised tearfully. 'Maharaj, Kshema has recently embraced Buddhism and is currently journeying with the sangha.'

'She has made a wise decision. Choosing the path of peace under the Buddha's guidance is wiser than living in a palace tainted by the tyranny of a son.' A deep sigh escaped him. 'Bring me the poison after Chellana leaves the cell.'

'I'll try, Maharaj,' Kosala prevaricated. 'But I can't promise anything.'

He looked piteously into her eyes. His voice trembled as he said, 'Bring me the large ruby-studded ring I had gifted you on the birth of our first child. Hidden beneath the bezel is a poison chamber. Fill it up with the deadliest poison you can find. I want you to bring me the ring tomorrow.'

Kosala nodded quietly and escaped from the cell, the sound

of her footsteps reverberating down the corridor. Leave alone fetching poison for Bimbisara, it was beyond her to cause the slightest harm to her husband whom she cared for so deeply.

**Chellana**

With her eyes swimming with unshed tears, Kosala entered the junior queen's chamber. Her eyes darted back and forth, betraying the turbulence of the emotions brewing inside. Chellana realized the elder queen was deeply distressed.

Chellana loved Kosala, who had always shown kindness and generosity towards her. There was no trace of jealousy in the way she acted. Instead, she radiated an aura of patience, kindness and love. This had created a strong, sisterly bond between the two. While the junior queen experienced jealousy towards Kshema, she never felt that way towards Kosala.

Bimbisar was extremely angry when Chellana had ordered the dasis to throw away Ajatashatru moments after he was born. She had no desire to raise a child who was prophesied to cause his father's demise. Instead of assigning the child to the care of dasis, Bimbisar had handed him over to Kosala's care, confident in her ability to raise him with gentleness and patience.

Bimbisar's faith in Kosala was proven right. She showered Ajatashatru with love, giving him more attention than Chellana ever could. Understandably, Kunika's affection for Kosala was stronger than his love for his biological mother. To everyone's surprise, Chellana didn't feel even a twinge of jealousy. How could she be jealous of Kosala, who was loved by everyone in the palace? There was not a soul who harboured any feelings of animosity towards the senior queen.

Kosala earned more respect than the other queens and also shouldered a larger part of the responsibilities of Bimbisar's queens. She discharged all her responsibilities with grace. In the beginning, Chellana, who had been opposed to marriage, held a grudge against Bimbisar. With each passing day, her feelings developed, and she fell deeply in love with him. His captivating personality and exceptional sense of humour swiftly stole her heart. She couldn't help but feel a little resentful towards his obsession with the kingdom and Kosala. In all fairness, he gave her enough time, but Chellana desired to be the centre of his attention.

Rajmata Hemavati was a remarkable and formidable figure. She liked to control everyone and everything. To give credit where it is due, she was an incredibly capable lady who played a pivotal role in the accomplishments of both King Bhattiya and her son. She ruled the palace with an iron fist, demanding strict obedience from every soul within its walls. The thing that annoyed Chellana was her authoritarian attitude, which didn't leave any scope for dissent or personal freedom. The Rajmata was a narcissistic woman who stubbornly refused to acknowledge her own mistakes. Bimbisar's deep affection for his mother made him overlook any faults she might have had. He was not prepared to accept any criticism about his mother.

Rajmata Hemavati favoured Kosala for her steadfast loyalty and absolute obedience, while she nursed a grudge against Chellana because of her rebellious attitude. At first, the junior queen tried to voice her dissatisfaction to Bimbisar, but he chided her for being disrespectful.

'The Rajmata is a wise lady who knows what's best for the kingdom.' And that was that.

Eventually, Chellana found a way to deal with the Rajmata. She attempted to win over Bimbisar to counter his mother's hostile attitude. The closer Chellana got to him, the more the Rajmata resented her. The situation worsened after their son was born and Chellana instructed the dasis to get rid of him.

The Rajmata took advantage of this opportunity to drive a wedge between her son and the junior queen. Chellana's regrets had no impact on Bimbisar. They drifted apart even more, much to the delight of the Rajmata. Rather than allowing their relationship to heal, she plotted for him to marry Kshema, the daughter of the powerful king of Madra.

Chellana maintained her animosity towards Rajmata Hemavati until the end. While Bimbisar mourned his mother's passing, Chellana was relieved by it.

The vacuum left behind by the death of Rajmata Hemavati had a powerful impact on Kosala. She had always looked up to the Rajmata, who cared for her like a mother.

The position of Rajmata needed to be filled, and Chellana, as the mother of the Magadh heir, was the top choice for the role. The junior queen, however, had no intention of being weighed down by the responsibilities that came along with the position. Just a day before the appointment, she made her wishes known to Bimbisar.

It was a sultry evening. Once dinner was over, Bimbisar and Chellana found themselves on the grand balcony, taking pleasure in the calm view of the garden below. With a cup of madira in hand, they delighted in the gentle caress of the light breeze on their faces. Soft music filled the air as a dasi skilfully played an evening raga on the veena. Bimbisar lay back comfortably on a soft silk mattress, lazily playing with Chellana's hair. His mood was softened by the drink, making him more receptive to her ideas. She had been patiently waiting for the right moment to bring up the topic.

'Maharaj, I request you appoint Queen Kosala Devi as Rajmata,' said Chellana.

'Why do you want her to be the Rajmata? Every queen aspires to hold that post for the enormous powers it brings. You are the mother to the heir and the rightful candidate for the post,' he sat up and stared at her in surprise.

'The duties of a Rajmata demand wisdom and maturity. Queen Kosala Devi is far wiser and more responsible than I can ever hope to be. She is the ideal choice for the role.'

'But she is not the mother of my heir,' he pointed out. 'I'm not sure she would like to accept the post.'

'Kosala Devi is as good as Ajatashatru's mother. I may be his mother by blood, but she is the one who raised him and guided him through life. She is the Yashoda, and I'm Devaki,' Chellana argued. Pouring some more madira into his cup, she eagerly awaited his decision.

It took many debates and much persuasion before he finally gave in, but convincing Kosala was an even greater challenge. She was unwavering in her belief that Chellana should be the Rajmata. Eventually, she relented and accepted the post.

Kosala was the perfect choice for the post. Fair and affectionate, she ensured that all the queens had the same level of responsibility and treated them with kindness. More importantly, she never bothered Bimbisar with trivial concerns, allowing him to focus on the important affairs of the kingdom. Unfazed by challenges, she gracefully dealt with everything, displaying a wise and balanced perspective.

'Rajmata Kosala, you look upset. What is the matter?' Chellana asked, as she sank into the soft cushion.

Chellana could see the streaks of tears on her face.

'Chellana, I met the Maharaj just now,' she said.

'You went to meet him?' Chellana was surprised that Ajatashatru had given her permission to see Bimbisar. He had been consistently turning down her requests to visit him.

'Is he well, Kosala?' Chellana whispered almost inaudibly. Her heart pounded with fear as she prepared herself for the response.

Kosala couldn't hold back her tears any longer. She sobbed uncontrollably. Though Chellana tried to comfort her by offering a cup of water and gently stroking her hair, she kept crying.

Unable to handle her emotions, eventually she gave in to Chellana's questioning. The two of them had grown closer after Rajmata Hemavati's death, but Bimbisar's imprisonment had created a stronger bond between them.

Regaining her composure, Kosala took a deep breath and said, 'He wants to see you, Chellana. You must seek Ajatashatru's permission and go to the prison today.'

'It will be difficult to get permission today,' Chellana hesitated. 'You know he has been denying me permission.'

'I'm aware of that, but this is important,' Kosala insisted. 'Maharaj's poor health has taken a toll on his overall well-being. He is in a state of hopelessness and has completely lost the desire to live.' Her eyes welled up again. 'He wants to die, Chellana.'

'Is there no way out of this predicament?" Chellana was furious. 'Ajatashatru's madness is causing so much grief to all of us. He wanted the Magadh throne; he got it. What else does he want now?'

'It's all part of our fate,' lamented Kosala with resignation. 'Hurry! Send your request to Ajatashatru and then we will see what he has to say.'

Chellana was pleasantly surprised when her son agreed to let her visit Bimbisar. Ajatashatru's mood had mellowed after learning that his wife would soon give birth to his heir.

Chellana's nightmare started as soon as she stepped into the cell. She couldn't help but cringe in disgust as a wave of nausea washed over her. *Is this where my son has kept his father—a king who had vanquished powerful enemies?* Like sharp talons, guilt tightly gripped the queen's heart. *I have given birth to a monster. All the prophecies have come true.*

The sight of Bimbisar filled her with horror, causing her to faint.

'Maharaj!' Chellana whispered in a shaky voice on regaining consciousness. There was no movement or any response to her call. 'Maharaj!' she repeated, moving closer to the corner where he lay.

Was he breathing? Questions flooded her mind as she stared at the immobile figure. After a moment's hesitation, she placed her head on his chest, finding comfort in the rhythmic sound of his heartbeat. He was alive.

Bimbisar stirred, as though coming to life after a deep sleep. 'Kosala? Have you brought me the poison?' His mind was wandering.

Chellana looked at him in shock and disbelief. Did she hear correctly? He had asked Kosala to fetch him poison. A deep sorrow overwhelmed her.

'Forgive me, Maharaj! I'm the one who deserves to be imprisoned for bringing a monster into this world. I should be the one to endure the suffering, not you,' Chellana wailed pitifully.

'Hush! Chellana, is it really you?' his exhausted eyes struggled to focus on her face. 'Don't blame yourself, it's not your fault.'

'I should have ended his life the moment he took his first breath. Why didn't you allow me to kill him, Maharaj?' Chellana banged her head repeatedly against the unyielding stone walls. Blood trickled down her forehead. She believed punishing herself would somehow compensate for all the wrongdoings of her son.

'Don't punish yourself, Chellana,' Bimbisar protested, too frail to do much else.

The loud wail and the sound of her head hitting the wall caught the guard's attention. Immediately, he dashed in and swiftly removed Chellana from the wall. He brought her a cup of water from his ewer and said, 'Rani Ma, don't create trouble for us. Maharaj Ajatashatru will sentence me to death if he were to find out.'

He shouted at the other guard and staunched the blood on her forehead. 'I'm sorry, Rani Ma, we can't allow you to remain here any longer,' said the other guard. Together, they escorted Chellana out of the cell. Nothing she said could change their mind.

Wasting no time, she speedily made her way towards the council hall, where Ajatashatru was engaged in a crucial discussion with his ministers. Entry to the council hall was strictly monitored. Access was granted only to the ministers who were summoned for a meeting. By leveraging her rank, Chellana could easily enter the complex, but gaining entry to the council hall was an insurmountable challenge. Two heavily armed guards stationed outside the massive wooden door blocked her path.

'The king is holding a meeting with his ministers,' said a guard. 'I'm sorry, Rani Ma, but we must forbid you from entering the hall.'

Chellana drew herself up haughtily and snapped, 'Prahari, have you forgotten I'm the king's mother? This is an emergency, and I assure you he shall be informed that you stopped me from reaching him in time.'

Her words had the desired effect on one guard. He consulted the other guard, who appeared uncertain.

'Didn't you hear it is an emergency?' the queen said sharply.

She swiftly stepped into the council hall before the startled guards could stop her. Chellana's presence left the gathering flabbergasted; their jaws dropped in astonishment.

Ajatashatru quickly got up from his throne and hurried towards his mother. 'What brings you here, Rani Ma?' Brows furrowed in concern, he asked urgently, 'I hope my queen is well. The baby…'

Instead of being concerned about his parents, his primary worry was his wife, who was awaiting the birth of their heir. For a few moments, Chellana forgot she was a queen, and that she had to maintain a dignified presence before the council of ministers. The only thing she couldn't forget was the devastating sight of her husband's agonizing deterioration. Bimbisar's life hung entirely on the decisions made by Ajatashatru.

She laughed loudly, her laughter resonating throughout the hall. 'It's astonishing how you can experience profound love for your unborn son, yet display such heartlessness in hastening your own father's end. How can you be so cruel to the father who cradled you in his arms and showered you with unconditional love?'

Her words lingered in the air, prompting the ministers to give Ajatashatru disapproving stares. Many of them had once served Bimbisar, but they had swiftly changed allegiances to serve their interests. Most of them disapproved of his cruelty towards his father.

'You all are like rats abandoning a sinking ship. Have you all locked your fathers away to grab their land?' Chellana spat out her words at them. Shamefully, they hung their head in silence. 'Remember that aiding a wrongdoer is just as sinful as committing the act yourself.'

'Rani Ma!' her son thundered. 'Leave now…or...'

'Or what?' Chellana challenged him. With a determined look in her eyes, she pressed on. 'You will call the guards and order them to drag me to a dark and filthy cell where you will torture and starve me to death?'

'My father deserved what he got.'

'Is that so? Or is it the greed for the Magadh throne that drove your actions?' Chellana shook her head sadly. 'It is my mistake. Every astrologer I consulted predicted you would cause your father's death. I should have heeded their warning and killed you the moment you were born.'

The mother and the son locked eyes. The tension between them escalated until he averted his gaze. 'He never loved me. The kingdom always came first,' he tried to justify his actions.

'Is that the reason he hurried to the garbage heap where you were discarded and rescued you when I had abandoned you? Is that why he sucked out the pus from your infected finger, without a hint of disgust? Why else would he adamantly refuse to leave your side during your sickness. Shall I narrate a few more incidents?

'I...'

'Are you not afraid, Kunika?' Chellana addressed him by the name he had in childhood. 'Aren't you worried that, one day, your eagerly expected son might treat you the same way?'

Ajatashatru's face crumpled, his eyes brimming with sadness, as he averted his gaze.

There was nothing more the queen could do. Despite her attempts, she had failed to stir his conscience. Chellana walked out of the council hall. Burdened by fatigue, her shoulders drooped while her feet moved slowly across the floor. A vulture ominously circled in the sky, its piercing cry disrupting the silence, causing her heart to break into countless pieces.

**Kshema**

Ever since Bimbisar and Kshema got married, he made several attempts to convince her to visit the Buddha, but she consistently refused. She believed she was the most beautiful woman in the palace and had no intention of joining Queen Kosala and others on their visits to the Buddha.

'Visit him once,' Bimbisar insisted. 'It's an unforgettable experience, Kshema.'

'I'm not seeking nirvana, Maharaj,' Kshema laughed.

Not one to be deterred, Bimbisar decided to entice her by another method. Aware of Kshema's fondness for scenic spots, he hired poets to recite verses that depicted the breathtaking beauty of the Buddha's monastery. The vivid descriptions of the monastery convinced Kshema to pay it a visit.

Even though she went to the monastery, the queen had no intention of paying her respects to the Buddha.

The Buddha understood that her vanity was hindering her from approaching him, so he employed his psychic abilities to create the vision of a woman who was even more stunning than Kshema. The woman was fanning the Buddha.

As the queen looked on, the Buddha made the beautiful woman age right in front of her eyes. The woman went through different stages of life—youth, middle age, old age, and death. When Kshema saw the once beautiful woman ageing and eventually dying, she realized that her own fate would be no different. The fleeting nature of beauty left a deep impact on her.

Kshema humbly bowed down to the Buddha, and sought his blessings. She embraced Buddhism and became an ardent follower of the Buddha.

Bimbisar was pleased to see the transformation in his queen. Kshema was distraught when Ajatashatru imprisoned his father. Incapable of handling the situation in the palace, Kshema made her way to the Buddha's sangha and appealed to him for sanctuary. Nothing mattered anymore. Neither her beauty, nor the riches nor the luxuries. All that mattered was peace. The queen discarded her royal clothes and jewellery, and dressed in a homespun robe; she became a bhikkhuni.

# 29

# The Final Act

It rained that night. As the petrichor filled the air and permeated through the open window, a sense of relief washed over the parched land. The delicate petals of the flowers released their fragrance, creating a beautiful symphony of scents in the air. It brought a renewed sense of optimism to many people in the palace.

Chellana lay tossing on her bed, her mind flooded with a constant stream of images, each one capturing the dejected expression on Bimbisar's face. No matter how dire the situation, her unwavering spirit had always guided her out of her troubles. This time, however, she could find no answer to the problem.

When she visited the prison, Bimbisar appeared disoriented. He had mistaken her for Kosala, and he had asked if she had brought him the poison. Knowing that every second mattered for his survival, she was determined not to waste any time. With his health deteriorating at an alarming rate, she was prepared to go to great lengths to get him out of the prison. Time was running out.

After a long and exhausting night, the weary queen finally succumbed to a fitful sleep. On waking up, she felt a strong sense of déjà vu, as if she had experienced this moment before. Outside, the night sky transformed into a stunning display of orange and pink hues, bringing a renewed sense of hope with the breaking dawn.

'I have to convince Kunika,' she resolved. 'He must release his father. Today.'

The sky had cleared up, and the joyful chirping of birds filled the air. As the sun climbed higher in the sky, she wasted no time and headed towards Ajatashatru's chamber, the soft morning light showing her the way. She knew her son was most receptive in the early hours, so she chose that time to approach him.

The sight of his mother entering the chamber caught Ajatashatru off guard. He was shrewd enough to guess the reason of her visit so early in the morning.

'Suprabhat, Rani Ma!' he greeted her with caution.

Affectionatly, she responded, 'Suprabhat, Kunika.'

'I hope you have not come here with the same request as yesterday. Rani Ma, you know my answer. It is best if we don't bring up the topic of father's release. It would serve no purpose other than ruin our day.'

'Your father is almost dead. He will not survive another day, Kunika. I wonder how long he will live, even if you release him from prison. You have the throne and crown. You are the ruler of the kingdom. What can you lose if he lives? It is unlikely that he will seize control of your kingdom. Why are you so fearful?'

Ajatashatru held up his hand to stop her. 'I'm afraid you have to leave now,' he said.

'Do you not tremble at the thought of your sins? Will you be able to sleep peacefully if your father dies in prison?' she asked, her eyes searching for signs of remorse. There were none.

Like her, he had not slept well that night. Nightmares of Bimbisar's dead body and his mother's accusations haunted him. But he was too proud to yield.

'You don't have to worry about my welfare. Leave me to face the consequences of my actions.'

'I'm your mother, Kunika. Who else will worry about the consequences of your actions?'

As he was about to summon the guard, the chamber door swung open and a dasi burst in.

'Maharaj!' she blurted excitedly. 'A prince has been born!'

The king's face lit up with joy as the words sank in. He turned to his mother and announced, 'Rani Ma, rejoice! You are a grandmother now.'

'I have nothing to rejoice about until you release your father from prison,' she retorted.

Without wasting another moment, Ajatashatru dashed out of his chamber and headed straight for his queen's birthing chamber, with Chellana struggling to keep pace with him.

The young queen was sitting on her bed, waiting for her husband. The midwife cradled the squirming newborn in her arm.

'My son!' shouted Ajatashatru as he raced toward the baby. 'I have a son who will inherit the Magadh throne,' he proudly declared. 'Let the celebrations begin.'

With the squirming bundle in his arms, Ajatashatru couldn't help but feel a sense of wonder as he gazed at his son's precious face. While an overwhelming feeling of love surged through him, his face crumbled at the thought of his father. In an instant, his self-control and willpower vanished into thin air. As he looked into the baby's eyes, he felt his heart melt with love. Is this how a father feels? He wondered.

'Your expression reflects the same awe your father had when he first held you in his arms,' Chellana's voice broke his train of thought. A sudden realization dawned on him.

Without uttering a word, Ajatashatru silently passed his son to the midwife and hurriedly departed from the chamber, leaving everyone surprised. As he made his way out, he quickly snatched the axe that was securely fastened to the chamber's wall. Chellana knew where he was going. As she folded her hands, a sense of calm engulfed her. She sent a heartfelt prayer soaring towards the sky. It was all going to end well.

Her feet carried her swiftly towards Kosala's chamber, eager to convey the good news.

**The curse comes true**

The prisoner lay in a dark, damp cell, untouched by the sun's rays. The cells were constructed to hold captive the king's most formidable enemies—rebels who plotted against him. Escape from here was impossible, condemning the inmates to a living hell.

His withered body convulsed under a threadbare blanket, his fingers icy cold despite the sweltering heat outside. The barely audible sound of his breathing and the slight rising and falling of his chest were the only signs of him still being alive. His entire body was in a state of stillness, a skill he had mastered through regular meditation. The air too was still but for his breathing and the occasional scurrying of mice.

The once broad shoulders and sinewy body that had set many hearts aflutter were now reduced to a mere skeleton covered in weathered skin. Bimbisar, who was once known for his golden complexion, now appeared ghostly pale. The tawny eyes that once had the power to terrify even the most courageous individuals were now dimmed by cataract. They frantically searched the tiny cell, their movements wild and erratic, desperately hoping to find a way out of this confinement. His once carefully tended crop of wavy hair and neatly trimmed beard were now unkempt and dirty—a tangled mess. Downcast, his moustache drooped below his lips. Once pampered by a masseuse, his hands had calloused skin, while the nails were not only chipped, but also had rough, uneven surfaces.

Bimbisar woke up in his cell. His mind was clear that morning. The distant sounds of music and celebration caught his attention. His ears perked up. He angled his ears, trying to hear better. Soft, barely audible music filled the cell with its gentle notes. The sound of music was joy to his ears. The haunting melody of the veena triggered a rush of memories. He could visualize the agile fingers strumming the strings. The notes had a distinct quality that only Vanmala, the court musician, could bring out. When was the last time he had heard those enchanting notes?

Bimbisar immediately recognized the familiar strains of his favourite raga. He knew each note by heart, having played it so often on his veena. He had not been mistaken. This music was indeed intended for a joyful event in the kingdom. In the past, he had been the soul of every festive gathering. Imprisoned in a cell, with his energy rapidly depleting, he had no idea about this event. No one cared to inform him. It was safer to forget deposed kings. Those guilty of overthrowing kings are so insecure, they can go to great lengths to prevent people from remembering or honouring their victims. Paradoxically, he found the situation amusing and let out a chuckle. Suddenly, the chuckle turned into a bout of coughing.

His hands shook uncontrollably as he struggled to prop himself up. An intense pain shot through his body, making him grimace as he cautiously set his scarred feet on the floor. The scars served as a constant reminder of the brutal treatment meted out by his captor. But the wounds deep in his heart remained invisible. He was no longer angry; just hurt by the injustice of destiny.

It was the curse. It hung over him like a dark cloud. Didn't the Anga queen curse the rulers of the Haryanka Dynasty, condemning them to be killed by their own sons? Resigned to his fate, he prepared to face death. The wait for the inevitable was excruciating. Each morning, he prayed for death to take away his wasted form. But death refused to oblige.

Painstakingly, he inched closer to the iron bars, the sound of his breath echoing in the dark cell. Intent on upholding his dignity, he shuffled along taking small steps, barely lifting his feet off the ground. He was careful not to do anything that would provide the guards an opportunity to humiliate him. These were the same men who had once bowed down to him and idolized him as their saviour. They had prayed for his health and happiness, but now they delighted in tormenting him.

'Is there a celebration in the palace?' His voice came out as a faint whisper, so soft that it was impossible for the guards to make out the words. 'Is there a wedding or a royal birth? Pray, tell me the occasion that calls for the celebration.'

'Did you say something?' asked the kinder of the two guards, coming closer to the bars. 'It must be important enough for you to have dragged yourself from the bed to the door.'

Bimbisar let out a heavy sigh. Gathering his strength, he licked his parched lips. 'Are those sounds of rejoicing in the palace?' He asked in his feeble, cracked voice, pointing a trembling finger towards the sounds. 'Can you hear that—the melodious tunes and the joyful laughter filling the air?'

'The old man wants to know if there's rejoicing,' the guards taunted, their laughter echoing in the corridor.

Squinting at them with watery eyes, he begged, 'Please, tell me if I'm right.'

'It is a celebration alright! You have a grandson now.'

'My grandson?' The lump in his throat grew larger, choking him. 'My grandson,' he repeated feebly.

'That is right. A prince, destined to become the future king of Magadh, was born today.'

He hobbled back to the cold wooden bed, wincing in pain.

In spite of his terrible condition, he felt an overwhelming sense of happiness. It was truly an auspicious event. He was a grandfather. The Haryanka Dynasty would continue shaping the course of history. He raised his hands in blessing. He no longer wanted Kosala to bring him the poison. The thought of seeing his grandson filled him with a renewed will to survive. He wanted to live.

Outside the cell, the two guards discussed the possibility of being allowed to join the celebrations for a few hours.

'I heard the king has approved a grand feast for all the soldiers. You can expect madira and some money as well,' said one guard.

'If only the old fellow died,' replied the other guard, longing for release from his duty outside the cell.

'Perhaps he will die in the next few hours,' replied his companion, sounding hopeful.

'There is no chance of that happening. Didn't you notice him hobbling towards the iron bars, despite his face contorting with pain?'

'This fellow is a survivor. Imagine, despite the starvation and torture, he refuses to let go of the slender thread of life. Anyone else in his position would have died long ago.'

'He is strengthened by his belief in the Buddha,' whispered the guard.

'We sealed the window from which he could observe the Griddhakuta, yet he survived. I wish he were dead. It's painful to witness his suffering. Running a sword through him would be a quick and merciful way to end his pain.'

'We have tried everything but failed to bring about his death. The king had expected him to die. In fact, his orders were explicit. The prisoner should be put to death.'

'Do you think the king will be angry when he learns that we

have failed to execute the prisoner?' Suddenly, the guard's face lit up. 'We could kill him now, and be rid of him.'

'I suppose we could do that,' agreed the other guard. 'But I don't have the heart to run a sword through the old man. He was a king, after all.'

'Suffocating him would be neater. I don't want to soil my hands with the old man's blood,' suggested his colleague. 'Instead, I could choke him to death. All you have to do is hold him still. Once he is dead, we can inform the prison warden and join the others for the feast.'

'Let's put an end to it once and for all,' the other guard said firmly. 'But I believe a king should meet his end in a manner befitting his status, with a sword, and not by suffocating or strangling. That is for cowards.'

That very instant, the guards saw Ajatashatru striding purposefully towards the prison, an axe in hand. The prison warden and a group of soldiers trailed behind, attempting to match his strides.

'There is no room for hesitation or contemplation now. The king is rushing towards us,' groaned the guard.

'You are right, brother. We have no choice,' his companion gestured towards the motionless prisoner.

'If we don't kill him, we will be punished for not carrying out the king's order. And dereliction of duty is punishable by beheading.' One guard unlocked the door of the cell and rushed inside. Without wasting a moment, he seized Bimbisar and stuffed a rag into his mouth, while the other guard ran a sword through him.

The last remnants of life drained away. The old king's body twitched before finally becoming limp.

Bimbisar was dead.

'The prisoner is dead, Maharaj,' the guard reported. With

blood dripping from his sword, he bowed low in front of Ajatashatru, expecting to be rewarded.

Aghast, Ajatashatru stared at the lifeless body of his father. The strong affection Ajatashatru had felt for his newborn son caused a transformation in him. He had rushed to release his father from prison. Unfortunately, he had arrived too late. No amount of grieving by the repentant son could bring Bimbisar back to life.

In a fit of rage, he screamed at the guards, 'What have you done? You fools! Fetch the vaidya immediately.'

Fear immobilized the guards; they were rooted to the spot.

'Go!' commanded Ajatashatru.

Pandemonium broke out as the warden tried to pacify Ajatashatru and the guards rushed to fetch the vaidya, but everyone knew Bimbisar was beyond help.

The aggrieved son fell to the ground, his anguished cries echoing through the dungeon, but it was already too late to seek forgiveness. Tears streamed down his face as he cradled Bimbisar's body, rocking it gently in his arms. 'Baba! Please open your eyes. Please speak to me,' he wailed.

The curse of the Anga queen had come true. This was just the start of a series of tragedies that would plague the Haryanka Dynasty.

# Epilogue

After the death of Bimbisar, Magadh entered a turbulent period. Kosala, Bimbisar's devoted first wife, died of grief. Enraged by the loss of his sister and brother-in-law, Prasenajit reclaimed the gift of Kashi that he had previously given to Kosala. In response, Ajatashatru declared war on Prasenajit. The conflicts between Magadh and Kosala were not resolved until Vidudabha deposed his father, Prasenajit. Ajatashatru emerged victorious in the battle against Vidudabha and seized control of the Kosala kingdom. During his reign, Ajatashatru consolidated power, expanding the territories of the Magadh Empire to include multiple kingdoms. He ruled from the fortified city of Pataligrama, which later came to be known as Pataliputra, along the Ganga River.

Ajatashatru, the ruler of Magadh, is credited with developing two innovative and formidable war machines that proved pivotal in his sixteen-year conflict with the Lichchavis, culminating in Magadh's victory in 468 BC. One such creation was a powerful catapult capable of launching massive boulders deep into enemy ranks. The other one was a deadly chariot equipped with large maces or swords protruding from its wheels, enabling it to slash foes while in motion. These innovative war machines played a crucial role in Magadh's triumph over the Lichchavis.

Amrapali, the once radiant symbol of wealth and splendour, found herself irrevocably transformed by the tragic betrayal of Bimbisar. Surrounded by grandeur and extravagance in her resplendent palace, she realized how her riches had trapped her in a gilded cage. Rejecting materialism, she chose a life of simplicity as a Buddhist bhikkhuni. Influenced by the Buddha's teachings,

Vimal Kondanna, the son of Amrapali and Bimbisar, embraced Buddhism and became a monk.

Despite his accomplishments and renown, terrifying visions tormented Ajatashatru; he suffered from chronic insomnia. He lived in the constant fear of his son being responsible for his death—a fear that consumed him till he passed away. His anger towards the Buddha subsided, and he became a committed disciple. He also organized the first Buddhist council in Rajgriha. In addition, Ajatashatru commissioned a multitude of stupas across the capital and restored eighteen Buddhist monasteries. Ajatashatru not only extended the boundaries of the Magadh empire but also had a spiritual awakening.

The practice of patricide, started by Ajatashatru, continued over many generations in the Haryanka Dynasty.

Udayin continued the practice of patricide by slaying Ajatashatru, and stepping into the tumultuous legacy left by his father.. Within the dynasty, the pattern of patricide developed into a tragic ritual. Aniruddha perpetuated this cycle by killing Udayin, only to meet a similar fate at the hands of his son, Munda.

This unbroken cycle of power and patricide finally ended with Nagadarshaka, the last ruler of the Haryanka Dynasty, being overthrown by the very people he governed.

Each instance of violence not only marked a shift in power dynamics but also exposed the pitfalls of ambition, underscoring the fact that history is a tapestry of both glory and gore.

# Acknowledgements

*Bimbisar's Curse* was a project fuelled by passion. The abundant praise for *Ambapali* (2023) encouraged me to document the Magadh king's significant involvement in her story. The more I researched, the more I realized the potential for his story. Though he received no recognition in literature, the obscure king of Magadh played a crucial role in establishing the Magadh Empire. Bimbisar was worthy of a complete book.

The idea for the book came to me while I was on a long-distance flight. It got me excited, and I dived into the research. Detailed historical records of the period Bimbisar lived in are scarce. It was an era when bards and storytellers thrived. Over time, a significant part of the oral narratives changed or was lost. However, there is considerable mention of Bimbisar and the historical period he belonged to in Buddhist and Jain scriptures. Many historians have also written about the king, who transformed a small inherited territory into a powerful empire. That was the starting point for me.

Writing *Bimbisar's Curse* was challenging. Unlike medieval Indian history, there isn't sufficient information on ancient India. I felt as if I were plumbing the depths of the ocean in search of rare pearls. Often, I had to give wings to my imagination to plug the gaps or embellish the story. To create depth, I needed to develop a series of supporting characters. Similarly, I had to rely on multiple sources to imagine and recreate life as it was back then. As I penned this book, a quote by Hilary Mantel came back to me:'The past changes a little every time we retell it.'

I am thankful to Dibakar Ghosh for having faith in the book.

Our conversations added a fresh perspective to the narrative.

To the editors at Rupa, thank you for your deep understanding of my story and its characters. Your perceptive inputs and guidance have improved this book in ways that exceeded my expectations. Amrita Chakravorty, many thanks for the captivating cover design.

I am grateful to my husband, Ajoy, who has been a constant source of support through the entire book-writing journey.

Finally, I want to thank my readers for picking up this book and making time to read it. Your support vindicates the hours I spend writing, even when it gets lonely and demanding.

# Glossary

| | |
|---|---|
| aarti | A sacred ritual performed with a lamp |
| amatya | An advisor to the king |
| antariya | Traditional lower garment worn in ancient India |
| apsara | Celestial nymph/maiden |
| arya | An honourable man |
| asava | Fermented preparations of medicinal plants used in treating ailments |
| ayushman bhava | May you live long |
| bajuband | Armlet |
| chandrahaar | Traditional Indian necklace with multiple layers of gold beads and moon-shaped pendant |
| chaturanga | An ancient board game like chess |
| chudamani | Traditional hair adornment in gold |
| dasi | Maidservant |
| dasi putra | Maidservant's son |
| ganika | Prostitute |
| guptchar | Secret agent |
| hawan | Sacred Vedic fire ritual |
| jharoka | An ornate window or balcony, primarily found in Indian architecture, particularly in palaces and forts |
| jhumka | A traditional jewellery worn in the ears |
| kanchuki | Bodice |

| | |
|---|---|
| kanthahaar | Necklace |
| karambha | Refers to food made of barley or rice and clarified butter |
| katibandh | Waistband |
| kheer | Flavoured rice pudding |
| ki jai | Victory |
| kirtan | Devotional songs |
| madira | Wine |
| magadh Laxmi | Magadh's goddess of prosperity |
| mahajanpada | Great kingdom |
| mahamantri | Chief minister |
| mahamatya | Chief minister |
| mashaal | Torch |
| nagarvadhu | Bride of the city |
| naresh | King |
| nritya samragni | Queen of dancing |
| odhni | A cloth worn over the head and shoulders |
| paan | Betel leaves |
| parijat | Night jasmine |
| parishad | Council of ministers |
| prahari | Guard |
| pranam | Term of salutation |
| purohit | Priest |
| putravati bhava | May you have sons |
| raj dharma | King's duty |
| rajguru | Royal advisor |
| rajnartaki | Royal danseuse |

| | |
|---|---|
| rajpurohit | Royal priest |
| rangoli | Traditional Indian decoration created with colours, particularly during festivals. |
| sabhagriha | Assembly hall |
| samrat | Emperor |
| sangha | Buddhist monastic order |
| satlari | Seven stringed necklaces |
| senapati | Chief of the army |
| seniya | Commander of an army |
| setthi | Wealthy merchant |
| shulkadhyakshya | Tax collector |
| suprabhat | Good morning |
| sur Samrat | King of melody |
| sura | Wine |
| uttariya | Traditional upper garment worn in ancient India |
| vaidya | Physician |
| vijayee bhava | May you be victorious |

www.ingramcontent.com/pod-product-compliance
Lightning Source LLC
La Vergne TN
LVHW100519110826
845146LV00002B/697

* 9 7 8 9 3 7 0 0 3 8 1 4 1 *